THE HAUNTING OF HILHURST MANOR

VINCENT VALENTEAN

For my brothers, Dan and Rob

1

Nolan Hillhurst sat alone in the grandeur of his Beverly Hills mansion.

His burly body was completely enveloped by a darkness that consumed the opulence around him. The trappings of wealth and success, garnered through a long and successful career, seemed to blend into the shadows as though they were simply a natural formation in a dank cavern. The enormous room, designed for laughter and lavish parties, now felt more like a void that was swallowing him whole.

He was lost and alone in the dark, and he didn't see any possible way to escape from it.

Shadows clung to the high corners of the space, casting long, eerie stretches across the cold marble floor. His only companion was an oversized television screen flickering silently in the dim light. It cast a pale glow that barely reached the edges of his face, a fading light at the end of the tunnel of his misery.

Nolan's gaze was unfocused, eyes glazed over as scenes played out on the screen. The images and sounds playing out before him melded into an indistinct blur. He knew every frame of this film, every line, every singular action taken by the leading man.

And he should. It was him.

He'd made his career as a star of the screen, an action star, to be precise. He's portrayed himself as a strong, stoic badass who could take on any challenge and rise unscathed on the other side. But Nolan Hillhurst, the man, was a far cry from the various men of power he'd performed as over the years.

He wasn't standing triumphantly now, music booming as he accomplished goals mortal men could only hope to achieve. Instead, his body was sprawled awkwardly in a plush armchair that had seen better days. One arm dangled lifelessly off the side, his fingers loosely gripping the neck of a nearly empty Jack Daniels bottle.

His other hand held a smartphone to his ear. The device's light was stark against the deep shadows that filled the room.

The space around him spun. It was as though he were trapped forever within a slow, sickening swirl of darkness and fragmented light. Anchoring him to the world of light was the calm and soothing voice of his agent, Lenny. He spoke to him on the other end of the line, trying to reassure Nolan that his best days were in no way behind him.

When Nolan responded, his words were slurred, thick with remnants of alcohol and despair. "I messed up, Lenny... I messed up bad," he muttered. His impaired voice carried a deep, sorrowful moan of regret that still somehow rang with the edge of bitterness. "It's all my fault. Miranda's gone. I drove her away. I loved her so much, too much, and now..."

Lenny's response was practiced and calm. It was the tone of a man used to smoothing over rough edges and putting out the fires his big-name celebrity clients often started around themselves. "Nolan, you're a catch," he said, trying to build Nolan's confidence back up. "You're *the* catch. An incredible specimen. There are plenty of fish in the sea, my friend. So, let's not dwell on the past. Let's look forward to the future."

Nolan took those words for what they were. Nothing more than empty platitudes. They were clichés that Lenny was regurgitating to him on autopilot to placate him enough to get to the actual reason for his call. Lenny claimed to care about his clients, but Nolan had long ago realized that the thing Lenny actually cared about was the money he could make from his clients. And sometimes, that involved picking them up out of the gutter and dusting them off to push them into the next screen test.

It was obvious to Nolan that this was exactly what was happening right now.

Further attempting to steer the conversation away from personal disasters, Lenny shifted gears to business. Nolan was surprised at how quickly he adopted this pivot. He assumed there would be more hand-wringing and cliché dropping before Lenny had the stones to try to divert from Nolan's life crumbling to pieces.

"Speaking of new opportunities," Lenny said cautiously, testing the waters. "I've got a couple of movie offers on the table that you should consider—"

"Stop it!" Nolan barked. He wasn't having any of it. His sharp, jarring tone echoed slightly in the vast, empty room as he cut Lenny off mid-sentence. "I can't think about work right now, Lenny. My life is falling apart. Can't you see that? I don't care about new roles or scripts. I need... I need..."

His voice trailed off as he felt choked by a sudden wave of nausea that swept up through his stomach, causing his head to spin more violently. The phone slipped, pressed between his shoulder and ear as he reached for the bottle again. The real world was getting a little too close for comfort right now, and Nolan needed to seek solace in the burn of alcohol.

"Nolan, listen to me," Lenny said. His tone was tight and

insistent. It carried a tinge of concern that Nolan believed wasn't entirely feigned. "You need to pull yourself together, man. You're Nolan freaking Hillhurst. This isn't you. You're stronger than this, and you've always been. Think about your career, your fans, your future—"

"Enough!" Nolan shouted, his face flushing with heat and fingers clenching into powerful fists. He could feel a tempest of anguish and rage building into a hurricane within his chest, pushing down even the spinning nausea for a brief moment. He flung his phone off to the side, not even watching to see where it landed. He heard the device clatter against the hardwood floor and the unmistakable sound of the screen shattering upon impact. It didn't concern him in the least. Material possessions were replaceable when one had the means he did.

But love, memories, and passion weren't something you could buy in a store. It wasn't something he could order up on Amazon and get a next-day delivery on. He'd replaced most of the electronics and furniture in the house at one time or another after a particularly nasty fight or spot of bad news that caused him to fly off the handle. Somehow, breaking things always seemed to help. It allowed Nolan to reclaim some of his control and power. It reminded him that he was strong.

Nolan had always valued strength above all else. It was his greatest passion. "Stronger," he would tell himself anytime he started to feel weak. It was the mantra he repeated to himself every time he lifted a barbell or rose from a squat in the gym. It was even tattooed on his arm, his personal motto.

But that wasn't going to work here. There was no way to feel strong right now, no way to grunt and lift his way through this pain. There was nothing he could break or smash to pieces that would let him feel any semblance of control over his life anymore.

He leaned forward, burying his face in his hands. Nolan propped his elbows awkwardly on his knees. His entire burly body shook as sobs began to wrack through him. The sound was hollow and haunting in the empty mansion and entirely unfamiliar to Nolan. He never cried. He considered it the ultimate weakness, a complete lack of control.

Nolan hated sneezing because it was an involuntary reaction. He hated anything he couldn't control. He got legitimately mad every time he sneezed to the point where he'd chastise himself for his weakness. Crying, then, was practically a mortal sin.

He hadn't cried at the funeral of his mother. He hadn't cried tears of joy at seeing his bride walk down the aisle. He hadn't even cried at the ending scene of *Field of Dreams*. But now he was full-on sobbing. This added a feeling of unquenchable rage and humiliation to his sorrow.

As the television continued to play tales of Nolan's heroism to an audience of no one, the shadows seemed to creep closer. It was as though they were somehow drawn to the despair pouring out of him like sharks smelling blood in the water.

Nolan let out a harrowing scream. It was a sound of sheer sorrow that echoed through the hollow chambers of the mansion. He laid his head back against the chair, eyes drooping under the combined weight of his despair and the dizzying effects of the alcohol. Within moments, the world blurred into nothingness, and he slipped into a merciful unconsciousness.

Hours later, Nolan jerked awake after choking on his own saliva in his whiskey-fueled sleep. For a moment, he had no idea where he was. His mind was foggy and disoriented as he harshly regained consciousness. The room spun around him as he coughed, the remnants of his earlier inebriation still clouding his senses.

The mountainous man blinked slowly, trying to piece together where he was.

"Miranda?" he called out weakly, his voice cracking as he reached out beside him, hoping against reason that she might miraculously be there. But his hand found only the cold, empty air.

As he sat there, the fog of his memory began to clear, cruelly reminding him of his imposed solitude. He whimpered at the realization. The sound was soft and childlike, belying his imposing frame. Loneliness pressed down on him like a physical weight. It felt suffocating and inescapable. He wasn't sure what dreams he might have had while passed out in his chair, but no matter how bad they might have been, they couldn't have been worse than the misery he was feeling now.

He needed to know the time. That was something achievable that could anchor him to reality. He reached for his phone, but his fingers grasped at nothing. Panicking slightly, he looked down, spotting the device on the floor. It was illuminated by the flickering light of the TV. The screen was shattered. Its face was a spiderweb of cracks that rendered it totally lifeless.

He cursed loudly, his frustration echoing off the walls of his media room.

Attempting to stand, Nolan found his body frustratingly uncooperative. The first attempt sent him sinking back into the chair. He groaned as the overture of a massive migraine was tuning up within the confines of his skull. On the second try, his knees buckled, and he collapsed to the floor with a deep thud. Gritting his teeth, he mustered all his strength, and, on the third attempt, he finally stood, albeit unsteadily.

He swayed there for a moment, gripping the back of his chair for support. Nolan's eyes fell on the bottle of Jack Daniels on the floor. It was lying on its side, a dark pool of whiskey spreading out along the surface of the floor.

It was an expensive bottle, but Nolan didn't care in the least. He scoffed at the spilled liquor, more annoyed by the fact that it was empty than anything else. He'd simply have to go get another.

With a heavy sigh, he began to stumble toward the kitchen, toward his liquor cabinet, which was always well stocked. In the past, Nolan walked through this house as though it were his castle and he was some medieval king. But now, his hand trailed along the wall, grasping for support. He couldn't even remain upright on his own. It was certainly a low point for the proud action-movie hero.

His movements were clumsy, nearly causing him to pitch to the side as he navigated the darkness.

"Miranda!" he shouted, his voice echoing off the high ceilings, filled with pain and regret. He knew she wasn't there, knew she couldn't hear his mournful apology. But a part of him just needed to get the words out.

"I'm sorry!" he screamed into the emptiness. He wished the wind could take his words and carry them out of this place to wherever his wife might be, delivering apologies for deeds he could never undo.

His cries went unanswered, swallowed by the vastness of the empty mansion. Each step felt heavier than the last. It was a painful reminder of his newfound isolation. That oppressive loneliness was made all the more poignant by the shadows that seemed to watch and whisper from every corner.

Nolan felt the streak of tears tracing cold paths down his cheeks. He gritted his teeth, once more angry that he was letting his emotions and body rule him. That weeping turned bitter as he staggered toward the kitchen through the suffocating darkness until a frustrated cry of anguish tore itself out from between his lips.

Nolan took a deep breath, as though trying to pull that scream back in through his mouth. A second later, a peculiar sensation began to prickle the back of his neck. It was an unsettling feeling that told him he wasn't alone.

Soft thumping sounds echoed through the vast hallways as if something, or someone, was moving at a deliberate pace. Nolan's heart thudded heavily in his chest, his eyes darting frantically across the darkness. He looked into the shadows, trying desperately to pierce the pitch black that enveloped him.

"Who's there?" he called out threateningly. His voice was rough with a cocktail of fear and bravado. His hands curled into fists by his side, eager for a fight.

He actually hoped someone had been dumb enough to invade his home. He wanted to hit something, and the heavy bag in his expansive gym wasn't going to do it. He wanted to hit something living. He crouched, trying to ignore the room spinning around him as he steadied his thick legs beneath him. Nolan fought the urge to reach back out and grasp the wall for support. If someone was there, they weren't going to see him stumbling around. They needed to see a powerful man who was ready to confront whatever dared to intrude upon his solitude.

But beneath the veneer of confidence, fear gnawed at him. This was a relentless reminder of his human frailty that he always tried to ignore. But now, in the still of night and in his weakened state, he wasn't able to tell his fear to quiet down. He couldn't push it back down into his heart, shielded behind the hardened stone and steel he'd often imagine himself composed of. However, he could still keep it from his voice. He wasn't going to let someone sneaking up on him get the satisfaction of hearing his booming voice shake or crack with terror.

He forced the trepidation from his voice as he shouted again into the darkness.

"I'm not afraid of you!" he cried out into the shadows, his

tone fierce like a gladiator, though his words slurred slightly. "Come out!"

His challenge was met with another creak. It was a subtle, eerie sound of movement that seemed both distant and perilously close. The thump of footsteps, or perhaps the settling of the old mansion, beckoned him deeper into the shadows.

He started to feel hope blossom in his heart, pushing through the fear. Hope that it might be Miranda returning, perhaps to collect her belongings, or better yet, to reconcile and put an end to the madness.

"Miranda, is that you?" Nolan called out. There was a softness to his tone now, one that even he didn't recognize. He called out to what he hoped was his wife in a soft, placating way, as one might call for a timid animal. "Please, if it's you, we can fix this…"

There was no response within the heavy silence that filled the gaps between his calls. Squinting into the darkness, Nolan inched forward. He kept his hands outstretched like a blind man, groping for something—anything—that might guide him or warn him of obstacles unseen.

His fingers brushed against the cool, smooth surface of a wall. They were guiding him as he moved with tentative steps. Every shadow seemed to flicker with the possibility of being more than just a trick of the light. The mansion, with its corridors and cavernous rooms, felt alive, as though it were breathing quietly with him.

Nolan continued to call out, his voice now tinged with a mix of hope and fear, echoing down the empty hallways. The reality of his loneliness only became more inescapable with each unanswered call. For a moment, he wondered if he was imagining things, wondering if maybe he had cooked up this feeling and those sounds, if only to tell himself he wasn't alone.

Because what Nolan Hillhurst feared more than anything in the world was being alone. When faced with only himself for company, Nolan had learned long ago that he didn't care for the person he found there. But as he continued to stumble and grope his way through the night, he told himself that he wasn't imagining things. He couldn't be. He heard what he heard, felt what he felt.

As if on cue, the thumping resumed. It was a soft but distinct sound that seemed to draw him farther into the depths of the house. Nolan followed, driven by dread and hope.

He rounded the corner with a violent war of emotions waging in his mind, rattling his skull and adding to the pain of his upcoming migraine.

Nolan jumped as something brushed against his leg. It was a soft, fleeting touch that sent him tumbling to the floor in his inebriated state. The impact with the cold, hard marble sent a jolt of pain through his hip, and he cursed loudly. Struggling to focus his vision in the dim light, Nolan finally made out the source of the disturbance. It was a pure-white cat, its fur practically glowing ethereally in the darkness.

It was Snowball. He was Miranda's stupid cat. She loved that thing more than she'd ever loved him, and it had been the subject of many past disputes.

Nolan's eyes narrowed with intense dislike as he stared at the animal. Miranda had doted on that selfish, loathsome, predatory little beast. Memories of the affection she'd showered upon the feline only fueled his lingering resentment.

Now, as Snowball's eyes met his, their predator-like gleam piercing the night, a wave of drunken rage surged through Nolan. Blinded by anger, he reached out and grabbed the cat by the scruff of its neck, lifting it off the ground as he staggered to his feet.

"It's your fault she's gone," he hissed at the struggling

animal, its body twisting and turning in an attempt to escape his grasp.

The cat hissed and scratched at the air between them, valiantly trying to fight against a creature so many times its size.

Nolan stumbled back toward the front door, intent on throwing the cat out into the night. He resolved to himself that if Miranda had chosen to leave, she could damn well search for her pet herself. He certainly wasn't going to care for it. The stupid animal only served as a reminder of her. It had gone from a simple annoyance to a source of pain now, and it had to go.

As he neared the door, a shadow darted from the darkness, moving with startling speed. Before he could react in his inebriated state, a cold, hard object struck the back of Nolan's head. A shuddering shockwave of pain reverberated through his skull and threw his world into disarray.

The blow knocked him off balance, and he fell forward, the cat yowling beneath him as his heavy frame landed on top of it. He heard and felt a loud crunch beneath him, and suddenly, Snowball wasn't struggling anymore.

But Nolan couldn't even comprehend what he'd felt. The room was spinning wildly as he lay there, disoriented and trying to grasp what had just happened.

Before he could gather his senses, the object struck him again, crashing down on the back of his head with relentless, brutal force. Again and again, it came. Each blow extinguished just a little more of the light in his eyes.

Nolan's consciousness faded, the last vestiges of life slipping away from him until he was nothing at all. In those final moments, the mansion, which had once been a source of pride, a symbol of his success and vitality, became his tomb.

2

In the opulent expanse of his Beverly Hills office, Lenny Silvermane sifted through a pile of contracts and press releases. His scowl marked both his growing frustration and concern.

The room in which he sat was a testament to his success as one of Hollywood's top agents. It was adorned with sleek, modern furnishings and walls lined with framed posters of the various blockbuster movies his clients had landed with his guidance.

However, the glamorous setting did little to lighten his mood today as he looked up at the woman standing across from him.

Miranda Sterling stood by the window, her silhouette framed against the sprawling cityscape. Five years had passed since her husband Nolan's tragic death, and time seemed to have hardened her irreparably.

"It's been five years, Lenny," she said, shaking her head as she looked out over the view of Los Angeles in the distance. Her mouth was open, and her eyes purposely shifted away from Lenny. "Five freaking years and I still can't bring myself to shed a single tear over that bastard. Does that make me a bad person?" She looked at him now, her face a blank mask of introspection.

Lenny wasn't sure how to respond to that honestly. But he knew how he was required to respond.

The Hollywood agent, who had represented both Miranda and Nolan, shook his head, setting aside the paperwork.

"You're not a bad person, Miranda," he said, standing from his seat to walk over beside her. "Your relationship with Nolan was... complicated." He was choosing his words carefully.

It was rare that Miranda spoke of Nolan at all. When she did, Lenny had made sure that he handled the moment delicately.

Miranda scoffed, turning from the window to face him. "Complicated?" she asked, a scowl forming on her face as her hands found her hips.

Lenny thought that perhaps he hadn't been delicate enough this time. "Complicated is putting it mildly. Even after five years in the ground, that bastard is still making my life a living hell." Her voice was sharp now, frustration palpable. "The only people worse than that asshole are his fans. The disgusting things they've said to me over the years... All because of him.

"Come on, Miri," Lenny said, waving his hand in the air as though she were overreacting. "They're online trolls. Why care what they say? They mean nothing!"

"Because it's not just the damn trolls, Lenny!" she insisted, pointing a manicured finger at his chest. "And you damn well know it! I've become a pariah. No more roles, no more calls! Hollywood left me to rot all because my bastard husband dropped dead. Some even get bold enough behind closed doors to call me a damn murderer."

"That's ridiculous," Lenny interjected firmly. "Nolan died of a heart attack—or at least, that's what we made sure the media reported." His tone was reassuring, but his gaze didn't meet hers as he spoke. "When I found his body, I did what I had to do to make sure that the more gruesome details of that night never got out. Lord only knows what happened, what he had gotten into, but I didn't want any of his mistakes blowing back on you!"

Miranda's lip curled in disgust. "Well, it did," she spat, walking over to the small bar in Lenny's office and pouring herself a neat scotch. She took a larger-than-normal sip and shook her head in frustration. "I have no freaking idea what happened that night, and frankly, I don't care. I'm just glad he's gone."

Lenny winced and looked at his office door, hoping none of his staff had been standing close enough to hear that. He knew all too well that Miranda's indifference to the details of Nolan's death was overshadowed only by her relief at his absence. Still, it was a sentiment she rarely expressed so openly.

Lenny knew he needed to steer the conversation in a more productive direction. It reminded him of his last phone call with Nolan. He'd tried to move him beyond his personal anguish and toward professional concerns, which had been mounting. He hoped Miranda would be more receptive to that tactic than her late husband had been.

"Holding on to this grudge isn't helping, Miranda," Lenny said, lowering his voice and leaning closer.

Letting her wallow in her emotions wasn't productive. Let her do that with her therapist. Lenny's concerns for her were far more practical.

"Your career is losing serious steam, and we need to get you back out into the spotlight. You're not getting any younger, and the window for leading roles isn't going to stay open forever."

Miranda nodded. Lenny knew the reality of the situation

wasn't lost on his client. She knew the stakes were high, and her time to turn things around was running out.

"What should I do, then?" she asked, setting her glass back down on the bar and shrugging. "How the hell do I distance myself from this mess? I've been trying for five long years. Five wasted years! Five years when roles that should've been mine went elsewhere because of the stink of Nolan Hillhurst clinging to me." She crinkled her nose and clutched at the flesh of her forearms as though she could actually smell and feel that stench emanating from every pore.

Lenny paused, considering her question. He knew they needed a strategy that would not only revive her career but also redefine her public image.

"First, we start with a rebrand," he said, his voice rising as he went into pitch mode. He held his hands up in front of him, moving them as he talked, as though presenting these concepts to Miranda in physical form. "I'm talking about new interviews, a few well-placed articles to clear your name, perhaps even a charity event to show your softer side. It's time the world saw Miranda Sterling again. And not as Nolan Hillhurst's widow. As the talented actress and superstar you've always been! You were a star before Nolan, and you'll be a star long, long after his memory fades."

Miranda's eyes sparkled with hope and determination. He could always tell when a pitch landed. And despite their ability to take on another persona entirely when the camera was on, actors typically had terrible poker faces. She nodded, and some of her youthful vigor seemed to return.

"All right," she said with a sturdy nod and a smile that showed off her perfectly straight, white teeth. "I trust you, Lenny. I always have. So, let's do it. It's time they remembered who the hell I really am!"

Lenny smiled and pumped his fist enthusiastically to put perfect punctuation on Miranda's words. He had to lay out a plan now, and his mind had kicked into overdrive, putting the pieces together. He subtly eyed Miranda's thin yet toned frame up and down. Her face still had the allure of youth, despite her age pushing forty. But that wasn't going to last. Plastic surgery could only hold back the hands of time for so long.

"The next step is to distance you completely from Nolan," Lenny said, pacing in front of her now as though chasing his thoughts. He found that this often excited people and made them believe in him and whatever vision he was trying to sell. "That means no more mentioning him in public, no more talking about his death in interviews, and it's time to liquidate some of Nolan's assets."

"I'm all for that," she said. "I only held onto them this long because I thought selling them off would have looked…well, suspicious."

"You were right to do that," Lenny said, making a placating gesture with his palms. He had to keep her spirits up. "But you've waited long enough. Everything has to go. I don't care if we sell it or auction it off for charity. But his cars, his possessions, and especially the house all need to find new owners."

Miranda's expression darkened at the mention of the house. Lenny was worried he was losing her enthusiasm, but there was no reason to hold on to that place anymore.

The mansion had once been a symbol of the glamorous life she'd shared with Nolan. It was a statement to the public that the two of them were a power couple, an *it* couple. They had been dubbed Nolanda by the press, and that had been a moniker that had served them well from a publicity standpoint for years. But Nolanda had to disappear forever so that Miranda could rise in its place as a solo act.

"You know," Miranda said softly, turning back to the bar

and pouring herself another drink. "That house was once my palace on a hill."

Lenny was struck at how she was able to sound simultaneously nostalgic and bitter. "But since Nolan's death, I haven't stepped foot in there. I left it to rot, just like him."

Lenny had been there for Miranda's last visit to that mansion. It had been on the day of Nolan's death before the coroner had arrived to take the body.

"I remember," he said with a nod, looking up as if revisiting that time and place in his mind. "You did a good enough job that day, appearing upset."

Miranda paused and scoffed. "It wasn't hard to pretend to be upset," she confessed. "But I wasn't upset over him. I hope he's burning in hell. The real tragedy was what happened to Snowball. Nolan's big, dumb, jackass body fell on my poor baby when he died. Any tears I shed that day were only for Snowball."

Lenny nodded in understanding and even gave her a small laugh. He considered for a moment the optics of trying to unload all of Nolan's assets publicly. The house would likely be a hard sell, seeing as it was the site of an icon's death. Lenny wasn't a real estate expert, but he knew enough to understand that this made for a hard sell.

"Perhaps just listing the house on the market isn't enough," he suggested thoughtfully. "Maybe you need to sell the place personally. A personal touch might change the narrative, make it more appealing to potential buyers."

Miranda considered Lenny's suggestion. Lenny nearly lost hope as he saw the very idea of returning to that house send a visible shiver down his client's spine. Yet, the need to sever all ties with Nolan's memory was a compelling force that he hoped she would see.

"Maybe you're right," she agreed reluctantly, with a sad

half-shrug. "A personal sale might finally put that place and that man in my rearview mirror."

Lenny nodded and exhaled in relief. He was pleased with and proud of her resolve. "It's all about taking control of the story, Miranda," he said, trying to really solidify the idea in her mind. "It's the first step to crafting a narrative that distances you from Nolan's shadow and re-establishes you as an independent force in Hollywood."

"And you think it'll work?" she asked with a raised eyebrow. The last of her doubts were bubbling to the surface now, and Lenny needed to sweep them away.

"Miri," he said with all the sincerity he could muster. "You're beautiful, you're talented, you're well connected, and everyone loves a comeback story. Once we put all the unpleasantness behind us, the rumors will dry up and you'll rule this town again!"

Miranda's face lit up, and Lenny knew he had closed this sale once and for all.

"All right, I'll do it," she said.

Lenny was pleased to hear a newfound determination in her voice.

"Let's set up a viewing. I'll host it myself. Maybe if they see me there, moving on, they'll be able to see themselves there."

"That's the spirit," Lenny said, walking over to the bar and pouring himself a drink. "We'll make it an event. We'll invite select realtors, do a press piece on it. It's not just a sale; it's a statement."

They clinked their glasses together and toasted to this new chapter. After another long sip, Miranda held up a questioning finger as if to stop Lenny's train of thought.

"So, once we're fully free and clear of Nolan, what's next?" she asked. She didn't sound hesitant anymore. She was hopeful, excited even.

Lenny had to stoke the fires of that excitement and keep

her focused on their end goal. "Once Nolan's memory fades, you won't be a tabloid darling anymore," he said simply, spreading out his arms as though presenting her with the world itself. "After you've publicly moved on, it's time for me to contact every person I know in this godforsaken town and tell them that they need to be a part of Miranda Sterling's major comeback! I'll sell it to them the way only I can do and start lining up a whole boatload of auditions for you."

Miranda's eyebrow arched skeptically at that. "Auditions?" she echoed incredulously. "I haven't had to audition for a role in fifteen years, Lenny. People at my level are offered roles based on who we are, not what we can prove in a casting room."

Lenny tried to approach the situation with delicacy, understanding her pride and her position. He needed to present this concept to her in a way that she would understand without deflating her excitement at the plan they were laying out.

"Miranda, right now, in the eyes of the studios, you're seen as damaged goods," he said gently. He saw her eyes widen ever so slightly in anger. He quickly continued, "It's not fair, but it is what it is, and we need to accept that reality. Once we've put Nolan's shadow behind us, the roles will start coming again. But for now, you need to audition like everyone else. You need to remind the studios why you're a star."

Miranda's face tightened, and Lenny watched as she wrestled with the grim reality he had laid out. She moved to one of the seats in front of his desk, sitting down and stewing silently. He could tell that the idea of auditioning like a novice gnawed at her pride. At nearly forty, she was acutely aware of Hollywood's unspoken rules about age. The industry was not kind to women as they aged, and Lenny knew Miranda was desperately fighting against being pigeonholed into "mom" or "cougar" roles.

She ran a hand over her face, feeling the tautness of her

surgically maintained skin. So much of her wealth had been funneled into cosmetic procedures to keep her looking the part of a leading lady. It was a valiant and expensive effort to hold back the relentless march of time, and Lenny had supported it wholeheartedly. But deep down, she had to know as he did that the clock was ticking.

Lenny noticed her distress and softened his tone further. "Miranda, think of this as a fresh start," he said, walking in front of his desk and leaning casually against it as he looked down at her. "It's a chance to redefine who you are. You can show them that you're more than the rumors. You're more than Nolan's widow. You are Miranda freaking Sterling, a damn talented actress who deserves to be seen for her skills and dedication!"

Miranda sighed. She no longer displayed the explosive excitement Lenny had noticed in her before, but it was clear that her resolve was firming.

"You're right, Lenny," she said finally, looking down into her drink at the wavy reflection on the surface of the liquid. When she looked back up at him directly, it was clear that her resolve had solidified and she was committed to the cause. She sat straight-backed with unflinching, direct eye contact and a confident smile on her face. "If auditioning is what it takes to get back on top, then I'll do it. I'll show them that there's more to me than my past. I'll show them I still have what it takes!"

Lenny smiled, relieved by her acceptance. "That's the spirit," he said encouragingly. "We'll start with some small roles, build your portfolio again. And soon, they'll see you're still a force to be reckoned with."

"You know, Lenny, parting with that house is like shedding the last of my old skin," Miranda said. She sighed and sounded exhausted by the weight of the memories held within those walls. "It's been such a burden, always dragging me back to those dark days with Nolan. But getting rid of it, actually moving on like this—I need it."

Lenny leaned forward, his face kind and understanding of her plight. "It's more than just a sale, Miranda," he said softly. "It's a declaration to the world and a pivotal step for you personally. Handling the sale yourself will send a powerful message. Miranda Sterling isn't just moving on. She's taking control."

"Control," Miranda said to herself with a slow shake of her head. She no doubt remembered Nolan's issues with that word and concept. She had been under Nolan's control for far too long. Even five years after his death, he was still finding ways to control her life and career. "I think I'm ready for some control of my own."

3

Ava Monroe settled into the plush couch that sat against the back wall of her home office. The pink walls seemed to shimmer as though this were the realm of a Barbie doll come to life or some kind of cartoon princess, which was definitely the vibe Ava had been going for.

She kept the phone pressed tightly against her ear. The reporter on the other line was eager, her voice a chirpy, insistent presence as she probed for juicy details about Ava's latest film project.

"It's truly an honor to be part of such a dynamic team," Ava said, dripping with the same sweet sincerity that had made her Hollywood's fastest-rising star. "I'm so thrilled with the direction we're taking."

Ava was the perfect celebrity interview, both for the reporters themselves and for concerned agents and publicists. She had a warm smile, kind, sincere eyes, and she was always incredibly polite and gracious to whoever interviewed her.

Despite the fact that this particular interview was being conducted via phone, she was still perfectly made up, with every hair in place, and she was wearing one of her trademark pink summer dresses as though the paparazzi were about to burst into her home.

Ava kept her tone perfectly modulated to convey excitement. Yet, as the words left her mouth, she winced internally. While reporters and publicists loved her Hollywood interviews, Ava was the only person in her immediate orbit who hated them.

She'd never liked fakeness, which she often found ironic given her profession and where she had chosen to live. She wished she could just talk like a normal person and be completely, genuinely sincere—not this fake, bubbly mask of sincerity she was forced to don in front of the press.

Each rehearsed phrase felt like a betrayal of her true self. But that was the game in Hollywood. Puff pieces that demanded a veneer of perpetual delight and gratitude were the unfortunate currency of the Hollywood press. And if she wanted to continue the level of success she had been enjoying for several years now, then she needed to pay up.

She'd learned early on, back in her days as a teenage model, that success in this industry was about more than just raw talent. It was about playing your part in the grand spectacle. Back then, she thought she understood the workings of the great Hollywood machine. But time had taught her how naïve that understanding had been.

One couldn't truly understand what it was like in the belly of the beast before they'd been swallowed up by it.

Looking around her office, Ava visually traced the lines of luxury that defined her sprawling home. Walls lined with awards and framed magazine covers spoke of her great success and material wealth. Yet, sitting here, giving another hollow interview, Ava couldn't shake the feeling that she had lost a part of herself along the way.

Her thoughts drifted to her personal relationships—the myriad of fake friends and industry acquaintances she'd accumulated since her big break. These were people who smiled and offered warm hugs in public but wouldn't hesitate to stab her in the back if it meant climbing one rung higher on the ladder of stardom.

She missed the time when she could trust the people around her, when she had friendships that were genuine. When people spent time with her simply because they wanted to and not because they were trying to gain social clout or because they had become a fan. But those days were never to come again. Ava knew that even long after her star would fade, she'd never be able to return to a normal life again.

She glanced at the office door, her gaze pensive. Beyond that door, somewhere in the vastness of their house, she knew Chase was probably lounging on a couch. Her husband likely had a drink in his hand as well. He might even be brooding over her interview, his mind weaving dark thoughts about how these fluff pieces might be feeding into the narrative of her success.

It was a narrative that had diverged sharply from his own over the last year.

Their career trajectories could not have been more different. When they had met, they were still Isabelle and Ethan. Just two young hopefuls unspoiled by the industry's harsh realities. Ava longed for those days, for the carefree exuberance and genuine passion that Ethan had embodied. But as they transformed into Ava and Chase, something vital had been lost.

Chase's career had taken a nosedive as Hollywood shifted away from the archetype of the burly male action hero to embrace new ideals.

Projects were now more frequently led by women or featured men who were half Chase's size. These were actors who brought a different kind of intensity to the screen. This change had inadvertently marginalized Chase. He was an obsolete commodity. It had left him grappling with a fading identity in an industry that no longer revered his particular brand of masculinity.

As the interview wrapped, Ava forced a final cheerful goodbye, though her heart was heavy. She hung up the phone and leaned back, closing her eyes. The silence of the room embraced her for a long moment. It was a relief to let go of the false cheeriness of her public persona. In these quiet moments, she often wondered if the price of her fame was too high. Lately, more than ever, she wondered if the sacrifices she was forced to endure every day were irrevocable.

Ava stepped out of her office, her heels clicking softly on the polished tile floor as she made her way downstairs. The walls, adorned with expensive modern art and portraits from her modeling days, chronicled the rise of Ava Monroe. Each frame, each piece of art, was a milestone in her journey from hopeful actress to Hollywood starlet.

The house, sprawling and elegantly appointed, had become her sanctuary. Now, by extension, it had become Chase's as well. And that was quickly becoming a point of contention for the young couple.

They had married just a year ago and agreed that he would move into her home. The reason for that, Ava had told herself, was because it was far more accommodating than his. However, in those rare moments when Ava was being honest with herself, she admitted the reason she'd pushed so hard for her home over his was simply because she was comfortable there and didn't want to leave.

Initially, everything had seemed harmonious. It was a seamless blending of their lives. They were happy. The two of them were Hollywood's new *it* couple, and it seemed as though everyone wanted a piece of them. They attended movie premieres together, standing side by side on the red carpet, basking in the flash of cameras and the adulation of fans.

But as time had passed, the balance had shifted. Chase's premieres became less frequent while Ava's career continued to soar. The photographers who had once clamored equally for both began to favor her, their shouts for Ava drowning out Chase's name. As a couple, they were still popular, but it quickly became clear that it was mostly due to Ava's rising star power. Chase knew it, too. And a bitterness had risen within him that Ava didn't know how to contend with.

Descending the final stair, Ava entered the living room. Chase was there, as expected, completely engrossed in an old action film. She knew this was one of his favorites. It was called *Doom and Boom,* and it starred Chase's hero, Nolan Hillhurst. Ava hated those films. She thought they were mindless garbage with no discernable story outside the big explosions and testosterone-inducing flashes of gunfire.

The room was dim, lit only by the glow of the massive TV screen. The film was currently showcasing one of its many elaborate fight sequences, complete with first explosions, revving engines, and rattling gunfire.

"What are you watching?" Ava asked, her tone light, attempting to bridge the gap that had been widening between them. She knew damn well what the movie was, but she'd been struggling lately to connect with her husband and engage him on a level he was comfortable with.

Chase remained silent, with his gaze fixed on the screen. He pressed a button on the remote, and the title of the movie popped up briefly. He offered no other acknowledgment of her presence. Ava felt deflated by his reaction to her simple question. But she wasn't entirely deterred yet. She was going to try another approach.

"How about we go out to dinner tonight?" she asked cheerfully, with a bright smile on her face. She hoped a change of scenery might lighten his mood, and she watched her husband's face for any sign of a positive reaction.

"No," Chase replied flatly, his eyes never leaving the television.

Ava's smile faltered, and she felt a pang of rejection at his curt response. It seemed that with each passing day, his depression and discomfort only grew, and she was becoming less and less successful in her attempts to cut through it.

Pushing past her own discomfort at the situation, she decided to continue trying to open up a conversation. Before she could think of another topic they might explore together, her nose crinkled at an unpleasant, musty, and increasingly all-too-familiar scent hitting her nose.

"Baby, have you… showered yet today?" she asked. The question was gentle, tinged with concern rather than judgment.

Chase's depression had become palpable, marked by neglect of personal hygiene routines that one would normally work into their daily life. He'd always been so proud of his appearance. He was extremely clean and always smelled nice. It was one of the things that made him such an exceptional cuddler. His hair was always styled and conditioned to perfection. His smile was always white and straight. His breath was always minty fresh. He had been every girl's dream in that respect.

"No," he said, the word short and devoid of any further engagement.

Ava felt her heart sink. She had known the answer before she had asked. It was more than obvious. Chase had completely neglected not just her but himself. She guessed it was probably three days since he'd engaged in any kind of self-care. She judged that by the sweatpants he'd been wearing for that entire length of time, coupled with the smell, his greasy, unkempt hair, and the stubble that had grown along his face.

"Baby, we talked about this," she said patiently. "You need to do human things. You have to shower and take care of yourself. It's not good to wallow like this."

"Okay," he responded simply. While it was technically an acknowledgment of what she was saying, Ava knew her husband well enough to know what it actually was: a not-so-thinly veiled brush-off.

Ava felt heat rise in her cheeks as concern started to give way to anger. She simply stood there, momentarily at a loss, as she tried to bring her emotions under control. If she lost it, then she was either going to start yelling or crying, and neither was productive right now.

Chase's indifference stung more than she cared to admit. She found herself once again missing the relationship between Isabelle and Ethan, those two souls with dreams unmarred by the harsh realities of their industry. Now, as Ava and Chase, they seemed to drift further apart, their connection frayed by unspoken frustrations and the silent battles Chase fought within himself.

With a quiet sigh, Ava turned her back with a heavy and aching heart. She knew she'd only be able to hold back the swell of her emotions for so long. Eventually, the dam would break and the waters of her rage and pain would explode out. She needed to avoid that right now. She wasn't sure she could handle it.

As she turned and walked away from the living room area, Ava brought a hand up to her mouth to stifle a sob trying to well up from within her chest.

The divide between them felt wider than ever, each one-word answer from Chase a reminder of how much had changed. She missed the man he used to be—the vibrant, passionate Ethan who had captured her heart. The man sitting before her now seemed like a shadow of that person, lost in the flickering images of a life dominated by horrific depression. A life that no longer included her.

She'd wanted him to go to therapy, even offered couples counseling for the two of them, but he'd turned her down time and time again.

"Are you gonna just stand there?" he called out to her, his voice numb but with the edge of irritation pushing along the boundaries of his depression.

Ava's jaw clenched as she absorbed the chill in Chase's voice. She could feel the growing spark of anger within her threatening to ignite.

"Are you planning on moving from that spot at all today?" she asked, turning back into the room to look down at her lounging husband. As soon as she had asked the question, she knew it had been a mistake. She hadn't been in control of her emotions, and her tone had come out far sharper than she had intended.

Chase finally turned to face her, his blue eyes meeting hers with a blank, emotionless stare. "I'm comfortable where I am," he replied flatly, his voice devoid of the warmth she once knew.

"Are you, really?" Ava challenged, unable to mask her frustration. "Because for the last few months, you've seemed anything but comfortable in this place."

Chase scoffed quietly at her, shaking his head with a sardonic grin. "Of course, I'm comfortable," he said with a sarcastic smirk that seemed to revel in the cruelty of whatever he was about to say next. "How could I not be comfortable in this monument to Ava Monroe's greatness?"

Ava blushed. She knew something like that was coming. The house had become something of a sore spot between them lately. It was Chase's favorite weapon to bring out against her. She assumed that was because he knew he actually had a point here. It had been Ava who had pushed for Chase to move in with her, and she hadn't made a huge push to redecorate to create a space that accurately represented the two of them.

The sting of his comment hit Ava hard. She had tried countless times to make him feel at home, to make him feel like a part of this life they were supposed to be building together. She had reached the point where she was willing to make concessions.

"We can redecorate if it would make you feel more comfortable," she said, her voice softening. It was a plea for understanding, but Chase's expression hadn't changed in the least.

"There's no need," Chase retorted dismissively. "We need to keep up appearances for your career, right? I'm just another accessory. Like a cute pair of shoes or a handbag."

"That's not true," Ava protested. Her voice was rising now. She was getting swept up in the emotion of the moment and getting defensive. He couldn't actually believe that she saw him that way.

Chase was quick to counter this, as though it had been a trap he'd set that she willingly walked into. "Really?" he asked with a laugh, shaking his head and sitting up straight to fully turn toward her now. "For the last few premieres and parties, your publicist and stylist picked outfits for me that specifically complemented the color of your purse and shoes. That sounds like an accessory to me."

His words were sharp, each one underscored with a mix of sarcasm and hurt. She hadn't even realized her team had done that. But the more she thought about it, he was right. He must've been holding on to that for a while, holding it back until he just couldn't anymore.

Ava felt a wave of guilt wash over her as she realized how her success and the demands of her public image might have overshadowed their relationship. The pain in Chase's voice was a clear indication of how disconnected he felt. It was a disconnect not just from the world they inhabited but from her and their relationship as well.

She had sacrificed a lot for this career. She'd given up her privacy, her social life, and her friends, but she was not going to let the Hollywood monster take Chase from her. That was where she drew the line.

She stepped farther into the room, coming to stand between Chase and the TV. Her anger was dissolving now, quickly transforming into concern.

"Babe, I never wanted you to feel like you're just an add-on to my life," Ava said, being genuinely sincere. There was none of the fake sweetness she'd been forced to adopt. She wasn't trying to talk to him as Ava Monroe; she was just Isabelle in that moment. "You're my husband, my partner. I want us to be equals, to support each other."

Ava hoped the earnestness in her statement was evident to her husband. She desperately wanted to bridge that gap between them, but this bridge had to be built from two sides to meet in the middle. She couldn't do it on her own.

Chase looked away from her, the muscles in his jaw working as he processed her words. For a moment, the old spark, the one that had ignited their love, seemed to flicker in his eyes.

"I want that, too," he said quietly, almost as if he was telling this to himself. "But right now, I just feel like I'm fading into the background."

Ava reached out, her hand hesitating before resting gently on his arm. She lowered herself to sit beside him on the couch and forced her face to keep any reaction to the stale stench emanating from him invisible.

"Let's fix this together," she said, looking deep into his eyes as though they could figure it out right there and right then with a little effort and some belief in the love that had gotten them this far. "Tell me what you need. What will make this right?"

The room filled with a tense silence as Chase considered her offer. Ava knew that this moment was a crossroads for them. She held her breath as she considered the next words that came out of his mouth could mend or further fray the threads of their union.

Chase paused, his demeanor shifting as he seemed to deflate more into the plush cushions of the couch. His posture seemed to surrender. He shook his head slowly, and when he spoke, his voice was hollow. "There's nothing to be done, Ava," Chase said, sounding dead inside.

It shattered Ava to pieces to hear him just let go like that.

"Our careers...our lives... They're just in two wildly different places."

Ava's heart clenched at his resignation. She felt tears starting to form in her eyes, and she told herself once more that she was not going to let the life and career of Ava Monroe take her husband away from her. They were not going to be another Hollywood divorce statistic, a footnote on page three of every tabloid. She wouldn't let it happen.

"Just because things are going well for me doesn't make you any less a part of this relationship," she insisted. The desperation in her voice was palpable as she tried to make him see this from a different angle. It didn't matter what the outside world saw. It didn't matter what the press said. All that mattered was the two of them and the bond they'd always shared.

Chase looked at her, and although he nodded, his voice betrayed his true feelings. "I know that," he murmured. However, his tone—the lack of conviction—said otherwise.

Frustration surged within her, breaking through her sadness. She couldn't help but voice it now. "Why can't you just be happy for me?" Ava asked, her voice rising. "Every time my agent calls with a new opportunity, I can't even feel excited anymore. I just get this pit in my stomach because I know you're going to react like—"

"Like a jealous child?" Chase cut in sharply, standing abruptly until he towered over her. His face was flushed with emotion, changing so quickly from the indifferent mask he'd worn moments earlier. "I'm not the one acting like a child here. You're the one who constantly needs your ego reinforced. You surround yourself with your own pictures as if you'd ever forget what you look like with all the primping you do in front of the mirror."

He glanced around, his eyes harsh and judgmental.

"This isn't a partnership, Ava. This is your house, not ours. I'm just a passenger in your life, and I don't have one of my own!"

Before Ava could formulate a response, Chase stormed out of the room, leaving her sitting on the couch with only the lingering smell of his dirty sweatpants behind as a reminder that he was ever there at all.

The door slammed behind him with such force that a framed photo on the wall shuddered and fell, the glass cracking as it hit the floor. Ava winced at the sound and stood to survey the damage. Walking over to the broken frame, her eyes gazed down at the carefree face in the exposed photo. It was her own face, though she scarcely recognized it. It was from a time that seemed both distant and painfully close.

She knelt to pick up the photo, her fingers trembling as she touched the cracked glass. The image looked back at her. It was an eternal reminder of the woman she had been and the man who had once looked at her with so much love and admiration.

Tears blurred her vision as she whispered affirmations to

herself. "I need to find a way to fix this," she said. "I am going to save our marriage."

She set the broken frame on a table and looked around the room. She saw all the lavish décor and the walls adorned with accolades to her success. She had carefully chosen every single decorative item with the utmost care.

But Ava realized that her home, this monument to her career, needed to change. It needed to become *their* home. It had to become a place where Chase could feel at home. A place they could call their own together.

Determined, Ava began to formulate a plan. She would start by creating a more balanced environment. It needed to be one that reflected both of their lives, not just hers. She nodded to herself. This was a tangible first step—one that she hoped would lead them back to each other.

4

Miranda Sterling sat at a corner table at a swanky Hollywood café. Her eyes discreetly scanned the bustling room. She knew all too well that in her line of work, privacy was a luxury seldom afforded, especially in such public settings. To anyone glancing her way, she appeared the epitome of composure, a celebrated actress enjoying a quiet moment alone. But beneath her poised exterior, turmoil churned.

Lenny's plan to revitalize her career had seemed so alluring at first. He'd actually managed to get her excited to sell off a bunch of old junk and start auditioning like some nineteen-year-old waitress. But when it came time to actually put that plan in motion, to implement Lenny's grand vision to reignite her fading star, she found that it was a lot easier said than done.

Earlier that day, she had driven to the Hillhurst Estate. The grand mansion she had once called home loomed magnificently in front of her, shining like a polished pearl in the mid-morning sun. She had told herself on the way over that she was ready to walk inside again. To stand in the place where her husband had died, in a house that held so many horrifying memories for her, all in an effort to exorcise this place from her life once and for all.

But as she stood outside, her gaze had lingered on the towering façade, and a sense of trepidation had overwhelmed her. The mansion, with its sprawling gardens and imposing architecture, had once symbolized her success and the bond she'd initially shared with Nolan. But now, it stood like a monument to darker times. Its luxury was unable to mask the memories of the man she had lived with. A man she wished she could just forget.

Her hands trembled slightly. She tried to close her fingers into a fist and bring this physical manifestation of her inner conflict under control. But that was beyond her power. She had talked to Lenny about control and her need for it. But it seemed as though, even in death, Nolan still held control over her in this place. Miranda hated the feeling, and she wanted desperately to get back in the car and show this God-forsaken place her taillights once and for all.

But she needed to prepare the house for the upcoming sale. It was her job to ensure everything was perfect for the open house, where she would, of course, have to be present. The interaction with her was going to be a selling point touted by her real estate agent to attract more potential buyers. It was a great idea, in theory. But in practice, she would have rather crawled through broken glass than done any of this.

Standing there, with the morning sun doing little to penetrate the aura of gloom that seemed to envelop the property, Miranda had found herself rooted to the spot. She was entirely unable to move forward.

Despite the daylight, the air had felt thick, almost suffocating. Looking up at the house, it was as if she were standing at the entrance of a dark, foreboding cave. It was certainly a far cry from her former residence. She couldn't do it. It was impossible. She had turned around, gotten back into her car, and driven away from that horrible spot as fast as she could.

Sitting in the café, Miranda ground her teeth together. She couldn't stop the frustration she felt upon revisiting that memory from bubbling to the surface as she took another sip of her tea. The warmth of the beverage did little to soothe her frayed nerves.

What was it that held her back? Was it fear?

Certainly, the mansion had seen its share of dark days. Shadows of her terrible past seemed almost palpable as she stood before it.

Or was it guilt?

Miranda had never mourned Nolan's death. There was no love lost between them, especially toward the end. Yet, in her more vulnerable moments, she couldn't help but feel a twinge of guilt for what had ultimately become of him. She would routinely ask herself if she were somehow responsible for the way his life had spiraled out of control and ultimately ended under circumstances that still brought a chill to her spine.

And now, here she sat out in public, shopping bags at her feet, ready for yet another phase of Lenny's master plan to get her back out into the world. He'd told her that good press was going to be of the utmost importance. That meant hanging around other actors and actresses who had a lot of good buzz surrounding them.

And Lenny was swinging for the fences on this one. He had called up his biggest client, the current darling of Hollywood, and asked if she'd meet Miranda for a drink out in public. She'd said yes, thankfully, and now Miranda was waiting to get the rub from a woman nearly half her age.

As she set her teacup down, her fingers steadied. Today, she had faltered, unable to face the house alone. But tomorrow, she resolved, would be different. She would return to the Hillhurst estate, ready to confront whatever specters lay waiting. It was the only way forward, the only way to truly free herself from the shadows of her past.

Lost in her reverie, Miranda was suddenly pulled back to reality by a familiar voice calling out to her. She looked up to see the person she'd been waiting for. Lenny's biggest current client. The darling of Hollywood herself, Ava Monroe.

The bubbly, young blonde was dressed all in pink, flashing Miranda a huge, open-mouthed smile as she approached. This girl definitely had that "it" factor. Her presence absolutely lit up the room. Of course, she'd met Ava before. She even liked the girl, as much as one Hollywood actress can actually like another. But they had never met up one on one. Miranda was curious to see how this would go.

The young starlet embodied everything Miranda had once been. She was thin, young, naturally beautiful, and free from the burdens of cosmetic enhancements that Miranda now relied on to maintain her appearance.

Ava was dressed effortlessly in a stylish pink sundress paired with strappy sandals, a hat, and round sunglasses that added a touch of mystery to her vibrant demeanor. She carried several shopping bags, evidence of a productive outing, and flashed a flawless pearly white smile as she approached.

The café, which had hummed with subdued chatter, now buzzed louder as other patrons took notice of Ava's entrance. Whispers spread, and nearly every cell phone in the vicinity was aimed at her, capturing her every move. Miranda stood and greeted her with a hug, soaking up every click of a phone camera in the immediate vicinity. This was the true purpose of this meeting, and it was going off without a hitch.

Ava was the center of attention, the current golden child of Hollywood who drew attention to herself everywhere she went. She embodied both charm and talent that far surpassed Miranda's own fame in its prime.

Despite the sting of jealousy that squeezed Miranda's heart, she mustered a gracious smile as they sat, one as polished and practiced as her public persona required.

"Ava, so good to see you, girl!" she said, directing her to the chair across from her with a gesture that was both welcoming and composed.

"Hey, Miri, I'm so sorry I'm late!" Ava exclaimed as she sat at the table. Her voice was like a cheerful melody that seemed to make even mundane social apologies sound delightful.

"Don't worry about it, Ava," Miranda responded with a warm smile of her own that she knew was nowhere near as captivating. "I understand California traffic better than anyone." Though Miranda's smile remained steadfast, her mind raced with contrasting emotions.

Ava set her bags beside her, immediately drawing the attention of their server, who hurried over to take her order. His approach was noticeably more prompt than the service Miranda had received upon her own arrival. This did not go unnoticed, of course.

"So, how have you been, Ava?" Miranda asked, feigning interest in the girl's life.

Of course, this conversation was faker than pro wrestling and nearly as painful. Miranda had her part to play, and Ava knew she did as well. They both understood the way the game worked. "I see you've been busy shopping." Miranda gestured toward the bags with a lightness she barely felt, steering the conversation into safe, neutral territory.

Ava's laugh was light and genuine, with practiced poise. Miranda noted how every time Ava moved, it was into another photogenic pose. The girl was good. She knew every phone was out and pointed at them, and she was going to ensure that any photo of her that appeared in the tabloids and gossip blogs would be stunning.

"Yes, a bit of retail therapy never hurts," Ava said, offering up a reply that was little more than empty words with no real substance behind them. "But tell me about you, Miri. How are things?"

Miranda appreciated the diversion from heavier thoughts, mirroring Ava's poses to make for more balanced photos. Spouting out empty platitudes in a public setting like this was just the distraction she needed.

"Oh, you know, the usual whirlwind. Keeping busy," she responded, her tone breezy and carefully controlled.

Like most good Hollywood banter, that was partly true, albeit empty. She wasn't about to sit there with this girl and delve into the deeper currents of her life. God forbid someone heard them. Cameras were becoming more and more sensitive with each passing year.

Miranda had always performed the dance of Hollywood well. She had long ago mastered the never-ending façade, the smile that didn't quite reach the eyes, the carefully neutral comments. It was a game of chess where every word could be a move, every silence a strategy. As she sat across from Ava, she was reminded why one must always guard their secrets closely in this glittering, treacherous world.

In her early days, Miranda had been schooled in the harsh realities of the industry. Every performer was in competition. That meant all alliances were temporary, and friendships often had ulterior motives. Sometimes, they would deteriorate into feuds. Seeing Ava in that same position, young and radiant, a reflection of what she once was, Miranda couldn't help but feel both a pang of nostalgia and a surge of caution.

Miranda sensed an opportunity to shift the focus away from herself and leaned in slightly, her voice casual yet tinged with genuine concern.

"So, Ava, how have you been holding up?" she asked, the question mundane and repetitive. But they had to fill the time somehow. "Everything going smoothly?"

To Miranda's surprise, Ava's smile faltered for just a moment. It was a crack in her otherwise flawless façade.

"Oh, everything's great, really," Ava said, her polished, plastic smile spreading back over her face instantly. But she had broken and let the real person out for a brief second. A major rookie mistake in such a setting. Miranda was starting to think Ava might not have been as skilled as she'd given her credit for. "Just staying super busy," she continued, her voice a bit too cheerful as she overcompensated for the lapse in her decorum.

Miranda's eyes narrowed slightly, adept at catching the subtle signs of discomfort in others. Hollywood protocol would be to ignore this and continue as though nothing had happened. But Miranda couldn't help but feel oddly…curious.

"You seem a bit off," she said, her own smile fading into a serious expression of concern. "Is there something wrong?" She made sure to prod gently, keeping her tone light so as not to indicate that anything might be the matter to anyone else in the establishment.

Ava winced, a slight flinch that she quickly masked by adjusting her sunglasses. It was a telltale sign that Miranda had struck a nerve.

"It's nothing, really," Ava insisted, brushing off the concern with a wave of her hand. "Just the usual craziness, you know?"

Miranda nodded, giving Ava a moment to compose herself and put her walls back up. Miranda chided herself for breaking the unwritten rule and trying to get real there for a moment. But she felt she needed to follow all of this up with one of those meaningless platitudes that all too often get tossed around in such situations.

"I understand," she said with a knowing smile and a nod. "But remember, if you ever need to unload or just take a break from the craziness, I'm here. No judgment, just support."

Ava paused, looking at Miranda with a mixture of appreciation and relief as she removed her sunglasses. There was a look of genuine surprise on Ava's face as she studied the woman in front of her. Miranda thought she saw a little apprehension in the girl's eyes, as though she were considering letting down her guard.

"Thanks, Miranda," she said slowly. "That means a lot, especially coming from someone who understands the pressure."

Miranda sipped her tea, watching Ava carefully across the table. The café buzzed softly around them, a cocoon of clinking glasses and conversation. Miranda put that plastic smile back on her face and tried to move the faux conversation along as best she could.

"So, how are things going with Chase?" she inquired, her tone casual but eyes sharp. It seemed a logical next topic.

Chase and Ava were Hollywood's current *it* couple, though everyone in the industry knew that Chase's celebrity had dwindled to the point where his fame stemmed more from being Ava's husband than from his action movie roles.

Miranda had never been particularly fond of Chase. He was polite, sure, and had the charm typical of someone in his line of work, but he reminded her too much of Nolan.

What was more, he practically worshipped the ground the bastard had walked on. His admiration for Nolan had been evident from the moment they had met. He had started asking her questions about her late husband that bordered on fanatical obsession.

It certainly wasn't Miranda's favorite subject, and it had soured her early on Ava's husband.

But still, she expected Ava to smile and laugh and say that things between them were wonderful. That was the proper response one gave in these situations.

But upon her mention of Chase, she noticed Ava's smile falter. The younger woman's gaze dropped to the table, shadowed by a flicker of discomfort. Ava reached for the teapot, perhaps more out of a need for something to do with her hands than an actual desire for tea. She poured herself a cup, and the liquid's steam curled like a smokescreen between them.

"Things are fine," she said tersely, taking a sip.

Her tone, however, betrayed her words, hinting at underlying tensions that Miranda couldn't ignore. How bad could it have been to break through Ava's façade several times now? Convention dictated that Miranda take the answer at face value and move on, but there was something in the way she had said those words that unnerved her.

Perhaps it was because Chase had reminded her so much of Nolan, but Miranda felt her heart go out to the blonde starlet at that moment. She remembered back when she was in the grip of a hellish marriage, how she wished she'd had someone older and more experienced to offer her guidance. And though every fiber of her being told her to leave it alone and stick to the typical Hollywood banter, Miranda felt as though she couldn't let it go.

She leaned in, lowering her voice to the point where no one save for Ava could hear her. "Is everything all right at home?" she probed gently. She dropped her smile completely and gave Ava a serious look, trying to convey that she was being real here, outside the Hollywood game.

A single tear escaped Ava's eye, tracing a path down her cheek. She reached up quickly to wipe it away, her face flushing red with embarrassment. The moment hung between them, charged and revealing. Ava's usual poise was shaken, hinting at troubles far deeper than mere scheduling conflicts or typical marital spats.

Ava cleared her throat, setting the teacup down with a little too much force. "It's just been a bit rough lately," she admitted, her voice barely above a whisper. "Chase... he's struggling with the changes in his career. It's... putting a strain on us."

Miranda nodded sympathetically. She understood all too well how the pressures of this town could seep into personal lives, turning private sanctuaries into battlegrounds. She also understood how fragile the egos of some could be, especially alpha types like Chase and Nolan. Nolan's insecurities had been at the heart of every issue they'd had as a couple.

"This industry can be cruel," Miranda murmured. "It changes so fast, and if you don't keep up, it can leave you behind. It must be tough for him—and for you—being in the spotlight together."

Ava sighed, looking out the window, as if searching for answers in the bustling street.

"Yeah," she said with a nod. "It's like... I want to help him, but sometimes, I feel like anything I do just makes it worse. He feels like he's in my shadow, and I don't know how to fix it."

"Has he gotten violent?" Miranda asked seriously, reaching out to touch Ava's hand.

Ava sharply pulled her fingers away at this and shook her head. "No," she said quickly and with assurance. "God, no. Nothing like that. He'd never do something like that. He's a big guy, but he's a gentle giant. He's a sweetheart. He'd never, ever raise his hand to me. That's just not in his nature.

"But he's depressed. Like he won't shower or shave. He can't get off the couch. He's getting snippy with every little thing I say. He has no drive to do anything. I've been trying to do something to get us back on track, but it's just not happening."

Miranda nodded. Ava's issues were a lot different from the ones she personally had experienced, but they were still issues, nonetheless. However, now Miranda felt silly for pressing.

Miranda reached across the table again, placing a reassuring hand over Ava's. She didn't pull away this time.

"You're doing your best, Ava," Miranda said kindly. "Sometimes, that's all you can do. Maybe he needs to find his own path again, something that gives him purpose."

Ava met Miranda's gaze, her eyes reflecting gratitude for the understanding. "Thanks, Miri," she said with a relieved sigh. It was such a real untethered moment that seemed so wildly out of place in this town. "It means a lot to have someone to talk to who… you know, gets it."

Miranda laughed, a sound rich with the wisdom of someone who had navigated Hollywood's choppy waters for years. "Believe me, girl, I practically invented troubled Hollywood relationships," Miranda said, laughing to hide the discomfort she was feeling at the memories this conversation was digging up. But unlike Ava, she wasn't going to let that shine through. She'd buried this baggage too deep for far too long to slip up now.

And so, Miranda kept her tone light, but her eyes showed a depth of understanding and kindness, which she felt Ava needed right now.

Ava offered a sad smile, her demeanor so wildly different from the beaming Barbie doll who had first walked in here. Miranda wondered now whether people were still snapping photos. She hoped that Ava would remember what they were there for and not start full-on crying at the table or something.

"It seems just about anything these days drives us further apart," Ava said with a sad shrug. "It's movie premieres, the damn paparazzi, even our home." That last word hung heavy with meaning.

Miranda seized on it. "What's wrong with your home?" she inquired; her interest piqued.

"It was originally mine," Ava explained, stirring her tea absentmindedly. "I had it built specifically with my style and preferences, you know? Chase feels like he's just a guest there.

Like it's not really his home. He isn't a part of it in his mind. And, like, I guess I understand why he might feel that way." Ava sighed with frustration. "I've even considered remodeling it completely to make him feel more at home. But I'm just not sure where to start."

Miranda suddenly saw a golden opportunity. An opportunity not just to offer advice but to possibly resolve both Ava's issue and her own.

"Well," she said slowly, wading gradually through the waters she sought to lead Ava into. "Maybe instead of remodeling, you should consider finding a new home together? You know, one that reflects both of you from the start?"

She tried to make the suggestion sound organic and thoughtful. The last thing she wanted was for Ava to see what was going to come next as opportunistic.

Ava nodded, though her face didn't change. It was clear that this was something she already considered. "I've thought about that, actually," she admitted. "But I just don't have the time to sift through home listings right now."

Miranda could feel the burden of Ava's busy schedule in her words. She just sounded so tired. The irony of the situation was that Miranda had nothing but time on her hands lately and was desperately trying to become even half as busy as Ava was.

"Well, maybe you don't have to," Miranda responded, watching Ava's head tilt with question and interest. "As luck would have it, I was about to put Nolan's house in Beverly Hills on the market. I worked hard to make sure the home blends Nolan's more masculine style with my softer, and if I do say so myself, fashionable touch."

Ava's eyes lit up, a spark of excitement cutting through her earlier despondency. She reached across the table, taking Miranda's hand in hers as a massive smile spread across her face. This was so different from the poised, practiced, and polished smile she'd worn when she had first arrived. This was the real deal. The genuine article. This was actual joy and hope brightening the girl's face. And Miranda thought it was a thousand times lovelier than any fake Hollywood smile could ever be.

"Are you serious?" Ava asked, her voice filled with hope. However, there was still some hesitancy there, as though this might be too good to be true.

Miranda nodded, smiling warmly. She wanted to convey a helpful and inviting presence right now. One that Ava would place her trust in.

"Absolutely," Miranda said. "I was getting the house ready to be shown just this morning. It's a beautiful place, and I think it could really be a fresh start for you two."

Ava's response came quickly and enthusiastically. She practically leaped out of her seat upon hearing this. "Chase always admired Nolan," she said quickly.

Miranda, of course, knew that from her previous annoying encounters with the young man, but she pretended it was a revelation and raised her eyebrows in mock interest.

"I mean, he loves him. Practically worshipped him even. Buying his hero's house and making it our home might be just what we need to fix things!"

"Then go home and talk to Chase about it," Miranda encouraged. "If he's interested, we can start the process as early as tomorrow."

Ava stood up, gratitude written all over her face. She looked down at Miranda like she was her fairy godmother. There was so much appreciation and relief on her face that Miranda actually felt guilty. She wondered if she was using the poor girl. But she quickly told herself that wasn't the case. Both Miranda and Ava had a need. And fate just so happened to present an opportunity where those needs coincided.

"Thank you, Miranda," Ava said as Miranda rose to meet

her standing. She threw her arms around Miranda in a tight, grateful hug, completely ignoring the gawking onlookers. "I need to get home and discuss this with him right away."

The opportunity had seemed to light a fire under Ava. Her earlier weariness had been completely replaced by a newfound determination.

"Of course, I understand," Miranda said, breaking the hug and giving the girl another smile. "I'm just happy to help."

As relieved as Ava clearly was, Miranda was feeling an even more profound sense of relief. As Ava gathered her bags and hurried out of the café with another thankful outpouring and a promise to call her soon, Miranda allowed herself a small, satisfied smile.

It was possible, probable even, that she might unload Nolan's house without ever having to step a single foot inside it ever again. That was a prospect that lifted a great weight off her shoulders. Watching Ava leave, Miranda felt a complex blend of relief and anticipation.

If all went well, this could be a new beginning for Ava and Chase and a timely resolution for her own lingering ties to the past.

5

Chase stared blankly at the television screen, looking through the screen rather than at it. The rapid-fire action sequences of the movie playing before him did little to distract from the growing discontent brewing within his heart and mind.

The explosions and choreographed fights that used to thrill him now seemed like cruel reminders of a career that was slipping through his fingers. Once, these films had been an escape, a way to forget his real-world struggles. Now, they were a mirror reflecting his own stagnation.

He took a bite of a protein bar; it was as bland and unappealing as his current prospects in the film industry. He chewed slowly. The bar's chalky texture matched his mood a little too perfectly.

Despite his waning career, Chase maintained his strict diet and workout routine. He kept his muscles taut and ready for a hero's role that Hollywood no longer seemed interested in offering. He wasn't sure why he bothered. It wasn't as if the casting directors were knocking down his door anymore.

Chase's hand absentmindedly stroked his unshaven chin.

The stubble was rough and nearly long enough to be called a beard. He let out a sigh, considering the futility of keeping up appearances when it felt like no one cared anymore.

The new Hollywood heroes were a far cry from the icons he had admired. He'd grown up infatuated with larger-than-life figures like Sylvester Stallone, Arnold Schwarzenegger, The Rock, and Nolan Hillhurst in particular.

Those men were titans. Their physical prowess was always on full display, defining an era of cinema that celebrated brute strength and machismo. They had made their mark, secured their legacies. They were legends now, their stories etched in the tale of Hollywood forever. They were immortalized with stars on the Hollywood Walk of Fame, celebrated with awards and accolades, and fondly recalled by legions of fans.

Chase, however, felt like he was just getting started when the industry shifted under his feet. He'd never have his own star on the Walk of Fame. He'd never be celebrated with awards and accolades. And what few fans he did have were already starting to forget he'd ever existed.

Actions stars now were different. Hollywood had gravitated to leaner individuals who were more versatile in the kinds of vulnerability they portrayed on screen. They were ninety-five-pound women or effeminate men in skinny jeans. That painted a stark contrast to the bulging biceps and larger-than-life personas of his idols. Hollywood had changed its formula, and it had left Chase behind. He now found himself struggling to fit into this new mold. But it seemed as though the industry had no more room for the likes of him.

He glanced down at his bicep, flexing it almost instinctively. It was massive and powerful, a testament to years of rigorous training aimed at sculpting a blockbuster physique. That body was meant for high-budget action films. It was destined for roles that required a man to hold a helicopter from taking off or single-handedly dismantle a terrorist cell.

But those scripts were fading, replaced by narratives that demanded a different kind of hero—one he wasn't sure he could transform into. Nor did he want to. Chase was who he was for a reason. He had something that was utterly alien to the rest of Hollywood.

Authenticity.

He was authentically him, and he made no apologies for that. He was offended when his agent suggested he go on a major cut diet to slim down and adopt a more fluid or feminine appearance. He said at the time that if the movie industry didn't want him as he was, then it wasn't going to get him.

He'd thought he was calling Tinsel Town's bluff, assuming this action transformation was just a temporary trend that would ultimately reset itself. But he had been wrong in that regard. And because of that, because of his rigid need to be true to himself, his opportunities dried up completely.

There was still a part of Chase that was proud of himself for standing up to the system and remaining true to himself. However, that part of him seemed to shrivel and die a bit more with every empty and meaningless day that passed.

The sound of a key turning in the door snapped him out of his own head.

That meant Ava was home. Chase quickly switched off the TV, not wanting her to see him like this again. After the fight they'd had earlier that morning, he felt weird at the very idea of her finding him zoned out in front of action flicks that highlighted his failures.

He straightened up as she walked in, forcing a smile that didn't quite reach his eyes. Ava was carrying several shopping bags, but something about her seemed off. Chase couldn't put his finger on it. It was perhaps some kind of mixture of excitement and nervousness. He assumed that some new wonderful opportunity had fallen into her lap today. Just another banner day in the life of Ava Monroe, international superstar.

But at the same time, he'd been replaying their argument over and over in his head, and he felt bad about the way he'd treated her. He told himself that, for now, he needed to at least try to act engaged and interested in whatever new, wonderful thing had buzzed into Ava's life.

"Hey," he greeted her, his voice a little rough from disuse. "How was your day?"

Ava paused, setting down her bags, her eyes meeting his. She paused and swallowed, as though trying to collect her thoughts enough to form words. There was clearly something she wanted to say. And it was something important, judging by the look on her face. Chase braced himself, unsure of what was coming. However, he remained hopeful that whatever it was might bring a change to the monotony that his life had become.

Chase noticed Ava's hands twisting together, her fingers interlocking as if they were trying to find comfort in each other. He watched with gnawing anxiety taking root in his chest as he prepared for what might come next. His mind raced with the possibilities, each more unsettling than the last.

What if she had reached her limit? What if this conversation was the beginning of the end?

Despite the struggles, despite the feelings of inadequacy that often clouded his days, Chase's love for Ava remained unwavering. He knew they were at a crossroads, and the fear of losing her was palpable. He wanted to be better, wanted to shake off this shroud of depression and be the man she deserved, but it was so damn difficult. It was like a shadow pressing down on his back, pushing him into the dirt. He tried to force happiness and interest in her accomplishments, but all he could feel of late was sadness and frustration.

He silently chastised himself for not being more expressive, for not showing her every day how much she meant to him. Had he let his own insecurities damage what they had beyond repair?

His eyes briefly scanned the room, passing over the myriad of portraits and photographs that celebrated Ava's career. Everywhere he looked, there she was—radiant, successful, the very essence of what he felt he was not. Recently, Chase had realized how much he had come to define himself through her, how her world had enveloped his own. And that had caused an inescapable bitterness to take root in his heart.

But still, despite it all, he loved her more than words could express. That bright and shining love was always present, even when buried under the dark weight of his insecurity and depression. The thought of navigating life without Ava was unthinkable. She was his anchor, his north star in a sea that had grown increasingly stormy.

"What's wrong?" he managed to ask, his voice tinged with concern.

Ava looked up at him, her eyes searching his. "I want to talk to you about something," she said, her voice steady but soft.

The words were simple, yet they sent a ripple of tension through Chase. He nodded, his throat tight as he managed a strained, "Okay." His voice betrayed his inner turmoil, cracking slightly under the weight of his apprehension.

"Let's go into the great room," Ava suggested, leading the way.

Chase followed close behind. Her stride was purposeful, yet there was a gentleness to her tone that offered him a sliver of comfort.

They walked together in silence, the short journey to the great room feeling longer than usual. Once there, Ava sat down on the couch, her movements graceful yet deliberate. She patted the cushion beside her, an invitation for him to join her.

Chase took a deep breath, trying to steady his raw nerves. He swallowed hard. The action was nothing more than a futile attempt to push down the anxiety that seemed to have lodged itself in his throat. He sat beside his wife, close enough to feel the warmth radiating from her, yet emotionally, he felt miles away. He was entirely swept up in a maelstrom of his own fears and doubts.

Chase met Ava's gaze again, trying and failing to keep the apprehension off his face. His mouth had gone dry, yet his palms were sweating. He needed to break the silence between them, needed her to move on with whatever she was about to say so that he could end this horrifying uncertainty.

"What's wrong?" he asked once more, his voice low and hesitant. He was desperate for answers, yet at the same time terrified of them. His depression made him incapable of being optimistic in situations like this.

Ava took a deep breath, her palms flat against her lap in a gesture of openness. "Things between us have been rough for a while now," she started, her voice steady but her eyes not hiding the concern.

Chase couldn't find words to respond. He only nodded. It was impossible not to acknowledge the truth in her statement.

"And I know you've been going through a lot mentally," she continued, keeping her voice level and her emotions steady. "I can't help but feel that a lot of it centers around our careers and the... I guess you can say imbalance between them?"

Chase instinctively started to shake his head, even though she had hit the nail on the head. The subject of her superstardom had come up in just about every fight they'd had recently. Denying it was beyond pointless. But his refusal to admit it had been something of a reflex to shield both Ava and himself from that painful truth.

Ava seemed to know this, too, and she raised her hand to stop him. "It's kind of you to try to protect me from that reality, but I'm not blind or deaf, Chase," she said. "I see how my success is affecting you. And it's heartbreaking to witness. I don't want to upset you, baby. I love you."

Chase fell silent, simply shrugging and shaking his head slightly. He wanted to disagree, to argue that she was wrong, to convince both her and him that he was unaffected. But deep down, he knew the truth. Ava's rising star was indeed casting a shadow over him, feeding his inner turmoil and resentment.

"It's all right," Ava reassured him softly, clearly sensing his struggle. "I understand those feelings, and it's okay to feel that way. If the roles were reversed, I think I'd feel the same."

She paused, choosing her next words carefully.

"But your career isn't over, Chase," she said, sounding utterly sure of this. "These Hollywood trends come in waves. You know that." She was clearly trying to inject a note of optimism into the doldrums of his life, but he understood the reality of his situation.

Chase scoffed and shook his head at the emptiness of her statement. "By the time this wave comes back around, I'll be aged out of these roles and cast aside," he said. There was a biting edge to his voice that he hadn't intended.

Ava sighed and cast her gaze down at her lap. He could see she had a lot of empathy for his plight, but it was also clear that she was understandably frustrated with his inability to pick himself back up. Industry issues like this were out of their control, and there was nothing she could do to help in this regard.

"I can't control what Hollywood does, babe," she said simply, looking back up at him with a gentle smile replacing her momentary aggravation. "But what I can do is try to make our home life better."

Their home life. Chase looked around at the great room they were sitting in. So much of it was pink, and there were monuments to his wife everywhere. Calling it their home was a bit of a stretch.

"I know living here, in this house, hasn't been easy for you," she said gently.

Chase had made his discontent with their surroundings evident of late, so it was good that she was at least acknowledging his plight. Chase recalled his earlier conversations with Ava. He'd so often voiced his discomfort more harshly than he intended. It was a source of both misery and guilt in his life. Surrounded by the tangible proof of Ava's success while his own career floundered, he felt the weight of his grievances more acutely.

Chase sighed as he looked around the supposed shared space. "Sometimes I just feel like I'm living in your shadow," he said, keeping his voice level. It was the first time he had voiced this concern without being accusatory or angry. "It's like I'm living in a monument to your success. It hasn't been easy for me. There's just none of me represented in this house. And when my career hit the rocks… It's just a lot sometimes."

It felt good to get that out in the open without there being a major fight attached to it. He hadn't snapped these words or barked them at her. He'd simply explained himself in a calm and rational fashion. Now, rather than get defensive and snap back at him, Ava seemed to take his words in and process them in a way she hadn't before.

Ava nodded in understanding. Her eyes were patient, if a little sad. Chase hated to imagine what the reality of the situation was doing to her internally. There was probably a lot of sadness mixed with guilt and maybe more than a little bit of anger stirred in there. But she seemed to swallow all of that to move the conversation in her intended direction.

"We've got a lot of problems to get through," she admitted, shaking her head slowly.

However, that statement gave Chase hope. Saying they

needed to get through these problems meant she wasn't about to leave him.

"I think the best way we can move forward together is by choosing one problem to solve first. If we try to fix everything at once, we'll fail."

Chase nodded in agreement. What she was saying certainly made logical sense. Chase exhaled in relief as he listened to Ava. His muscles had been so tight with the anticipation of a different kind of conversation since she had gotten home. Now, they began to relax slightly. This wasn't a lead-up to a divorce. It was a pathway to a solution. Chase was more than willing to explore any potential solutions Ava might suggest. Though his mind had lately been a dark pit of despair, the prospect of a tangible, approachable goal offered a glimmer of light.

"The biggest problem right now with our home life is our home," Ava continued, gesturing around the opulent room that so clearly bore her signature style. "Maybe it was selfish of me to expect you to just live here. This was always my house, built for my life before we were married."

Chase watched her closely, noting the earnestness in her expression and feeling the weight of her words. Ava was acknowledging something significant, something he had been trying to make her see for weeks now.

"I think we should find a new home together," Ava proposed. "One where we can both be happy. A place that feels like *ours*, not just mine or yours."

Chase blinked in surprise. She had offered to redecorate this house before, but Chase had always refused. For some reason, the very thought of that made him uncomfortable. It was like he was changing her in some way if he agreed to that. But a fresh start, a new home for them both that they could design and live in together… That was more than just a generous offer; it was a necessary step if they were going to salvage what they had built as a couple.

He took a deep breath, the decision settling in his mind. "I'd be willing to talk about moving," he said slowly, "if we can find a place that we both like." He gave her a smile that was only half of what he actually felt. He was overjoyed in his heart, but he didn't want to seem overly eager. He knew that leaving this house wasn't going to be easy for Ava, and he wanted to be delicate about how he handled the scenario.

Ava's face brightened with a radiant smile. The very same smile he'd fallen in love with many years ago.

"That means a lot to me, Chase," she said, clearly relieved that he was willing to do this with her. "I know it's not easy, but I really think it's the right step for us. And I actually already have a place in mind that I think you'll really like."

Ava's face was full of optimism, but Chase felt his heart sink at her words. Despite her assurances of partnership, it felt like just another one of her decisions. Her choosing the house they'd move to without his input felt like yet another Ava Monroe decision that was being made *for* him rather than *with* him. He couldn't shake the feeling that this would be yet another posh manor crafted to suit Ava's tastes, leaving little room for anything of his.

That would be like rearranging deck chairs on the Titanic. Nothing more than superficial changes that ultimately signified nothing.

Ava's eyes widened as she caught the clear flicker of resistance on his face. "Just hear me out, okay?" she said, holding her hands up defensively to cut off any resistance he might give. "If you don't like the idea, then we can find something together when we have the time."

She paused, clearly gauging his reaction before continuing. Chase softened his expression and gave her a simple nod, urging her to continue.

"I had tea with Miranda Sterling today," she said simply.

The name immediately struck a chord with Chase. Miranda Sterling was the widow of Nolan Hillhurst, the man whose films had fueled his dreams of becoming an actor.

He had met Miranda once, at a film premiere he could barely remember now. Star-struck, he had bombarded her with questions about her late husband, oblivious at the time to how his enthusiasm might be received. She had responded politely enough, but even then, he could sense her discomfort. She'd taken the first opportunity to make a subtle withdrawal masked by courteous smiles.

Chase's initial resistance waned slightly, replaced by a flicker of curiosity. Miranda Sterling was connected to the very world he had once longed to conquer, a world that had inspired his career aspirations.

Ava's eyes met Chase's with an unwavering earnestness as she continued. "Miranda is selling Nolan Hillhurst's old mansion in Beverly Hills," she revealed, her voice excited.

It was the kind of excitement a parent might convey when telling their children they're going to Disney World. Chase held his breath at this news. Was this truly going where he thought it was going?

"It's still just as he left it. The house was designed with a full gym, a lap pool, and just about everything someone into fitness could want."

Chase blinked, his mind struggling to process the information. The room felt as though it were spinning around him. Nolan Hillhurst had been his hero. Meeting the man had been one of the great dreams of his life. Of course, those dreams had been dashed five years ago when an untimely heart attack had put him in the ground. But the possibility of living in Nolan's house, walking the same halls—maybe even restoring some of the greatness the mansion had witnessed—was overwhelming to him.

Ava watched him closely, noticing his silence and the astonishment flickering across his face. "Are you okay?" she asked gently, a note of concern threading through her words.

Chase stammered, his thoughts scrambling to align. At first, all he could manage was a subtle shake of his head. He was utterly unable to find the right words to convey the emotions coursing through his veins. "Are you sure about this?" he finally managed to ask, his voice hoarse with the burden of raw emotion.

"Yes, I am," Ava replied firmly, his face never wavering for a second. "But it's not just about moving there. We can rework the space together, turn it into a place that we both can be happy to call home."

The gravity of her gesture, the depth of her understanding, struck Chase profoundly. Here was Ava, ready to step into a new chapter with him, in a place that held so much personal significance. It wasn't just about relocating. It was about rebuilding, about sharing a part of himself that he'd felt was dead and decaying until this moment.

A laugh, genuine and relieved, escaped him in a smile. It was the first true, sincere smile he'd shown in weeks. The feeling of his lips spreading up his cheeks practically felt alien as the light of hope and happiness tore through the shroud of his crushing despair.

"Well?" Ava asked, mirroring his smile now as well but waiting for some kind of verbal confirmation.

Chase didn't respond verbally. He was too overwhelmed. Instead, he leaned in, closing the distance between them, and kissed Ava deeply. Her initial surprise quickly gave way to a warm embrace. Her arms slowly snaked up his chest to wrap around his neck as she returned his kiss with equal fervor.

At that moment, the weight of the past months seemed to have lifted. The shadows of doubt and insecurity dissipated under the bright promise of new beginnings. Chase felt a resurgence of hope, a rejuvenation of his spirit as he considered the possibilities that lay ahead. This wasn't just about moving houses. It was about so much more. It was reclaiming a sense of purpose, embracing a future where both their dreams could find room to flourish.

Ava's response to his kiss, her arms securing him in an embrace, reaffirmed their connection. There in the quiet of their current home, amidst talks of moving, they found a moment of profound recoupling. It was a special reminder of the strength of their bond. They were once more ready to face whatever challenges and transformations lay ahead.

Chase felt butterflies in his stomach, and his heart fluttered as they kissed. It was the kind of electric, love-filled kiss they hadn't experienced together in many months. As they separated, Chase realized this renewed sense of connection stemmed from a newfound hope for their future. This incredible gesture Ava had made for him ignited feelings he needed to meet with the enthusiasm and gratitude they deserved.

As they pulled apart, there was a moment of silence where they simply looked into each other's eyes. There was a quiet intensity in their conjoined stares, and Chase felt a part of himself wake up that he thought was long since gone. He suddenly became keenly aware of his unkempt appearance, having not showered or shaved in quite some time, and felt a wave of embarrassment.

"Wow, that was nice," Ava remarked, breaking the silence with a gentle smile and a hand on his chest over his heart.

Chase nodded, trying to search for the right words to convey what he was feeling. "I'm sorry for the way I've been," he said, frowning and averting his gaze out of shame. "I just felt so alone in all of this."

Ava slid her hand along his chest until she was touching his arm softly. "A lot of that is my fault," she admitted. "I promise to do better and to consider your feelings more in the future."

Chase smiled and gave a small laugh with a shrug. "You're already off to a hell of a start in that department," he replied, his tone lightening.

"This could be a new beginning for us. A fresh start," Ava suggested, her eyes bright with hope.

Chase agreed, and a mischievous look crossed his face. Suddenly, he felt a deep desire for his wife, for her closeness and affection. "How about we take this little reconciliation upstairs to the bedroom?" he proposed, his voice low and an eyebrow raised provocatively.

Ava's smile turned coy, and she scooted back on the sofa, appraising him playfully. "I would love that," she responded, biting her lip and looking him up and down.

He leaned in again, and she stopped him with a delicate, pale hand on his chest.

"After you take a shower."

Chase laughed, the sound hearty and genuine. It almost felt strange to feel the genuine laughter pushing out through his throat.

He grabbed his wife's hand, kissed it lightly, and headed toward the bathroom. He felt energized by the promise of not just a renewed relationship but a renewed life together. As he walked away, he glanced back at Ava. She watched him with an affectionate gaze that reassured him they were finally on the right path.

6

Two days later, Ava sat comfortably in the passenger seat of Chase's sleek black Corvette as they approached the grand gates of a massive Beverly Hills estate. The morning sun gleamed off the polished car as they neared the entrance. A heavy, barred gate swung open automatically at their approach, welcoming them to their potential new home.

Beyond the gate lay a stunning white mansion sprawling across well-manicured grounds. Despite the fact that no one had lived here for five years, it seemed as though Miranda had been dutiful in ensuring the property was maintained. This was more than just someone getting a property ready for sale. It looked lived-in and warm.

The only word Ava could use to describe it was inviting, as though the grounds of the manor itself were beckoning them closer.

As they drove up, the sheer breadth of the mansion came into view. The front façade boasted a rounded porch with majestic white columns that stretched up to frame the majestic entryway. Everything about the architecture of this façade spoke of opulence and grandeur.

Chase gave a low whistle, clearly impressed. He sat beside her in the driver's seat, his hair once more perfectly in place, his face shorn of any unsightly stubble. He looked like her husband again, and that, above all else, had thrilled her. The promise that this new home represented seemed to wake up something in her man, and he was once more the doting, protective, and attentive husband who had captured her heart so long ago.

"It's a lot bigger than even our old place," Ava commented, her eyes wide as she took in the sight.

Chase nodded, his gaze fixed on the mansion as he shifted the car into park. "Nolan Hillhurst's motto had always been that bigger was better and stronger was best," he remarked, a hint of awe in his voice. "He applied that to everything from his muscles to his cars. Apparently, that included his home, too."

Ava noticed they had been parked in front of the entrance to the grand home for nearly two whole minutes. It was almost as if Chase was reluctant or too awestruck to move forward. She touched his arm gently.

"We can go in, you know," she said, her tone teasing and playful.

Snapping out of his daze with a jolt, Chase looked over at Ava and flashed an embarrassed smile. "Sorry," he said, chuckling at himself as he slowly undid his seatbelt.

"Don't apologize," Ava replied, her voice light and playful. "It's cute that even after all this time in Hollywood, you still get starstruck."

Chase laughed, a sound filled with genuine amusement. He seemed momentarily at a loss for words. His usual confident demeanor was replaced by a childlike wonder. This was a side of him that Ava found endearing. It was something she rarely saw anymore.

As Chase opened the driver's side door, the enormity of the building loomed over them. Its white façade was gleaming in the California sun, welcoming them into what could potentially be their new home.

Ava opened her own door and climbed out into the warmth of another stunning California afternoon. She scanned the area for any sign of Miranda, but there was no trace of her. Instead, parked prominently in front of the mansion was a high-end Tesla, which struck Ava as odd.

She knew Miranda preferred the carefree style of a convertible, the type of car that allowed her to feel the wind in her hair. The absence of such a vehicle piqued her curiosity—where was Miranda?

As they stood, pondering this, the grand doors of the estate swung open. To Ava's surprise, it wasn't Miranda who greeted them but her agent, Lenny. He was standing on the porch with a welcoming smile and a wave for the two of them.

Chase groaned as he rounded the car to stand beside her, his tone laden with annoyance. "What the hell is he doing here?" he muttered under his breath.

Ava frowned slightly at Chase's reaction. She knew all too well that Chase had never liked Lenny. He viewed him as nothing more than a snake in the grass, an opportunist lurking beneath a veneer of charm. But that was what a Hollywood agent was supposed to be. She was far more accepting of the little concessions they needed to make to exist in Hollywood than her husband was.

Over the years, Ava had often defended Lenny, reminding Chase that as a Hollywood agent, pushing boundaries was part of his job description.

"Remember, he's Miranda's agent, too, and he was Nolan's,"

Ava reminded him quietly. She hoped that would ease some of his tension.

Chase only shrugged, a gesture of resignation. They both stepped away from the car to meet Lenny's enthusiastic greeting.

"Welcome to your new home!" Lenny exclaimed, his arms spread wide in a grand gesture. Of course, his smile was mostly directed toward Ava.

She wasn't surprised at all by Lenny's overt display of attention to her and not Chase. After all, she was his biggest current client, and he never missed an opportunity to try to impress her. However, she hoped today would be different. This visit needed to be about both her and Chase, not just her career or desires.

"Lenny, I'm surprised to see you here," she said, raising her eyebrows but keeping her tone warm.

"Oh, when I heard you were coming to tour this grand place, I told Miranda I just had to be here to help," Lenny replied, stepping toward her and leaning in to kiss her on each cheek, European-style.

He then turned to Chase in a more subdued tone. "Hello there." And he extended his hand.

"Hi," Chase replied simply, reaching out to shake Lenny's hand.

His grip was noticeably firm, and Ava caught the slight grimace on Lenny's face. She knew instantly that Chase had applied a bit more pressure than necessary.

She shot Chase a look that silently conveyed, "Play nice."

As Lenny recovered from the handshake, Ava took in the enormity and grandeur that surrounded her. It made her own not-at-all-modest home seem like a fixer-upper. But she wondered if the astonishment and wonder she was feeling was all because of the house itself or something else entirely.

This house, this moment, represented a potentially new

chapter for her and Chase. It was a chapter that could either revive their spirits or confirm their fears. Lenny's presence added an unexpected layer to the day's proceedings, reminding her once again of the complexities of life in Hollywood. It felt like her career was nudging its way into this highly personal moment for her and her husband. But this was a place where personal and professional boundaries often blurred, she reminded herself.

Ava's eyes scanned the surroundings, still processing the absence of their expected host. "Where's Miranda?" she asked innocently. "I thought she was joining us for the tour." There was a hint of disappointment in her voice, which Ava realized might potentially offend her agent. She quickly followed up with an explanation for her reaction. "I totally wasn't expecting to see you here, Lenny."

Lenny nodded, understanding her confusion, and playfully clutched at his chest. "Oh, are you disappointed to see me instead?" he joked, keeping his tone light and artificial.

Ava smiled politely and shook her head, letting her own fake Hollywood smile spread along her cheeks. "I could never be disappointed to see you, Lenny," she responded. Her tone was warm yet diplomatic. The perfect Hollywood response.

Beside her, Chase gave a low growl, barely audible, which fortunately went unnoticed by Lenny. Ava resisted the urge to give him a soft elbow in the ribs.

Lenny chuckled and nodded. "Miranda was called away at the last minute for a big lunch with a producer," he said apologetically. "It could be a huge audition for her, but she didn't want to cancel on you guys. So, I offered to come instead." He flashed a charismatic grin. "She didn't have to twist my arm to spend time with my favorite client. And by being here, I get to help two of my top talents at the same time. It was a no-brainer."

Chase crossed his arms over his broad chest, his skepticism

palpable. He raised an eyebrow curiously. "Isn't it a bit weird for a Hollywood agent to be playing real estate agent?" he remarked, his tone edged with suspicion.

Lenny responded with a dismissive laugh and a wave of his hand as though trying to brush Chase's words out of the air. "All kinds of agents are interchangeable, you know?" He gave Chase a wink and a smile that failed to land as intended. Ava was quick to note the slight tension it left hanging in the air.

Eager to move past the awkwardness, Ava decided it was time for her to interject. "Can we see the house now, Lenny?" she asked. Her voice was laced with enthusiasm. Ending the casual chit-chat and reminding Chase of the reason for their visit was sure to steer the visit back on track.

Lenny's demeanor shifted. He suddenly became very animated. His passion for the sale was apparent as he addressed the two of them, gesturing broadly at their new potential home. "This is the kind of home that comes around once in a lifetime," he proclaimed, his sweeping arm gesture only becoming more grand with each second. "Nolan put as much care and thought into sculpting the perfect home as he did in sculpting his perfect body."

Lenny gestured for the couple to follow him as he led the way enthusiastically. His steps were quick and sure as he approached the expansive front door.

"You'll see," he assured them. "It's more than just a house. It's a masterpiece, much like Nolan himself was."

Ava was relieved to see a small smile on Chase's lips at hearing so much positivity around his childhood hero. She hoped Lenny would keep up the Nolan praise. Chase's love of Nolan Hillhurst was certainly enough to overpower his dislike of Lenny Silvermane.

With a flourish, Lenny opened the door, inviting Ava and Chase to step inside. As they crossed the threshold, they were greeted by an impressive foyer that echoed the grandeur of the exterior. The house's interior was a testament to Nolan Hillhurst's larger-than-life persona, with high ceilings, expansive windows, and an open layout that promised both luxury and comfort.

As they followed Lenny into the heart of the mansion, Ava took in every detail. Her mind was racing with possibilities. Every corner held potential, every wall a blank canvas on which they could paint the story of their lives. Could this house transform from a symbol of someone else's legacy into a home where she and Chase could rebuild their lives together?

Lenny's enthusiasm was palpable as he spread his arms wide, akin to a showman unveiling some grand wonder of the world. "This was more than Nolan's home," he proclaimed, no longer focusing on Ava. He was now speaking directly to Chase.

He wondered if that was something Miranda had instructed him to do. She knew of Chase's love for Nolan and his legacy. Perhaps it was a sales tactic. Sell Chase on the home first to ensure the sale goes through. As far as tactics went, it was a pretty good one, Ava had to admit.

"It was his castle, his fortress, his place of power, his paradise." Lenny gestured around them with a flourish of his left arm. "Every inch of this place was designed with comfort and functionality in mind. The entire home is wired for smart technology—it's like living in Tony Stark's mansion from *Iron Man*."

Ava laughed at the comparison, amused by Lenny's dramatic presentation. She looked over at Chase, expecting him to share in the amusement, but he wasn't laughing. Instead, he was marveling at the vastness of the space, his eyes wide with awe. She wasn't sure he'd actually heard anything Lenny said to him. She knew from the look in his eyes that his mind was already made up. The rest was simple playacting.

"Come on, follow me," Lenny urged, leading them through the grand foyer toward a massive media room.

The room featured a sunken seating area with a luxurious couch positioned in front of an entertainment center so large it nearly took up the entire wall.

Chase, still caught up in his initial awe, asked his first question. "Does all of this come with the house?" he asked.

Lenny nodded enthusiastically. "It does," the eager agent replied. "Miranda wanted you to be able to get the full experience of this home and what it represents."

Ava opened her mouth to respond, a flicker of trepidation crossing her face. She wasn't sure she wanted all this stuff. She had hoped they could select their own furnishings and decorations together. Something that would truly make the space their own. But before she could voice her concerns, Chase interjected.

"I love it all," he said. "I want it all."

His enthusiasm swallowed up Ava's objections before they even left her mouth. He was so excited; she didn't want to rain on that parade. It was a topic of conversation they could broach later together.

"That's the spirit," Lenny said, patting Chase on the back.

It was a testament to how excited Chase was that he didn't recoil or react in any way to Lenny's touch.

Their tour continued to an adjacent game room, which boasted pool tables, air hockey tables, and arcade game cabinets lining the walls. The room was the epitome of a macho boy's dream, complete with neon lights and vintage movie posters. It was very much in line with what someone might expect from a Hollywood action star's retreat.

Ava felt a twinge of discomfort. The space was impressive, undoubtedly, but it was also clearly tailored to a specific taste. One that didn't quite match hers in any way. Miranda had said she put effort into making this place a blend of both her and

Nolan, but Ava had yet to see anything that represented Miranda whatsoever. She bit her lip, holding back her initial reaction. She didn't want to dampen Chase's excitement. This enthusiasm was something she hadn't seen in a long time, and she cherished it, despite her reservations.

As they moved from room to room, Ava remained quiet, trailing behind the two men. The more she saw, the more her emotions began to collide with one another in her mind. She loved seeing Chase so animated, so full of life. It was a side of him that had been subdued for too long, something she'd been desperate to get back. Yet, she couldn't shake the feeling that this house, magnificent as it was, might be too much a reflection of someone else's dreams and not enough of the shared vision they had agreed was their goal.

But the decision didn't need to be made today. And perhaps, with a little time and discussion, they could find a way to make this grand house feel like a home they both loved.

As Lenny enthusiastically began detailing the high-tech features of the kitchen, Chase's interest visibly piqued. He listed off gadgets like a smart refrigerator that could track food expiration dates and suggest recipes and food scales integrated directly into the countertops. This was ideal for someone as meticulous about nutrition as Chase.

Ava listened, trying to share his enthusiasm, but inwardly, she hoped there would be aspects of the kitchen that she could appreciate, too. It seemed once again that this space was tailored to Chase's preferences, and she felt left out.

As they approached the kitchen door, Ava's attention was suddenly diverted. Out of the corner of her eye, she thought she saw a blur of white darting around the corner of a distant hallway. Lenny and Chase were caught up in a discussion about meal prep efficiencies enabled by the kitchen's technology and didn't notice her pause.

Curious and a bit cautious, Ava slowly walked toward the

hallway, toward the source of that strange movement. What was it? Had some kind of animal made its way inside? The very idea of encountering an animal in the house was not particularly appealing, especially if it was some wild, feral, diseased creature.

As she neared the wall to peer around the corner, she instinctively placed her hand against it for balance. To her surprise, the wall felt unusually warm, almost like the skin of a living creature. Startled, she quickly withdrew her hand.

"What the hell?" Ava murmured to herself, trying to shake off the eerie feeling. With a hesitant sniffle, she reached out again, touching the wall more deliberately this time. It felt normal now, cool and solid under her touch. She laughed quietly at herself, attributing the sensation to her nerves, which were on edge from the overwhelming day and the unexpected setting of the house.

Turning her attention back to the corner, Ava cautiously looked around the wall. She was half-expecting to see a small animal, like a squirrel or raccoon, tucked away in a nook. However, there was nothing. Just an empty hallway stretching back toward other parts of the mansion.

Feeling a bit foolish—and relieved that neither Lenny nor Chase had witnessed her momentary fright—Ava shook her head and decided to rejoin them. As she walked back to the kitchen, Ava couldn't help but feel a mixture of excitement and unease. The house was impressive, certainly, but it was also beginning to feel a little too alive. It was, perhaps, a little too filled with the lingering essence of its previous owner.

She pushed those thoughts aside and stepped back into the kitchen, ready to focus on the positive aspects and the potential new start this place might offer them.

Upon her return, she found Chase and Lenny deeply engrossed in their conversation about the room's features. Chase had seemingly forgotten his utter distaste for the man who piloted Ava's successful career in all the excitement the house represented for him.

They hadn't noticed her absence, which left her feeling relieved that they hadn't seen her searching for animals and weirdly rubbing her hands along the walls. Yet she was also slightly put off by it. She felt invisible, as if her thoughts and feelings were secondary to the decision-making process.

Chase was peering into the refrigerator, marveling at its size. "I could fit weeks' worth of meals in here," he remarked with genuine enthusiasm.

Ava watched him with affection that was more than a little stained by her concern. She didn't have the heart to suggest they might choose their own appliances. How could she when he was this animated, this engaged?

They had reconnected so deeply the night before, their intimacy rekindled to a degree that reminded her of their early days. It felt the way it had when their relationship was fresh and every moment together was charged with passion and promise. She didn't want to lose that. She had a taste of it again, and she wasn't willing to let go. So, she closed her mouth and let her husband continue to gawk at every gadget and doodad in the space.

As the tour continued, they moved through the sprawling mansion, visiting each bedroom, the gym, the pool, the pool house, and the lush grounds. Every room they entered seemed to fuel Chase's excitement, and Ava found herself eventually swept up in his enthusiasm. Her earlier apprehensions were momentarily forgotten as she felt an empathetic joy at her husband's excitement.

However, as the tour wound down and they stood once more in the foyer, Chase posed a question to Lenny that sent a shiver down Ava's spine.

"Is it true that Nolan died in this house?" he asked, his eyes wide with curiosity.

Ava nearly jumped out of her skin at that, her eyes suddenly gazing around the room in horror as if she were about to stumble upon a dead body.

Lenny's expression sobered, and he gave a slow nod. "Yes," he admitted, his voice tinged with regret. "Poor Nolan suffered a heart attack right here in this foyer. It happened while Miranda was away visiting her parents. A tragic end, really. His heart had been weakened by years of steroid and recreational drug use. It's a real cautionary tale."

Ava felt a cold dread settle over her as she looked down at the foyer floor, half expecting to see a ghostly imprint of the action star who had once dominated the silver screen. She raised her eyes to Chase, hoping her expression would convey her discomfort with this grim piece of history.

But Chase's face showed only a confident excitement, untouched by the house's macabre past. "We'll take it," he said decisively to Lenny, then turned to Ava, his eyes seeking confirmation. "Won't we?"

Ava gaped open-mouthed, caught in a moment of deep conflict. She paused before offering any kind of answer. Her gaze swept from Chase to Lenny and ultimately to the floor where Nolan had died.

It felt like a weight was pressing down on her. It was a foreboding sense of anxiety urging her to flee from the house, to escape the shadows that clung to the ornate walls of the mansion. But then she looked into Chase's eyes, seeing a plea for affirmation. She couldn't deny him. She couldn't open this door for him and then slam it shut in his face just as his hopes reached their apex point.

Telling herself that her fears were just nerves, a natural reaction to such a significant change, Ava nodded slowly. "Yes," her voice slightly trembled as she spoke, reaffirming their decision to Lenny.

She tried to smile, but she couldn't stop her lips from shaking. However, neither Chase nor Lenny seemed to notice.

"We'll take it."

As they finalized the details, Ava tried to stifle the nagging doubts that whispered of misgivings, choosing instead to focus on the possibility that this house, fraught with history, might somehow become the sanctuary they needed to forge a brighter future together.

7

Miranda lounged by her pool, reclining in a comfortable chair and watching as the sunlight danced along the water. She took a deep breath, feeling the sun's warmth on her skin. The serene atmosphere of her backyard oasis was almost enough to calm the storm cloud of thoughts raging in her mind.

She thought back to her lunch with Ava from the previous day. The poor thing had been so distraught, so clearly upset, that Miranda couldn't help but feel a pang of sympathy. But now, as she replayed the conversation in her mind, she wondered if jumping in to offer up the house had been somewhat self-serving. After all, she was exploiting someone's personal misery for her own gain.

Miranda knew she was getting what she wanted out of the deal. She'd never have to see, step into, or be anywhere near the last remnant of Nolan left on this planet. The mansion had been a constant, painful reminder of her late husband, a symbol of their tumultuous past and his tragic end. Letting go of it meant severing the final tie that bound her to that chapter of her life.

A twinge of guilt crept in, a whisper of doubt that maybe she had been too quick to leverage Ava's vulnerability for her own benefit. But she brushed it aside quickly. She reminded herself that her actions were justified. Sure, she had gotten what she wanted, but it was also a viable solution to Ava's problem at the same time. If anything, she had done something truly good and helped someone who was, in a way, a friend.

Ava needed a new beginning, a fresh start away from the shadow of her current home and the strain it placed on her marriage. Miranda's offer had provided that opportunity. If she also benefited from it, then that was just a cherry on top. Miranda, too, needed a new beginning and a fresh start. It just so happened that their fresh starts fed off one another.

It wasn't predatory. It was symbiosis. It was mutually beneficial. It had been the right thing to do.

Miranda closed her eyes, letting the sounds of the water and the warmth of the sun soothe her. The deal was practically done, and soon, Nolan's mansion would be out of her life for good. She would finally be free from the lingering remnant of Nolan's presence, and that was something worth celebrating.

She reached for her glass of iced tea, savoring the cold, refreshing taste. As she sipped, she thought about how she would move forward. The sale of the mansion was a significant step, but there were still other remnants of her life with Nolan that needed to be addressed. Slowly but surely, she was reclaiming her independence, building a life that was once more entirely her own.

Ava's distressed face flashed in her mind again, and Miranda felt a flicker of concern. She hoped Ava and Chase would find happiness in the new house. Despite the transactional nature of their arrangement, she genuinely wished them well. Hollywood was a tough place, and maintaining any semblance of a stable, happy relationship was a monumental task.

Miranda sighed, setting down her glass. She had done what she could for Ava, and now it was up to her and Chase to make it work. The sun continued to shine brightly, casting sparkling reflections on the water. Miranda allowed herself to relax, confident that she had made the right decision for everyone involved.

Miranda reached for a margarita sitting on the table beside her chair. She raised it to her lips and took a sip, silently toasting to the end of an era. She savored the cool, tangy taste of the drink as it slid down her throat. She allowed herself a moment of peace, reclining farther into her chair and closing her eyes to the rhythmic sounds of the water gently lapping against the sides of the pool.

Her phone started to vibrate on the small table. She set the drink down and saw that it was Lenny calling. Miranda quickly picked up the phone, eager to hear what Lenny had to say. "Hello, Lenny," she answered, her voice calm but curious.

"Miranda, my favorite client!" Lenny greeted her enthusiastically.

Miranda rolled her eyes at his greeting. Despite everything she and Lenny had been through over the years, he still tended to "handle" her like any other client. She cut right to the chase.

"How did things go at the house with your golden goose?" she asked. There was a sharpness to her tone that was unintentional. She knew Lenny made a lot of money off Ava, far more than he made from her. Still, she couldn't help but feel a twinge of jealousy.

Lenny chuckled, though there was a slight edge to it. "You always know how to cut to the heart of the matter, don't you, Miranda?" he lamented. "Everything went well. Chase and Ava seemed impressed, and Chase was particularly taken with the place. They're going to take it."

Miranda exhaled in relief, and it seemed as though her entire body relaxed instantaneously. "That's good to hear," she said, forcing a lightness into her voice. "I'm glad they found it suitable."

Lenny's tone shifted, becoming more businesslike. "Yes, it's a great move for them," he said. "And for you, Miranda. This is a big step in moving on."

Miranda nodded, even though he couldn't see her. "Yes, it is," she said in agreement. "I'm more than ready to put all of that behind me."

There was a pause on the line, as if Lenny was choosing his next words carefully. "You did the right thing, you know," he said, as if he could peer into her mind and see the tumultuous tug of war that guilt and relief were playing in there. "Offering the house to Ava and Chase is a win-win for everyone."

"Sure," Miranda agreed, though the echo of that guilt still lingered. "How soon can we finalize everything?"

"Very soon," Lenny assured her. "I'll handle all the details, as always."

"Thank you, Lenny," Miranda said, genuinely grateful for his efficiency. Despite his occasional smarminess, he was good at his job. "I appreciate everything you've done."

"Anything for you, Miranda," he replied smoothly. "Enjoy the rest of your day. We'll have this wrapped up before you know it."

Miranda ended the call and set her phone back on the table. She picked up her margarita again, taking a longer sip this time. The cool liquid laced with perhaps a little more tequila than was necessary soothed her lingering anxieties.

As she lay back in her chair, watching the sunlight glisten on the pool's surface, she allowed herself to believe that maybe, just maybe, everything was going to be all right.

Her phone buzzed again, and she saw it was Lenny calling back. She quickly picked up with a hint of impatience in her voice. "What is it, Lenny?" she asked, wondering what he could have possibly forgotten to tell her.

"Just thought you'd like to know," Lenny said, his tone businesslike now, "Ava and Chase just sent in their offer on the house."

"Great," Miranda replied, trying to keep her tone neutral. "Send it to the real estate agent and close as soon as possible."

"Don't you want to know what the offer is first?" Lenny asked, sounding slightly taken aback.

"I don't care," she said back with exasperation. "I just want this done."

There was a moment of uneasy silence.

"I'll contact the realtor right away," Lenny said.

"Thank you, Lenny," Miranda said, more softly this time. "I appreciate it."

"Of course, Miranda. Enjoy your day," Lenny replied before they both hung up.

Miranda finished her margarita and set the glass down, feeling a sense of closure. She had done what needed to be done, and now she could move on. The house would soon belong to Ava and Chase, and she would be free to start anew.

With the sun dipping below the horizon, Miranda stood and stretched. She felt lighter, as if a weight had been lifted from her shoulders. She took one last look at the pool, its surface now darkening in the twilight, and turned to go inside. Tomorrow was a new day, and she was ready to embrace it.

8

Two weeks later, Chase found himself once more standing in front of Nolan Hillhurst's house. The enormity of it still felt surreal. He now owned the home of his hero, the icon of his life, the man he had idolized throughout his youth. As he gazed at the grand façade, memories of watching Hillhurst's films and dreaming of such a life flooded his mind.

Ava came up beside him, slipping her hand into his. "Can you believe it?" she asked, her voice filled with excitement.

Chase squeezed her hand and shook his head in disbelief. "I still can't believe this is real," he said, clearing his throat as he felt his emotions well up.

Ava smiled up at him, her blue eyes sparkling. "You need to believe it," she said with a cutesy crinkle of her nose that he had always found adorable. "Because our new beginning starts right now."

Chase reflected on how they had gotten there. They'd gotten through all the fights, the bitter jealousy, the feeling of inadequacy and loneliness that had nearly drowned him while living in Ava's home, surrounded by everything Ava all the time. He had once told her that he felt like he lived in her purse, just another possession to be taken out and used whenever she felt like it. That comment had hit her hard, and he had instantly regretted it. But it had also been the way he felt at the time.

Looking down at his wife, with her beaming smile, blond hair, and glistening blue eyes, Chase saw utter perfection. How could he have ever been so harsh to her? She had now given up her home to create a new one together with him. They were going to take this step together.

He leaned down and gave her a long, passionate kiss. Ava lost herself in the moment, wrapping her arms around his neck. Their passion had been reignited since they had decided to purchase this home. They had made love every night like they were eighteen again. All because of this gesture, this house, this palace.

As their lips parted, Ava whispered up to him. "You know," she said, "I still get butterflies in my stomach every time you kiss me."

Chase blushed and then, in a spontaneous display of affection, swooped her up in his arms, carrying her onto the porch with ease. She laughed and held on to his neck as he reached out with one hand to open the front door. Chase carried her across the threshold for the first time as the owners of this grand home.

Once inside, Chase looked at Ava and felt a profound swell of love. That caused him to grip her just a little tighter. It was as though he couldn't imagine being without her. The only thought running through his head at that moment was that he never wanted to put her down or let her out of his sight.

At first, Ava laughed and commented on his strong grip. "You're so strong," she said playfully. But her tone quickly changed as she felt his grip tighten. "Ow, Chase! You're hurting me."

Despite her words, Chase didn't let go.

"Chase, ow, what the hell? You're hurting me," Ava said, repeating herself.

Chase blinked as though he'd just heard her for the first time. But he knew that he'd heard her clearly the first time. So why hadn't he reacted? He quickly apologized and put her down.

Ava rubbed her thigh, wincing slightly. "That really hurt, Chase," she said, her eyebrows furrowed with concern. "What the hell were you doing?"

Chase looked genuinely contrite. "I'm sorry," he said, reaching a hesitant hand out toward her but stopping just short of touching her. "I didn't realize my own strength, I guess."

Ava sighed and shook her head. "It's okay," she said with a smile and a sigh. "You're just my big, strong man, is all." She was clearly trying to lighten the mood, and it had worked.

Chase gave her a smile and a shrug.

"Let's go check out the kitchen and decide where we're going to redecorate."

Chase followed close behind and felt an urgency to round every corner behind her quickly. He didn't understand why, but he didn't want to let her out of his sight for even a second. The sudden feeling of possessiveness didn't alarm him, though. Instead, it felt natural, almost…right.

As they walked through the house, the rooms echoed with the grandeur and opulence of Nolan Hillhurst's life. Each space was a testament to the action star's larger-than-life persona. The kitchen was no exception. It was a chef's dream, equipped with state-of-the-art stainless-steel appliances, marble countertops, and a massive island.

Ava moved through the kitchen, and she flashed him a toothy and infectious smile. "This is amazing!" she exclaimed, shaking her head as she looked around to examine the endless possibilities. "We could have so many dinner parties here."

Chase stood close, his eyes never leaving her. "Yeah, it's perfect," he agreed, but his mind was more focused on her than the room. He felt an intense need to keep her close, to protect her, to never let her out of his sight.

Ava turned to him, her face glowing with excitement. "What do you think about putting some new bar stools over there?"

Chase nodded absently, his thoughts consumed by the overwhelming urge to be near her. He watched as she moved around the kitchen, her movements graceful and confident. He felt a strange mix of love and possession, a desire to control and protect as he followed her.

"Chase, are you even listening?" Ava asked, turning around and nearly bumping into him. She squeaked in surprise. "Whoa! Jeez, I didn't realize you were so close. You scared me!"

He blinked and focused on her. "Sorry," he said, snapping out of his momentary reverie. "What did you just say?"

"I asked if you think we should get new bar stools," she repeated, with more than a hint of annoyance in her voice.

"Yeah, whatever you think is best," he said, trying to sound engaged.

Ava frowned. "Are you okay?" she asked, tilting her head as she examined him. "You seem a bit off."

"I'm fine," Chase replied quickly, forcing a smile. "Just overwhelmed, I guess."

Ava smiled and wrapped her arms around his waist. She buried the side of her face against his strong chest. "It's going to be great, Chase," she said, giving him a loving squeeze. "This is our home now."

Chase looked down at her, his heart swelling with love. "I know," he said as the entire room around her crystallized.

She was the only thing he saw. The house suddenly seemed inconsequential next to his near-obsessive need to have her close by.

"I just...I don't ever want to lose you."

Ava laughed softly, still snuggling into him. "You won't lose me," she said, her words slightly smushed into his chest. "We're in this together."

"Forever," Chase added.

She continued to hold on to him but didn't respond right away.

That unnerved him. He gave her a little squeeze of his own. "Right?"

"What?" she asked, looking up at him and trying to pull away, but he kept her there against him.

"I said forever, and you didn't respond," Chase said, feeling the edge of insecure panic rising in his chest.

"Of course, forever, silly," Ava said, pushing against him as though trying to break his grip.

Chase wanted to increase the pressure, to hold her tightly against him as though she might fly off if he were to let go, but he told himself that was silly and forced his fingers apart to release her.

Chase nodded as they separated. He understood that what he was feeling was out of the ordinary, but despite that admission, the feeling of possessiveness lingered. As they continued to explore the house, he stayed close to her. No matter where she went, his hand was always reaching for hers, his eyes constantly watching her.

The rest of the day passed in a blur of unpacking and planning. Ava talked excitedly about their future, about the changes they would make to the house, about the life they would build together. Chase listened, but his mind was preoccupied with keeping her close, ensuring she was always within reach. He didn't even care about the house anymore. At that point, it just felt like four walls. A place to eat and sleep. It was inconsequential to his growing need for Ava's presence.

Each room told a story of Nolan Hillhurst's life, filled with memorabilia and a sense of grandeur that was almost overwhelming. But Chase didn't care anymore. That didn't matter. Closeness was what mattered. Commitment was what mattered. Loyalty was what mattered. And he needed to make sure that his wife was giving him all three of those things with one hundred percent of her being.

Ava had been particularly taken with the pool area. "We could host some fantastic parties out here," she said, her eyes lighting up at the thought.

Chase nodded, his eyes never leaving her. "Yeah, it's perfect," he agreed, his voice softer.

That had been the second time she had brought up parties. He didn't like that idea, but he kept it to himself for now. Why did she need to invite other people into their home? Was he not enough? Did she need to fill the space with chattering sycophants and Hollywood phonies to create distance from him?

That wasn't going to happen in this lifetime, he told himself.

As they walked back inside, Chase's eyes fell on a large set of double doors just inside the pool area. He remembered from his earlier tour that it was Nolan's gym. He'd been so impressed with it initially. It was his favorite room in the house. It was the place in which Nolan had sculpted his impressive body, where he'd built that power and dominance that would ultimately be transferred to the screen.

"I want to take a look at the gym," Chase said to Ava, his voice tinged with excitement.

Ava smiled at him. "Go ahead," she said with a smile. "I'm going to go look through the bedrooms."

Chase paused, the urge to keep Ava within his sight

gnawing at him. "Maybe you should come see the gym with me," he suggested, his tone hopeful.

Ava laughed lightly, shaking her head. "That's your place, Chase," she said simply, gesturing with both arms toward the doors. "It's all for you. I have other things to do today."

Chase ground his teeth, his eyes narrowing. A wave of irrational anger surged through him. He felt the urge to scream at his wife, to demand her compliance, to grab her by the arm and pull her into the gym with him. But the feeling quickly subsided, replaced by an insatiable curiosity beckoning him toward the gym. It was as if the room was calling out to him.

"Okay," he said, forcing a smile. "If you need me, I'll be in the gym."

Ava laughed again, her eyes sparkling. "I think I'll be okay on my own."

"Just don't go anywhere, all right?" he said, trying to keep desperation from his voice.

Ava laughed. "Where would I go, babe?" she asked, her brows furrowed in confusion that pushed through her amusement.

Chase simply shrugged in response. "I dunno," he said, reaching up to rub awkwardly at the back of his neck. "I don't know why I even said that…"

"All right, well, enjoy your gym time, baby," she said. "I'll be upstairs." She turned and left, and Chase had to stop himself from calling out to her again.

He watched his wife for a moment longer, then turned and pushed open the double doors to the gym. He stepped inside and was once more amazed at the massive space. There were so many advanced machines, along with a slew of free weights, an open workout area for stretching, and everything a man needed to build himself into a true powerhouse.

He ran his hand along a long bar set up on one of the bench press stations, feeling the cold metal under his fingers.

He could practically feel the power in this room, the determination that had been used to create a body and a career someone could be proud of. He thought of his own career and how it had been falling into obscurity.

He then thought about Ava and her career. She was the hottest thing in Hollywood. Men all over the world lusted after her. How long would she want to remain with a shriveling nobody who was letting the industry pass him by?

The disappointment, the bitterness, the frustration—all of it seemed amplified in this room. He knew that this room held the key to power. To ultimate power. Power enough to keep his wife by his side and prove to the entire world that he was a man among men.

As he stood still in the gym, staring at his reflection in the floor-to-ceiling mirror that made up one of the walls, all ambient noise suddenly stopped. Chase couldn't even hear the sound of his own breathing anymore. All he could hear was a voice in the back of his mind, soft but determined to be heard. It just said one word.

"Stronger."

The word echoed in his mind, growing louder with each repetition. Chase felt a shiver run down his spine. He took a deep breath, trying to steady himself. The silence in the room was oppressive, almost as if the gym itself were alive. It was urging him to push his limits, to reclaim his former glory.

Chase moved to one of the weight racks and picked up a dumbbell, testing its weight in his hand. The voice in his mind continued its chant, relentless and unyielding.

"Stronger."

He began to lift the dumbbell, feeling his muscles strain and contract with each repetition. The sensation was both familiar and invigorating, a reminder of the days when he had trained tirelessly, driven by a similar desire for strength and success.

But that drive felt greater now. He was no longer a young go-getter trying to lay claim to the world. He was now a fallen star seeking to reclaim his spot on top of the mountain. And he was fighting to keep his woman, fighting to show her that he was her equal, superior even.

As he worked through his routine, Chase felt a strange energy coursing through him, like he wasn't alone. As though there was someone in there with him, watching over him, pushing him to be better, to be stronger. He also felt strong in this place. He had, of course, always been strong. But now he felt…mighty. He felt all-powerful. He felt as though he had the strength of ten men. And the more he pushed himself in the gym that day, the easier the workout became.

And so, he pushed himself beyond his limits, adding more weight, more reps, more sets to his already arduous routine. With every pump, he felt even stronger than he had a second before. He felt as though he were transforming, becoming one with the space, with the true power only a dominant alpha man could touch and hold.

Chase's movements became more fluid, more determined. He moved from one exercise to the next with purpose. His body was responding to the demands placed upon it at every turn. The voice in his mind grew louder, more insistent.

"Stronger."

It was no longer just a word; it was a command, a promise, a mantra, a destiny.

Time seemed to lose meaning as Chase immersed himself in his workout. The gym, with its pristine equipment and echoes of past triumphs, became a sanctuary. This was a place where he could shed the doubts and fears that had plagued him. He could feel the power growing within him, the determination to rise above the challenges that had threatened to consume him.

This was where he would shed the weak man who had felt

belittled and emasculated by the success of his wife. This was where he would reclaim her and his place at the top of their relationship.

Finally, as sweat poured down his face and his muscles burned with exertion, Chase stopped and stood in front of the mirror once more. His reflection stared back at him, a mix of exhaustion and exhilaration etched across every inch of his rippling, godly body. The voice in his mind was silent now, its message delivered.

Chase took a deep breath. The air in the gym felt cooler, more refreshing. When he exhaled, Chase even saw his breath for a brief second. He wiped the sweat from his brow and took a moment of pride. He had pushed through barriers, both physical and mental, and emerged stronger on the other side.

He knew the journey ahead would not be easy. There would be more challenges, more moments of doubt. But in this gym, in the heart of Nolan Hillhurst's legacy, Chase had found a source of strength that he could draw upon. It was a reminder that he had the power to shape his own destiny, to rise above the obstacles and reclaim his place in the world. And to keep his wife, his Ava, by his side for the rest of her life.

With renewed determination, Chase set the dumbbells back on the rack and walked toward the door. He was ready to face whatever lay ahead, secure in the knowledge that he had the strength to overcome it. Now that he was done, he needed to go find Ava. She'd been away from him for too long.

As he walked into the rest of the house, leaving a trail of dripping sweat in his wake, the words of that inner voice still echoed in his mind, repeating that same mantra that he would carry with him for the rest of his days.

"Stronger."

9

Ava woke up feeling disoriented. The bed she was in was hers, but the room felt strange and alien in the stillness of the night. She took a deep breath, reminding herself that it was her first night in the new house. It was normal to feel a little out of place. Eventually, the room and the entire house would start to feel like home. She glanced at her phone on the bedside table and saw that it was nearly three in the morning.

She had gone to bed early by herself after Chase had decided to get in another workout after dinner. That wasn't out of the ordinary for him, but that was usually when he was preparing for a role.

It had been an especially long session, and she was exhausted from the busy day they'd had. Earlier in the evening, she had poked her head into the gym to tell Chase she was heading to bed. He had been in the middle of an intense workout and had promised to join her after he finished. Ava had jokingly reminded him to shower before climbing under their nice, clean sheets.

He hadn't laughed or even acknowledged her. He had just returned to his workout as if she hadn't spoken. Ava had gone to bed disappointed, assuming Chase would want to christen their new bedroom together. They had been so passionate with each other recently, leading up to the move. It hurt more than a little that Chase seemed to prefer his gym over her tonight.

She reached out to the other side of the bed, expecting to feel Chase beside her. Instead, she found only empty space. Sitting up, she looked around, hoping to see him standing nearby or walking back from a late-night bathroom trip. But the room was empty, and the house was eerily silent. What was more, she noticed that his side of the bed was entirely undisturbed. Had he not come to bed at all?

The unfamiliarity of it all sent a chill down Ava's spine. She flicked the switch on her bedside lamp, but nothing happened. She groaned in frustration and checked to make sure it was plugged in. Grabbing her phone, she saw it wasn't charging, either. Was the power out?

Activating the flashlight on her phone, she noticed the battery was down to three percent. She also saw that the plug was firmly inserted behind her nightstand. "Great," she muttered to herself. "Just what I need."

She knew she needed to get up and check on things. She needed to find Chase and get him to check the circuit breaker or something. But despite that, a sense of foreboding kept her rooted in place. Ava swallowed hard, every fiber of her being resisting the idea of getting out of their bed. She told herself, though, that she was being ridiculous. She was just scared, being in a new house by herself in the dark.

Gathering her courage, Ava pulled the blankets off her legs and swung them over the side of the mattress. The cold tile floor made her gasp. It felt like she was stepping on ice. Despite that, she soldiered on, telling herself that she was not going to let her imagination run wild and push her thoughts to dark places. There was nothing to be afraid of.

Ava slowly made her way through the darkened room, her phone's flashlight casting eerie shadows on the walls. She found the light switch by the door and flicked it on, but the overhead light didn't work, either. She felt a pit form in her stomach, her spirit deflating as it seemed they were in the middle of a full-on blackout.

"Of course," she grumbled, frustration pushing aside her fear for a moment. Opening the door, she stepped into the hallway. "Chase?" she called out, her voice echoing slightly.

There was no response. The house felt like a dark, silent maze.

She carefully crept down the stairs, wincing at how cold the floor felt beneath her bare feet. She wished she had thought to look for her slippers.

"Chase?" she called out again, louder this time. The silence was unnerving, and her voice seemed to echo off the walls unnaturally, as though she had wandered into some vast cavern of twisting tunnels.

Ava made her way toward the back of the house, where the gym was located. Her phone's battery died just as she reached the door, plunging her into complete darkness.

"Dammit," she cursed softly, feeling the cold edge of fear creeping into her every movement.

Just then, she heard a faint sound. It was familiar, yet entirely unexpected. There was no mistaking it. A long, low mew, like that of an older or sick cat. Ava froze, listening intently, but the sound didn't come again. She remembered the white blur she had seen during their first visit to the house, as though some animal had made its way inside. Was it possible that they were sharing their space with a feral cat? Shaking her head, she tried to dismiss the thought.

"I'm just tired," she told herself. "Hearing things."

Another sound broke the silence—metal clanging against metal and a faint grunt of exertion. She turned toward the gym and saw a faint light seeping through the slightly ajar door. How could there be light in there when the rest of the house was dark? Pushing the door open slowly, she peeked inside.

Chase was there, shirtless and wearing the same black athletic shorts he'd had on earlier. He was lifting a heavily loaded barbell with ease, grunting with each rep.

"Chase?" she called out, stepping into the gym. The moment she spoke, the lights in the gym snapped off, plunging the room into darkness. She yelped in surprise. "Chase?" she repeated, her voice trembling now. She heard the barbell settle back onto its rack. Through the darkness, she saw Chase's hulking silhouette approaching her, his form massive and intimidating as he cut through the shadows, utterly uninhibited.

"What's wrong?" he asked, his voice weary.

"Why didn't you come to bed?" Ava demanded, trying to keep her voice steady. "And why is the power out?"

Chase looked around, as if noticing the darkness for the first time. "Huh, how about that?" he said nonchalantly.

"It's creepy," Ava insisted, shivering slightly.

"Don't worry," Chase said, stepping closer.

He reached out and gripped her arms with his strong, calloused hands. The moment he touched her, the lights snapped back on throughout the house, flooding the room with brightness. Ava found herself looking up into familiar blue eyes, eyes she knew so well.

Chase smiled apologetically. "I'm sorry for working out so late, babe," he said with a shrug. "I got in the zone, you know? There's nothing to be afraid of."

Ava nodded, feeling reassured by his words coupled with

his powerful touch. "Okay, but you need to shower before coming to bed," she reiterated, laying a hand on his sweat-soaked chest.

Chase's smile widened. "Sure thing," he said, his tone light.

They walked out of the gym together, heading toward the main foyer. As they climbed the stairs, Ava heard a slight hiss, once more like that of a cat. She turned around quickly, looking back into the shadows.

"Did you hear that?" she asked Chase.

"Hear what?" he replied, with his brow furrowed and his head tilted in a questioning gesture.

"Never mind," Ava said, shaking her head. "I guess I'm just jumpy."

They continued up to their room, and Ava climbed back into bed. But the strangeness of the night still lingered in her mind, and she had a hard time getting back to sleep. Chase had gone to the bathroom to shower, and she soon heard the water running. It was a steady, comforting sound in the otherwise silent house. She lay back on her pillow, trying to make sense of everything. The new house, the blackout, the strange noises—it all felt overwhelming.

She left the lights on in the room while she waited for Chase to come back. She was now more grateful than ever for their presence.

As she lay there, bathed in the artificial glow of the overhead light and two bedside lamps, she thought about how much had changed in such a short time. Their move to this grand house, Chase's seemingly renewed fitness kick, and the unsettling events of the night all swirled in her head. Ava tried to quiet those thoughts, to focus on nothingness so she could relax her mind and get back to sleep. However, she couldn't shake the feeling that something was off here. She just couldn't put her finger on what it was.

Chase emerged from the bathroom, freshly showered and looking more like himself. He flipped off the overhead light as he climbed into bed beside her, wrapping his arms around her in the warm, encouraging glow of their bedside lamps.

"Everything okay?" he asked, his voice gentle.

Ava nodded, but the unease remained. "Yeah, just a weird night, I guess."

Chase leaned over and kissed her forehead. "It's a big change," he admitted with a nod. "But we'll get used to it. I have faith in us."

He reached up to turn off the light by the side of his bed, and for some reason, it elicited a panic response in Ava. Her heart was suddenly beating faster than ever, and her breath caught in her throat. Unable to speak, she reached out to grab Chase by the arm.

"What?" he asked, his head snapping to her with concern.

"It's just...," Ava said, not wanting to say the words. She knew how childish they were going to sound. "I just...don't wanna be in the dark right now."

Chase gave her a patient look and a warm smile. "I understand," he said with a kind understanding.

Ava breathed a sigh of relief, instantly thankful for this man and the place he held in her life.

"But that's silly, babe. Turn off the damn light."

Ava's heart sank as Chase reached over and clicked off his lamp. She couldn't believe he would dismiss her like that, as though her wants, needs, or concerns hadn't mattered to him at all. Her mouth was hanging open as she scooted closer to her lamp, to the small circle of light that it still created. It was like a shield that was warding off the shadows of a house she didn't know or understand just yet.

"Babe," Chase said, lying down with his back to her. His voice was tight with impatience. "I said, turn the damn light off. Don't make me ask you again."

Ava wanted to protest. She wanted to ask Chase who the hell he thought he was talking to. She wanted to say that she had a right to have whatever lights on that she wanted. But she did none of that. Instead, Ava simply reached over and, with a shaking hand, turned out the light and plunged the entire room back into darkness.

10

Ava closed her eyes, replaying Chase's words in her head. It wasn't just the words that he had spoken; it was the tone in which he had spoken them. It hadn't been a request. It had been an order. A command, even.

So why, then, had she complied? Why didn't she stick up for herself? Ava knew the answer deep down inside, but she didn't want to admit it to herself. She had been afraid. There was something in Chase's voice at that moment. Something alien and terrifying. It wasn't that she felt threatened. It was more that she felt...intimidated by it.

Chase fell asleep beside her almost instantly. If he had any misgivings about the way he'd spoken to her, he certainly wasn't going to lose any sleep over it. His breathing was steady and rhythmic now, a clear sign that not only had he fallen asleep, but it was a deep sleep. Ava could only lay awake, staring at the ceiling. The room was dark, with the only light coming from the faint glow of the moon through the curtains. Shadows danced across the walls, and the unfamiliar shapes of the room seemed to close in on her.

There was nothing she could take comfort in, no familiarity in this space whatsoever. Even the man lying beside her felt completely foreign to her at that moment.

And try as she might, Ava couldn't shake the memory of what she'd heard in the shadows of this house. The cat's mew and hiss she'd heard earlier stayed with her, and she wondered if it was possible that her mind had played the same trick on her twice in one night.

It had sounded so real, so close. Ava tried to convince herself it was just her imagination, a trick of her tired mind, but the thought lingered.

What if there was something more to it? What would she even do in that instance? Set up a humane trap? Call animal control? What if there was a cat in here that had some kind of disease or rabies?

She sat up again, listening intently, as though she might be able to hear it again. She almost wished she would. If she had tangible proof that there was an animal somewhere in here, then she'd at least know for sure. The unsettling uncertainty was what was ultimately killing her.

The house was silent now, save for the occasional creak of settling wood. She shivered, feeling the cold air against her skin. An unnatural, frigid breeze had wafted in, like a draft coming in through the window. But the window had been firmly shut before she'd even gone to bed. And even if it was open, this was the summer in Beverly Hills. There was no breeze cold enough to create the chill running through her right now. It could have been the air conditioning. But the thermostat was all the way downstairs. She really didn't want to get up and check it herself. But she also didn't want to wake Chase up and ask him to do it.

Pulling the blanket tighter around herself, as though it were some kind of protective cocoon, she resigned herself to what needed to be done. Ava decided to get up and check the thermostat downstairs, and maybe, while she was down there, check on the rest of the house once more, if only to ease her troubled mind. A walk might even do her some good. It could familiarize her with the house more, making it feel less alien. A walk could even tire her out a bit, making it easier for her to fall asleep.

Quietly, she slipped out of bed, careful not to wake Chase. She grabbed her robe and wrapped it around herself before stepping into the hallway. The floor beneath her was no longer cold, and the lights in the hallway were working again. She clicked on the light after closing the bedroom door to illuminate her path.

Ava walked down the hallway, her footsteps soft on the tile floor. As she passed each room, she glanced inside, seeing only boxes and furniture waiting to be unpacked. Despite the relative normalcy found around every corner, her sense of unease grew stronger with each step.

Reaching the stairs, Ava descended slowly, her hand trailing along the banister for support. She made her way to the living room, where the large windows overlooked the darkened grounds outside. Everything seemed so still, so quiet.

She found the thermostat there and checked on the temperature. It was set to seventy-four degrees, which was a degree or two cooler than what she normally found comfortable. She hit the button to raise the temperature up to seventy-six, hoping that would improve the temperature in the house.

Ava then moved to the kitchen, checking all the appliances. Everything appeared to be in working order, despite the earlier power outage. She turned the light switch on and off a few times and was relieved to see them working perfectly.

Ava wandered out of the kitchen and down the hall, noticing the gym at the end. The door was once again partially open, and she noticed a light shining out from within. She sighed to herself, murmuring under her breath that she'd need to have a talk with Chase about turning off the lights when he left a room. As annoying as it was, this was thankfully a problem could be easily rectified. She just needed to go in there and turn them off herself.

As she approached the gym doors, she hesitated. The memory of Chase lifting weights in there, his hulking form emerging from the shadows, made her pause. Taking a deep breath, she pushed the door open and stepped inside.

The gym was as she remembered it, filled with state-of-the-art equipment and weights. The room was dark, but moonlight streamed through the high windows, casting eerie shadows across the floor. She looked around, half expecting to see something out of place, but everything seemed perfectly normal.

Ava walked over to the bench press where Chase had been earlier. She ran her fingers along the cold metal bar, feeling the smooth surface beneath her fingertips. The silence in the room was almost oppressive, squashing any ambient noise as though she existed in a vacuum.

The unnatural stillness made her uncomfortable. Ava turned to leave, but a soft sound suddenly cut through the eerie silence and stopped her in her tracks. It was faint, almost imperceptible, but there—like the whisper of a voice or the rustle of fabric. Ava's heart pounded in her chest as she strained to listen.

"Hello?" she called out softly, her voice barely above a whisper. "Is someone there?"

There was no response, only the echo of her own voice bouncing off the gym's walls. Ava shivered and took a step back, her hand clutching her robe tightly around her. She felt a sudden rush of cold air, despite the fact that she had just raised the thermostat. It made no sense. This draft was colder than the one before, passing through her body and chilling her to the bone until her teeth started to chatter.

She took another step back, her eyes scanning the room. After that initial disturbance, the silence returned, filling her with an even deeper sense of growing dread. Ava knew she needed to leave the gym, to get back to the safety of her bedroom and the comforting presence of Chase.

As she turned to go, the lights suddenly clicked off once again, bathing her once more in the very same darkness she'd experienced before. Her heel caught on a dumbbell, which sat on the gym's rubber-lined floor, and she fell roughly, smashing her tailbone in a seated position. It was then that she heard the sound again, louder this time. It was unmistakable now—a low, guttural growl that sent chills down her spine. She wasn't imagining it. This time, it was real. The hissing, gravelly growl of a feline sounded out from somewhere within the oppressive darkness, swallowing her with its intensity and inescapable emptiness.

Ava's breath caught in her throat, and she froze, her eyes wide with fear. "Chase?" she called out, her voice trembling. "Chase, are you there?"

But there was no answer, only the echoing silence of the gym. Even the cat's growl had retreated, leaving her once more surrounded by darkness, silence, and a chilling cold that felt like it was freezing her spine solid. Then it returned, that low yowl which seemed to come from every corner of the room at once. Ava's heart raced as she tried to back away. But she had no idea where the sound was actually coming from. Her mind screamed at her to run, to make a break for it and stumble her way back to safety… if there was anywhere in this entire house that could still be classified as such.

She turned and fled the gym, knowing the basic direction of the door. She passed through the threshold and turned back toward the gym, sliding the double doors shut behind her before turning to race down the hallway.

She reached the stairs from memory and took them two at

a time, her robe billowing out behind her as she moved. Ava burst back into the bedroom, the moonlight guiding her way. Her chest heaved with exertion and fear as she slammed the door closed, as if whatever she had heard out there was somehow in pursuit of her. The sound of the door crashing closed seemed to rouse Chase. He stirred in the bed, groggy and confused.

"Ava? What's wrong?" he mumbled, sitting up and rubbing his eyes. He reached for his lamp.

Ava was about to tell him that the power had gone out again, but the lamp clicked on with ease at his touch, filling the room with light. Ava let out a short, humorless laugh at the insanity of the situation. She wanted to scream, to grab at her hair with both hands and run from the house in a blind terror. But she knew she couldn't do that.

What she had experienced had a logical explanation. She just couldn't see it in her terrified state. She just needed everything to calm down. She needed Chase to stand beside her, to tell her that she wasn't crazy, and to help her figure out what had happened.

But for that to happen, she needed to find her voice again, and that was a lot easier said than done in her frazzled state.

"Babe," Chase said, more insistent this time. He didn't sound concerned the way she thought he might. Instead, he seemed almost annoyed.

Ava chalked this up to being woken from a deep sleep by a loud noise. It had to be jarring.

Forcibly slowing her breathing, Ava found that she was able to speak again. Her voice shook as she tried to explain. "I heard something, Chase," she said, pointing at the door with shaking fingers. "I was down in the gym, and the lights went out again. I...I swear I heard something like an animal. It sounded like...like a growl. But not like a dog's growl. Like a cat's growl."

Chase was eerily still as he processed her words. When he spoke, she thought he might tell her it was all right, that she was safe. She thought perhaps he'd question her about the source of the growl or ask for more information. But he did none of those things.

"What were you doing in my gym?" he asked, his voice tight with irritation.

Ava's mouth dropped open, and she scoffed. "Really, Chase?" she asked incredulously. "That's all you have to say to me? After I tell you all of that, the only thing you care about was that I was down in your stupid freaking gym?"

He didn't answer. He simply rose from the bed and crossed his arms over his chest, waiting for an answer to his question.

Ava grunted in frustration. "I went down there to turn up the thermostat because I was cold, and the light was on in there! Happy now? But I went in there and heard something growling, Chase! That's the important thing here!"

"A growl?" he asked with a raised eyebrow. "Are you sure?"

"Yes, I'm sure," Ava insisted, her eyes wide with fear. "It was real, Chase. There's something in this house."

Chase sighed and approached, seeming more annoyed than anything. Still, he pulled her into his arms, trying to soothe her. But this wasn't like other times he'd held her. It wasn't tender. It wasn't loving. It felt like an obligation on his part.

"It's a new place, Ava," he said simply, stroking the back of her head while going through the motions of offering a minimal amount of comfort. "It's gonna feel strange for a while. We're just not used to it yet."

Ava shook her head, pushing away from him and gritting her teeth as he broke his hold on her. Now, Ava's fear was quickly turning to frustration. "No, Chase!" she insisted, her fingers curling into fists. "This was different. It wasn't just the house settling or my imagination. There was something there."

Chase held up a hand as though to calm a rearing horse. When he spoke, his voice remained calm at all times, though she didn't find that reassuring. "Okay, okay," Chase said with a heavy sigh that once more set her agitation on edge. "I'll go check it out, babe. But I'm sure it's nothing."

Chase made a move for the door, and Ava reached out to grab him by the arm. A sudden fear for his safety caused her to cling to him desperately.

"No," she said, laying the side of her face against his arm. "Don't."

"It's fine," he said. "You'll see." He pulled his arm from her grip, perhaps a little more forcefully than was necessary. Without a look back at her, Chase made a beeline for the door.

"Be careful," Ava called out after him, her heart beating in her ears now.

She watched as Chase effortlessly flung the door open and headed out into the hallway. Ava watched him go, her fear growing with each passing second.

She sat on the edge of the bed, her hands clenched in her lap. The minutes ticked by, each one feeling like an eternity. Finally, Chase returned after ten excruciating minutes. His expression was calm, with maybe a trace of leftover annoyance.

"I didn't find anything," he said, sitting down beside her. "The gym's empty, and there's nothing out of place."

Ava's shoulders sagged with relief, but the unease remained. The fact that he didn't find anything didn't make her doubt what she had heard in any way. And how hard had he actually looked, anyway?

"I know what I heard, Chase," she insisted, wringing her fingers together. "I swear, it wasn't just my imagination."

Chase groaned in response. "Ava, it's late," he said with a weary sigh. "What do you want me to do? Go down there and start taking the walls apart? What's gonna make this better for you so I can get back to sleep?"

She couldn't believe he was being so callous in the face of her fear. Who was this man sitting beside her? The man she married, her Chase, would have never reacted like this, no matter what misgivings he was having.

Ava simply nodded, her fear starting to mix with a mounting exhaustion. "It's fine, Chase," she said simply, shaking her head. "Just…forget about it, all right?"

"Okay," Chase replied, pulling the covers back and climbing back into bed.

Ava felt her face grow hot at his casual dismissal. She had heard something, an animal, a feline, somewhere in this house. There was something alive down there. And if Chase wasn't going to help her find it, then she would need to find it herself.

11

Ava woke the next morning, groggy from a night of fitful sleep. She had continued to hear the mewing, hissing, and growling of that unseen cat in her dreams, and it kept jolting her back awake. Rolling over, she reached out to touch Chase, seeking comfort in his presence. But her hand met only cold sheets.

Ava frowned and picked up her phone, relieved to see it was now fully charged since the power had come back on. The screen displayed 7:30 a.m.

"Chase?" she called out, her voice weary and tinged with concern. There was no response. The house was eerily silent once more. It reminded her of what she'd been through the previous night, only now the comforting rays of the sun were filtering in through every window.

Sighing, she pushed the covers off and swung her legs over the side of the bed. The floor still felt warmer now compared to the icy cold it had been just a few hours earlier. Despite the warmth, she slipped into her fuzzy slippers and pulled on a robe, steeling herself to search for her husband.

As she stepped out into the hallway, the sunlight streaming

through the large windows made everything feel less intimidating. The golden light painted the walls with warmth. The shadows cast now were long and soft, unlike the harsh, swirling nightmare darkness she'd experienced last night.

She marveled at how different the house felt during the day. Last night, it had seemed like a maze of shadows and eerie noises beckoning her into the heart of hell itself. She wished she had seen how creepy it was at night before buying it.

"Too late for second thoughts now," she muttered to herself. She knocked gently on the bathroom door. "Chase, are you in there?" she asked, her voice carrying a note of hope.

There was no answer. She hesitated for a moment before opening the door and peering inside. The bathroom was empty, the air still and silent. Her worry began to grow, with a knot tightening in her stomach.

"Where could he be?" she whispered, closing the door and continuing her search. Walking into the kitchen, she called out again. "Chase? Are you in here?"

The kitchen was bathed in the soft morning light, but there was no sign of him. The counters were spotless, and the sink was empty, indicating he hadn't had breakfast yet. She wondered if he had left the house without telling her. Each unanswered call was only heightening her growing unease.

Feeling a bit more frantic, she made her way to the foyer and looked outside. Chase's car was still parked right where it had been yesterday. She stepped out onto the porch, the morning air crisp and cool against her skin.

"Chase, this isn't funny!" she called out, her voice tinged with desperation. "Where are you?" Ava's mind raced with possibilities. Could he possibly be in the gym again? It seemed unlikely since he had just been there not even four hours ago. But she saw no other alternative.

Her steps quickened as she made for the gym, her anxiety

mounting with each step. As Ava neared the door, she heard the unmistakable sound of clanking metal and grunting. Her face grew hot with anger. What on earth was he doing in there again?

She stormed into the gym, her voice sharp with frustration. "Chase," she barked at him, her fury evident, "what the hell are you doing in here?"

Chase looked up from the bench press, his face slick with sweat. "Just getting a workout in," he replied nonchalantly, barely acknowledging her presence. If he was alarmed or put off by her flustered and angered state, he didn't show it in any way.

"You were just working out four hours ago," Ava snapped. "Why are you back in here already? You're gonna hurt yourself!"

Chase set the barbell down and sat up, wiping his face with a towel. "You gotta put in the time and have the discipline to keep moving, babe," he said matter-of-factly. "You should remember that before you start to let yourself go."

Ava felt a sting of embarrassment as he reached out and poked her in the stomach with a sweaty finger. She blushed, more from anger than anything else. The way he looked at her with a hint of disdain made her feel small and inadequate.

"How long are you going to be in here?" she asked, trying to keep her voice steady. "Are you almost done?"

Chase shook his head, his expression unyielding. "I still have a ways to go," he said unapologetically and impatiently. He was tapping his finger against his knee now, as if waiting for her to leave him alone so he could get back to what he was doing.

"Fine," Ava said, turning on her heel. "I'll go into town for lunch and get some air."

Chase's expression changed, and he moved faster than she thought possible to block her path. One minute, he was on the bench, and the next, he was standing between her and the door. His sudden movement startled her, and she took a step back.

"Why do you need to go out?" he asked, his tone demanding with more than a hint of suspicion. His eyes narrowed accusingly.

Ava suddenly felt very small in front of her husband as he towered over her. She had never feared him before in their entire relationship, but something was different now. Something about the way he was asking made her uneasy.

"I just want to get out of the house," she said truthfully, her voice faltering toward the end of her statement.

"This house is our home now," Chase said firmly. "You should stay." He gripped her arms, his hands strong and calloused. The squeeze he gave was rough but not violent. It hurt nonetheless, and Ava resisted the urge to squeak in pain.

"Chase, you're hurting me," she managed to say, her voice trembling.

Chase's fingers sprang open, and his expression softened immediately. "I'm sorry," he said, suddenly seeming to come back to himself. His eyes, which had looked so unfamiliar, now seemed filled with remorse. "I didn't mean to."

Ava rubbed her arms where his fingers had left red marks. "What's gotten into you?" she asked, her voice a mix of confusion and concern.

Chase looked away, unable to meet her gaze. "Nothing," he said simply. "I'm fine."

Ava took a step back, her heart pounding in her chest. "Maybe we made a mistake," she said quietly. "Maybe we shouldn't have moved here."

Chase shook his head vigorously. "No, we just need to get used to it," he said simply. He didn't say it as though he was sharing an opinion. He said it as though it was an absolute truth of the universe. "It's a big change, that's all. We'll be fine."

Ava wanted to believe him, but the unease in her gut wouldn't go away. "I think I still need to get out for a bit," she said cautiously. "Just to clear my head."

Chase hesitated, looking as though he was about to protest again. Finally, his jaw seemed to unclench, and he nodded slowly. "Okay," he said, though he still sounded annoyed by this desire to go out into the world. "If that's what you think you need."

"It is," she said simply, but Chase was still standing between her and the door.

For a moment, it seemed as though he wasn't going to move. It was as though his words and his body were on two different wavelengths, acting independently of one another.

"Chase, can I get by, please?"

For a moment, he didn't move, as though he might suddenly go back on what he had said and bar her way for some unknown reason. But eventually, he relented and stepped aside. However, his movements were stiff and stubborn, as though he were fighting against himself to make them.

"Thank you," Ava said simply, turning to leave. But as she walked away, she could still feel Chase's eyes on her, watching her every move.

The intensity of that unseen gaze made her shiver. She hurried up the stairs and back to the bedroom, where she grabbed her purse and jacket. Before leaving, she glanced at her reflection in the mirror. Dark circles under her eyes and a worried expression stared back at her. It was so unlike her to just go out into the world like this. Unwashed, no makeup, and looking haggard and tired. But she needed to go, needed to get out and just…get some air for a while.

She descended the stairs quickly, almost tripping in her haste. She could feel the tension in the air, as if the house itself were watching her, waiting for her next move. As she reached the bottom of the stairs, she paused, taking a deep breath to steady the constant quake she was feeling in her joints.

Walking toward the front door, Ava called out one last time over her shoulder. "Chase, I'm leaving now," she said.

There was no response, just the echo of her own voice. She opened the door and stepped outside into the fresh air. It was a welcome relief from the oppressive environment of their new home.

Standing there on the porch for a minute and letting the early morning sun warm her skin, Ava looked down at her arms. She saw faint bruises were forming there in the shape of Chase's huge fingers. She shook her head, trying to dispel the growing sense of dread that wouldn't let go of her.

As she walked to her car, Ava hoped that some time away from the house would help clear her mind and figure out what was happening there. It was as though the problems she and Chase had once had were no more, but they had been replaced by a new and infinitely worse set of issues. Their problems before had filled her with a deep sadness. But what she was feeling now was something different.

It was fear. She was becoming afraid of her husband. That was something she hadn't thought was ever possible.

The drive into town was uneventful, but Ava's mind was a whirlwind of thoughts. She replayed the morning's events over and over, trying to make sense of it all. She wondered if the house itself was somehow to blame. It seemed like an absurd thought, but the last twenty-four hours had been completely absurd.

By the time she reached the edge of town, Ava felt a bit more composed. She let go of any thoughts she had about the house in some way influencing her husband. No one had lived in that place for five years, and they had bought it without sending in an inspector. The wiring probably needed to be replaced, and there must have been an issue with the AC. As for the sound of the cat that seemed to follow her through the halls of the home... Well, Ava still didn't have an explanation for that, other than it was possible a feral cat was somehow working its way through the walls.

She parked the car and sat there for a moment, staring at the storefronts and people going about their day. The normalcy of it all bumped up against the heinous turmoil she felt inside. She took a deep breath and closed her eyes, hoping to center herself before deciding on her next move.

Ava decided to stop at a small café she had always enjoyed. Pulling into a parking spot, she shut off the engine and took another deep breath. The aroma of freshly brewed coffee wafted toward her as she stepped inside. The warm, bright, inviting atmosphere was so different from the dark, frigid tension she had just left behind.

Ava found a table in the corner and sat down, ordering a coffee from the cheerful barista. In a stroke of luck, it seemed as though neither the barista nor any of the patrons recognized her. She breathed a sigh of relief. They probably never for a moment considered that Ava Monroe might appear in public in such an unkempt state.

As she waited, Ava pulled out her phone, scrolling aimlessly through her contacts. She needed someone to talk to, someone who could help her make sense of what was happening. But as she scrolled, she realized with a sinking feeling that there was no one she trusted enough to confide in.

Hollywood friends were often self-serving vultures, always looking for the next juicy piece of gossip to sell to the tabloids. Ava knew that any hint of marital trouble would be splashed across the headlines before she could even hang up the phone. She sighed, feeling more isolated than ever.

When her coffee arrived, she wrapped her hands around the warm mug, taking comfort in its heat. She took a sip, savoring the rich, robust flavor, and tried to collect her thoughts. The café was bustling with people, their conversations blending into a soothing hum that provided a small measure of comfort.

Ava continued to scroll through her contacts, her thumb pausing over several names before moving on. She couldn't shake the feeling of betrayal that would come if any of them decided to leak her problems to the press. She needed someone she could trust, someone who understood the pressures of their world but also cared about her as a person.

Her thoughts turned to Lenny, her agent. He had always been more than just a business associate. He had often been a confidant, a mentor, and, in many ways, a friend. He knew the ins and outs of Hollywood, and he had always looked out for her best interests. It was also in his best interest to keep any controversies surrounding his top client out of the press. Maybe he could provide some much-needed perspective.

Ava took a deep breath and dialed Lenny's number. As the phone rang, she felt a flicker of hope that he might be able to help her navigate this strange and unsettling situation.

12

Lenny sat in his plush office chair, the leather creaking slightly as he adjusted his position and leaned back. The framed accolades of the films he had helped bring into production served as constant reminders of his successes, yet today, they offered him little comfort. Today, he felt like a total failure.

He held a phone to his ear, the voice of a casting director buzzing on the other end.

"I'm telling you, Miranda Sterling is perfect for this role," Lenny said, his voice smooth and confident. "She has the experience, the gravitas, and let's not forget, she's got the perfect story for a comeback. After losing her husband so tragically five years ago, this could be the start of something new for her."

There was a pause on the other end of the line. The casting director, a woman named Karen, with a reputation for being incredibly discerning, seemed unconvinced. Lenny could almost hear the gears turning in her head.

"We were actually looking for someone a little younger,"

Karen replied, her tone noncommittal. "Someone who can give us that ingenue vibe."

Lenny clenched his jaw, holding back a snarl. He knew better than to make enemies of casting directors, especially one as influential as Karen.

"Miranda is the definition of ingenue," he countered, forcing his tone to remain pleasant. "She's timeless, Karen. She brings a depth and nuance that younger actresses simply can't match."

"Maybe she was the definition of ingenue ten years ago," Karen shot back, a hint of amusement in her voice. "But those days are long behind her."

Lenny could feel his frustration mounting. This was not going as he had hoped. He took a deep breath, trying to keep his composure. "I understand your concerns, Karen," he said slowly. "But Miranda Sterling has a presence that's undeniable. She's still got that spark. This could be the role that reignites her career."

There was another pause, and Lenny could almost hear the casting director weighing her options.

"What about Ava Monroe?" Karen asked suddenly, and Lenny winced. "She's got the look we're going for. Young, fresh, and she's got a huge following."

Lenny bit back a sigh. It wasn't that he didn't want to find roles for Ava. Her success was his success. But he knew that if this role Miranda was eyeing went to Ava, the older actress would be livid. And he knew Miranda well enough after all these years to know that she would undoubtedly take it out on him.

"Ava has a lot of projects on her plate right now," Lenny said carefully. "But I can check with her to see if she's interested."

"Do that," Karen said, her tone final, "and let me know. We need to move fast on this."

Lenny hung up the phone and buried his head in his hands. So far, his attempts at revitalizing Miranda's failing career weren't going well. He was caught between a rock and a hard place, trying to balance the needs of two high-profile clients with very different career trajectories. He leaned back in his chair, staring up at the ceiling, and tried to think of his next move.

Miranda had been his client for over a decade. He had seen her through the highs of her career and the devastating lows that came about after Nolan's death. She was talented, no doubt about that. And the roles he sought for her were right in her wheelhouse. He had no doubt in his mind that she would knock these opportunities out of the park if given the chance.

But Hollywood was a fickle place, and sometimes talent didn't matter in the end. The industry had a short memory, and it had seemingly forgotten all about Miranda Sterling. Ava, on the other hand, was the current darling of Hollywood. She was everything the town loved. Young and vibrant, with her career on a meteoric rise. She had been unspoiled, untainted by the industry. She still had some of her original personality, and it served her well in being relatable to moviegoers. She was like Jennifer Lawrence before she had become completely insufferable.

But that was what living in the Hollywood bubble did to a person. After a while, they began to think that their make-believe world was the real world, and actors inevitably lost touch with the people they pandered to.

The phone on his desk buzzed, snapping him out of his thoughts. He glanced at the caller ID and saw that it was another casting director. He took a deep breath, preparing to switch gears. "Lenny speaking," he answered, slipping effortlessly back into his professional demeanor.

As he navigated the new conversation, his mind kept drifting back to Miranda and Ava. He had to find a way to keep both of his clients happy. But how? He was juggling too many balls, and it felt like they were all about to come crashing down.

Finally, after what felt like an eternity, he ended the call with the casting director and leaned back in his chair again. He had managed to secure a promising lead for another client's project, but his thoughts kept returning to Miranda's situation. He needed a breakthrough, something to get her back in the game.

He felt as though, in many ways, he owed it to her. Lenny had a genuine affection for Miranda. One that came from a place of longstanding friendship and understanding. He needed to make this work for her. It had become his personal mission in life.

Lenny stared at the photos on his wall, searching for inspiration. One picture caught his eye. It was a candid shot of Miranda and Nolan from years ago. Both were smiling and vibrant, the world at their feet. It was a stark reminder of how much things had changed.

He picked up his phone and considered calling Miranda to give her an update. He'd have to reassure her that he was still fighting for her. But he hesitated.

What could he say that wouldn't sound like empty promises? He needed something concrete, a real opportunity to present.

Lenny's phone suddenly rang again, the sharp sound cutting through the silence of his office. He dreaded looking down at it, expecting to see Miranda calling for an update. But he was surprised to see that it was actually Ava calling him. He exhaled in relief and picked up the phone, taking a moment to ensure that there was no tumultuous remnant in his voice.

"Ava! How's my favorite client doing?" he greeted her boisterously. "How's the new house treating you?"

Ava's response was not what he expected. "It's... different from what I expected," she said, her tone uncertain and meek.

This wasn't the Ava Lenny knew. This unsteady, shaky voice could not have possibly belonged to the girl who lit up the room with a smile and took Hollywood by storm.

"Ava, what's wrong?" he asked, the concern in his voice evident. And it was a genuine concern.

Ava's problems were his problems. So much of the money coming into his agency rested on that girl. He had to make sure she was happy, focused, and avoiding drama at all costs.

There was a pause as Lenny could almost hear her trying to find the right words. That concerned him. He wondered what could have happened to darken her spirits so much. He recalled how excited she had been upon closing on the home. It was supposed to be a new beginning for her. So why was she so down?

"It's nothing," Ava said suddenly, trying to brush it off.

Lenny wasn't having it. "If something's bothering you, I need to know about it," he said. "That's what a good agent does. I'm here for you." Lenny mentally patted himself on the back for subtly reminding Ava of how valuable his services were.

Ava sighed deeply, and Lenny could hear the exhaustion in that exhalation. "The first night in the house wasn't great," she admitted.

"What do you mean?" Lenny asked, leaning forward in his chair.

"Chase has been obsessed with Nolan's gym," she said simply. "He's been locking himself in there for hours. It's like he's distancing himself but also being weirdly clingy about letting me go too far from him."

Lenny blinked in surprise, thinking to himself how much that sounded like Nolan and the way he'd fixate on both

Miranda and his workout routine. But Lenny wasn't about to say that. He didn't want to scare the poor girl.

"He's probably just excited to be living in the place his hero built," Lenny offered up as an explanation for the boy's odd behavior. Lenny bit back a curse that wanted to push through his lips. If that ridiculous lunkhead, in any way, dragged his star client into some kind of public meltdown or mess, Lenny would ruin him. Not that there was much left of his career to ruin. "As for the clinginess, he's probably also treasuring this new start for your relationship."

Ava paused on the other end, and Lenny imagined her chewing on her lower lips the way she often did when deep in thought.

"That makes some sense," she admitted finally.

Lenny, sensing a chance to move the conversation along, asked, "What else can I do for you today, Ava?"

There was a brief silence before Ava stammered, seemingly embarrassed. "I was just calling in for an update," she said, though Lenny wasn't buying that for a second.

He quickly realized that she had called him solely to talk about what was going on at home. He felt honored to be thought of as a trusted friend by his top client but also a little sad for her that her agent seemed to be the only person she could turn to right now.

"I've fielded a few requests for you to look over some scripts," he said. "I've cherry-picked the ones I think are worthwhile."

"Thanks, Lenny," Ava replied before hesitating, the bubbly spark she normally spoke with completely absent from her voice. "Do you think I should invite you and Miranda over to the house for a little housewarming dinner?"

Lenny froze, thinking about Miranda and her aversion to that place. He wasn't sure how much he should reveal to Ava, but he knew it would be bad if she asked Miranda about something like that directly.

"Miranda has a complicated relationship with that place," Lenny said cautiously.

"What do you mean?" Ava asked, her curiosity clearly piqued.

"It's where her husband died," Lenny said simply, deciding to give part of the truth without exposing all the horrible memories his old friend associated with her former home. "You know, that kinda thing stays with a person. It has those bad memories associated with it."

Ava sighed. "That makes sense," she said, sounding as though she had really been hoping that she'd be able to bring someone into the house, likely to break the tension she and Chase were going through. "But it's disappointing."

Lenny decided to offer her a little more information to help drive the point home. "It's more than just that," he added, trying to paint a more complete picture of the tragedy that happened on that day, "When Nolan died of a heart attack, he was actually holding Miranda's cat at the time. The poor thing was crushed to death under him when he hit the floor."

There was dead silence on the other end of the line.

"Ava, are you all right?" Lenny asked, concern creeping into his voice.

"I'm fine," she said quickly. "I have to go." She abruptly hung up without waiting for a response from Lenny.

That had been a jarring end to the conversation, but it was possible Ava actually did have to go. He hoped that if there were any further issues going down in that house that she would let him know. If things with Chase got bad enough, Lenny knew more than a few rough-and-tumble individuals who would be happy to pay the former action star a visit. They'd make sure he understood how to treat a lady like Ava Monroe.

He set the phone down, telling himself he had done the right thing before going back to his computer and continuing with his day. Of course, Lenny had no idea that on the other side of town, in a small café, Ava Monroe was having a panic attack.

13

Ava sat in the café, her hands shaking so violently that some of the foam from her latte spilled onto her hand. The hot liquid stung, causing her to drop the cup. It clattered onto the saucer, drawing the attention of a few people, including a nearby waitress who rushed forward.

"Ma'am, are you all right?" the waitress asked, her voice laced with concern.

Ava couldn't hear her. The only sound echoing in her head was the horrible mewing from the previous night, followed by the hiss and growl she'd so clearly heard. Lenny's words reverberated through her mind about how Miranda's cat had been in Nolan's arms when he'd died.

The waitress waved a hand in front of her face, and Ava suddenly noticed her. She couldn't make out the words but just assumed she was asking if she was all right. Ava nodded, and the waitress seemed satisfied with that response, though she still looked worried.

Ava's thoughts were consumed by the implications. Miranda's cat had died in the house the same night as Nolan. And she had heard the sound of a cat several times now, coupled with that flash of white darting around the corner during their initial tour of the property. It had to be a wild coincidence. There couldn't be anything beyond that.

But Ava started to think about how dark the house had felt last night and how cold the floor had been. She thought about Chase's strange, erratic behavior. She began to wonder if there could be something more to that place than met the eye. That thought lasted for only a brief moment. She quickly dismissed the idea outright. It was ridiculous.

"Ava Monroe, you can't start blaming your problems on the supernatural," she muttered to herself. There was a logical explanation for the cat noises she had heard. It had nothing to do with an unfortunate cat who was crushed to death in that place five years ago.

Ava quickly paid for her coffee and left, sitting in her car for several minutes before pressing the ignition button. She gripped the steering wheel as her mind continued to fixate on the cat and the noises she had heard. It echoed in her head until she slammed the heel of her hand on the wheel in frustration.

"That's it," she said aloud, resigning herself to get to the bottom of this mess. "I'm going to go back to the house and find the source of that noise. It's probably some poor animal stuck somewhere."

She often found that speaking aloud to herself helped her process information. But right now, with her mind worked into a horrified frenzy, Ava found that talking to herself only made her feel unhinged.

The drive home passed in a blur. When Ava got out of her car, she hesitated before walking into the house. It was like every hair on her body was standing on end. She finally told herself she was being foolish and walked inside. The truth was somewhere in that house. She just had to find it.

Chase was nowhere to be seen as she crossed the threshold, so Ava decided to start looking on her own.

She searched in every closet, every cabinet, even under the stairs. Finally, she got down on her hands and knees, making little *psst* noises to try to lure the cat out into the open.

"Here, kitty, kitty," she whispered, hoping the cat would hear her and not Chase. "Come on out. I'm here to help you."

When that tactic bore no actual fruit, she got two bowls, one with tuna and the other with milk. She set them down beside her and just waited. Frustration and desperation were building within her. She didn't just *want* to find this cat. She *needed* to find it to stop her mind from spinning terrifying stories. A real-life, tangible, living cat would be all the proof she needed that there was nothing crazy or supernatural going on in her house.

Ava moved through the house, peering into every dark corner and shadowed nook. Her heart pounded as she opened each door, half expecting something to jump out at her. But each time, she was met with nothing but empty spaces.

"Here, kitty, kitty," she called softly, her voice trembling slightly. "It's okay. I'm here to help."

She entered the living room, where the sunlight streamed through the large windows, casting long shadows on the floor. The room felt much less intimidating in the daylight, but the memory of last night's eerie events still lingered.

As she crouched down to look under the couch, she heard a soft thump from behind her. Ava spun around, her heart racing. She saw nothing out of the ordinary. It was just the room as it had been. She shook her head, trying to dismiss the growing sense of unease.

"You're just being paranoid," she told herself. "There's a cat somewhere in here. There's no ghost. Just a house with its own noises."

Despite her self-reassurances, she couldn't shake the

feeling that something was off. The house seemed to hum with a low, almost inaudible energy. She could feel it vibrating under her fingertips as she touched the walls.

Moving to the kitchen, she continued her search. She checked every cupboard and pantry, even the small storage spaces she hadn't noticed before. Each time she opened a door, she held her breath, hoping to find the source of the mysterious noises. At that point, she'd be happy enough to find a cat turd. Even that would set her mind at ease.

Moving into a hallway off the main foyer, Ava found a small storage closet. She opened the door and got down on her hands and knees, crawling around inside.

"What are you doing?" a voice asked from behind her.

Ava jumped, banging her head on the bottom of one of the closet's many shelves. She turned to see Chase looming over her. He was dressed in a pair of athletic pants, sneakers, and a tank top. That meant he had been in the gym yet again. As he looked down at her, his expression wasn't curious or even concerned. He was annoyed. His lips were pressed together, and his eyebrows furrowed in irritation.

"I told you last night that I thought I heard a cat meowing somewhere in the house," she said, trying to smile at the ridiculousness of it. But Chase didn't return her smile. "I was just looking for it, that's all."

"There's no cat," he said, his voice flat. "Cut it out."

"I know what I heard," Ava protested.

"There's no cat," Chase repeated more insistently.

"I think I saw it during the tour, too," Ava added.

Chase's face contorted with anger, his cheeks flushing red as he clenched his jaw with unrivaled fury. "There's no damn cat!" he screamed, smashing his fist through the wall and creating a huge hole there.

Ava gasped and jumped back at the sudden, violent

outburst. She fell back on her backside, sitting on the floor, looking up at him with an open-mouthed gape of horror.

Chase looked down at her with smoldering anger in his eyes. There was not a single shred of sympathy or remorse for what he'd just done. "I don't wanna hear another word about it," Chase said, making it clear that there was no room for debate. "Now stop it. Start making my dinner."

Ava was taken aback. Chase had never shown rage like that before, not even when they had been having issues. And he'd never commanded her in such a sexist way, as though she were some kind of servant. Ava wanted to question him, but the look in his eye told her that she shouldn't. She just nodded and gathered herself up, putting thoughts of the mystery cat out of her mind as she made her way into the kitchen.

An hour later, the two of them were sitting at the dinner table, eating the meal of unseasoned chicken, rice, and broccoli that Chase had told her to make. It was bland muscle food. Ava didn't like it one bit, but she had complied with his wishes out of fear. Every time she had thought about objecting, she remembered the sight of his powerful fist plowing through the wall.

Chase didn't seem to feel any remorse about their argument and talked with her jovially, as if everything was fine. Ava responded as best she could, but she was trying to make it clear that she was unnerved.

Finally, when Chase was done, he just got up without taking his plate, leaving it for her to clean up. She was surprised. Chase had always cleaned up after himself. He was a neat freak, far more so than her. But he had just left the plate there without so much as a second glance, vanishing out of the kitchen and moving once more in the direction of the gym.

Ava, in a haze, cleared the plates off the table and put them in the dishwasher. She told herself that she needed to go lay down. Her lack of sleep was finally catching up with her, and she was completely frazzled and exhausted.

As she walked past the spot where Chase had smashed the wall, she noticed something strange right away. There was no hole anymore. There was no drywall debris, not even a chip in the paint. She found that even more terrifying than the moment Chase's fist had smashed through in the first place.

"Chase?" she called out, her voice trembling.

After a moment, he appeared around the corner. "Yeah, babe?" he asked impatiently.

"When did you have time to fix the wall?" she asked, her voice shaking.

"What are you talking about?" he replied, looking genuinely confused.

"You put a hole in the wall an hour ago," she insisted, pointing at the undisturbed surface. "Now it's completely gone."

Chase laughed. She had always loved his laugh, but it sounded different now. It wasn't menacing or off-putting in any way. It was just…different. How does something as unique to a person as their laugh suddenly change?

"You're being silly," he said with an amused shake of his head. "That never happened." He kissed her on the head and walked away, leaving Ava to stare open-mouthed at the spot where the hole had once been.

She walked like a zombie into the living room, shaking her head and muttering to herself. Ava sank into the couch, her mind a whirlwind of confusion and fear. The hole in the wall had been real. She had seen Chase's fist smash through the drywall. The anger in his eyes, the raw force—it had all been real. But now, there was no trace of it. She rubbed her temples, trying to make sense of it all.

As she sat there, the events of the past few days played over in her mind. The eerie noises, Chase's erratic behavior, the unsettling feeling that something was deeply wrong here—it all felt like a bad dream. She knew she couldn't ignore it anymore.

"What the hell is going on in this house?" she asked aloud.

14

Ava sat in the room she was planning to convert into her office. Seated at her desk, she was scrolling through her laptop. The room was filled with the warm glow of the afternoon sun streaming through the large windows. It cast long shadows on the polished wooden floor. Her desk was cluttered with papers, scripts, and her laptop.

She was supposed to be looking through her next script, preparing for an upcoming shoot, which would start filming in a month. However, her mind was anywhere but where it should be.

The script lay untouched beside her, the crisp pages still pristine and unmarked. Instead of immersing herself in the lines and scenes she needed to memorize, she found herself unable to focus. The recent strange events and Chase's increasingly erratic behavior weighed heavily on her mind, making it impossible to concentrate on work.

She sighed, running a hand through her hair in frustration. Ava's gaze drifted back to her laptop screen, where she had typed "Nolan Hillhurst" into the search bar. She hit enter, and the screen filled with links and images related to the late actor.

There were the usual publicist-created interviews, polished and professional, showcasing Nolan as a dedicated artist and a loving husband. Various reviews of his films popped up, praising his physical prowess and commanding presence on the screen.

But it was the tabloid articles that interested her the most. Ava knew the gossip mongers often made up stories and ran with information from dubious sources. But sometimes, there were nuggets of truth buried within the sensationalism. She scanned the headlines, looking for anything that might provide insight into Nolan's life and, perhaps, clues about what was happening to Chase.

Her eyes skimmed over titles like "Inside Nolan Hillhurst's Troubled Marriage" and "Former Co-stars Speak Out on Hillhurst's Temper."

Each headline seemed more lurid than the last, painting a picture of a man whose private life was as tumultuous as his on-screen roles were heroic. Ava clicked on a few links, skimming through the articles, her heart pounding as she read the salacious details.

One article detailed a public argument between Nolan and Miranda at a Hollywood event, with eyewitnesses claiming Nolan had been drinking heavily and shouting obscenities. Another piece recounted stories from former co-stars who described Nolan as intense and sometimes difficult to work with. They described his temper as flaring unpredictably. These accounts were interspersed with grainy photos and dramatic captions, each one adding to the image of a man who was far from the perfect hero he had portrayed on screen.

Ava leaned back in her chair, her mind racing. Could there be something about Nolan's life and death that was affecting Chase? She couldn't shake the feeling that there was a connection, something just out of reach that she needed to understand.

Her thoughts were interrupted by the sound of footsteps approaching. She quickly closed the browser window and picked up the script, pretending to be engrossed in her work. Chase entered the room, his presence filling the space with an unsettling energy.

"Hey," he said, his voice gruff. "What are you up to?"

"Just working on my lines," Ava replied, forcing a smile. "Got to be ready for the shoot next month."

Chase nodded, but his eyes seemed to bore into her, as if searching for something. "Good. Keep at it," he said simply. "I want you to do well."

Ava nodded, her heart pounding in her chest. She could feel his gaze linger on her for a moment longer before he turned and left the room. As soon as he was gone, she let out a breath she didn't realize she'd been holding. She looked back at her computer, the tabloid article still fresh in her mind. She had to find out more about Nolan and the house. Ava just knew it was the key to understanding what was happening to Chase and to their lives.

Ava found an article specifically about Nolan and Miranda's troubled marriage. The headline screamed at her from the screen:

"INSIDE THE NIGHTMARE: Nolan Hillhurst's Marriage from Hell!" A dramatic photo of Nolan's muscles bulging and his face contorted in a scream from one of his action movies dominated the page. Her heart pounded as she began to read.

INSIDE THE NIGHTMARE: Nolan Hillhurst's Marriage from Hell!

Behind the glittering façade of Hollywood's golden couple, Nolan Hillhurst and Miranda Sterling, lurks a dark and twisted reality that few will ever glimpse. While the world sees a perfect pair, sources close to Miranda paint a picture of a marriage marred by control, fear, and abuse.

"He was always controlling," says a former personal assistant

who wishes to remain anonymous. "Nolan has to know where Miranda is at all times. He tracks her phone, questions her about her day, and even decides who she can and can't be friends with. It's like she's a prisoner in her own home."

Miranda, known for her grace and poise, seemed to lose her spark as the years went by. Friends noticed she became more withdrawn, rarely attending events without Nolan by her side.

"She used to be so full of life," recalls a fellow actress. "But after Nolan entered the picture, it was like the light was just gone out of her eyes."

Disturbingly, the story doesn't end with psychological control. Multiple sources allege that Nolan's temper frequently turns violent.

"I saw bruises on her arms more than once," says a close family friend. "When I asked her about it, she just brushed it off, saying she was clumsy. But I knew better."

One harrowing account comes from a former housekeeper. "There were nights when I'd hear them shouting at each other," she confides. "One time, I heard a loud crash and ran to see what was happening. Mr. Nolan had thrown a vase against the wall, and Miss Miranda was cowering in the corner. I quit the next day. I couldn't bear to see her like that."

Adding fuel to the fire are rampant rumors of Nolan's abuse of anabolic steroids to maintain his body. The actor, known for his towering physique and intense workout regimen, reportedly uses performance-enhancing drugs to maintain his bodybuilder frame.

"He's obsessed with being the biggest and the best," says a former gym buddy. "But the steroids made him unpredictable. One minute, he'd be fine; the next, he'd be flying into a rage over nothing."

The steroid use allegedly contributed to his erratic behavior and deteriorating health.

"You could see the changes," the gym buddy continues. "He'd get these crazy mood swings, and his body started to break down. But he wouldn't stop. He said it was the price of staying on top."

The culmination of these factors created a volatile and dangerous environment for Miranda Sterling.

"She lives in constant fear," says the family friend. "But she feels trapped. Leaving Nolan isn't an option. He made sure she knew that."

Ava's hands trembled as she finished reading the article. The image of Nolan and Miranda's marriage was far darker than she had imagined. She stared at the screen, the horror of what she'd just read settling over her like a heavy blanket.

Ava had read many tabloid articles in her life. Many of them had specifically been about her. Many of them were also complete fabrications. But something about this article was believable. She wasn't sure why, but she knew deep in her heart that this was 100% real. All of this happened verbatim.

She couldn't describe why or how, but something in her was just utterly certain that this was the undisputed truth.

She leaned back in her chair, staring blankly at the computer screen. The words of the article echoed in her mind, painting a vivid picture of the torment Miranda must have endured. The details, the quotes, the allegations—they all resonated with a disturbing clarity.

Ava felt a pang of empathy for Miranda, imagining the fear and helplessness she must have felt living with a man like Nolan. She also remembered what Lenny had said about this house holding bad memories for Miranda. That made a lot more sense with this added information.

Part of Ava wanted to call Miranda and ask about it, to hear her story in her own words and gauge the truth for herself. But Ava knew she couldn't do that. Something like this, if it were true, would be incredibly painful to talk about. She was nowhere near close enough to Miranda to ask her those kinds of questions. She sighed, knowing that even if she mustered the courage to ask, it would be crossing a line.

She then thought about possibly asking Lenny about it.

Lenny had been close to both Nolan and Miranda. He might have some insights. But she quickly put that idea out of her mind.

She didn't want to put Lenny in a sticky situation where he was forced to talk about one of his clients behind their back to another. Additionally, he could refuse to give her any information and then tell Miranda that she was snooping around. That would make her look even worse.

Ava rubbed her temples, trying to dispel the headache beginning to form. She started to think about the way Chase had been the last several days. The way he'd spoken to her, those explosions of rage. They were nothing like the Chase she'd known for years. That wasn't the Chase she'd fallen in love with. It couldn't be the Chase she'd married. Honestly, it sounded an awful lot like Nolan, as he was described in this article. One minute, he'd be fine, and the next, he'd be flying into a rage... That was the quote that rang out to her the most.

She wondered if maybe Chase, in an effort to boost his sagging career, had started taking performance-enhancing drugs. That could explain all the exercising and the sudden horrible rage fits. The thought of Chase, once so loving and gentle, now mirroring Nolan's dark path, sent a shiver down her spine. Could it be that the house, or something within it, was influencing him?

Ava bit her lip, contemplating whether she should confront Chase about it. But then she quickly put that out of mind. With how unpredictable he'd been, accusing him of drug use might not be the best idea. The last thing she wanted was to provoke another outburst or make him feel cornered. She needed to approach this delicately, but how?

She stared at the article one last time before closing her laptop. The house was eerily quiet, the kind of silence that made her skin crawl. Ava stood up and walked to the window, looking out at the manicured lawn and the distant hills beyond. The world outside seemed so normal, so serene, in stark contrast to the turmoil she felt inside.

She turned back to her office, the sunlight casting long shadows across the floor. She couldn't shake the feeling that something was terribly wrong in this house. It wasn't just Chase's behavior. There was a darkness here, a lingering malevolence that seeped into their lives and twisted everything. She needed to find a way to protect her husband, herself, and their marriage from whatever was lurking in the shadows of their new home.

Ava bit her lip in thought. She returned to her laptop and, on a whim, Googled "Nolan Hillhurst Death." The search results were a mix of tributes, obituaries, and fan memories. She clicked on one of the top results, an article from a popular entertainment news site. The headline read: "Legendary Action Star Nolan Hillhurst Dies at Home."

Legendary Action Star Nolan Hillhurst Dies at Home

The film industry mourns the loss of one of its brightest stars. Nolan Hillhurst, known for his towering presence and iconic roles in numerous action films, was found dead in his Beverly Hills home. The forty-five-year-old actor reportedly suffered a heart attack. Hillhurst's unexpected death has left a void in Hollywood, where he was revered not only for his on-screen heroics but also for his off-screen charisma.

Hillhurst's grieving wife, Miranda Sterling, issued a heartfelt statement: "Nolan was not just my husband; he was my best friend and confidant. His passing has left a hole in my life that no one could ever fill. His fans and friends will remember him for his strength, courage, and kindness. I will miss him every day."

Sterling, also an accomplished actress, has asked for privacy during this difficult time. In a tragic twist, the couple's beloved pet cat, Snowball, was also found dead, crushed under Hillhurst's body. Snowball was known to accompany Sterling during her downtime, often seen nestled in her lap during interviews and photo shoots.

The entertainment world extends its deepest sympathies to Miranda and all who were close to Nolan. His legacy will continue to live on through his unforgettable performances and the countless lives he touched.

Ava felt a pang of sympathy for Miranda. The actress's words seemed genuine, yet Ava couldn't help but wonder how much of that sentiment was true and how much was crafted for public consumption. She continued to comb through article after article, piecing together the narrative surrounding Nolan's death. The more she read, the more the initial tragedy seemed shrouded in a veil of unanswered questions and speculation.

Scrolling farther, Ava's eyes caught a more sensational headline: "Suspicion Surrounds Nolan Hillhurst's Death." She hesitated for a moment before clicking on it. As the page loaded, her heart began racing with morbid curiosity.

Suspicion Surrounds Nolan Hillhurst's Death

As Hollywood continues to mourn the loss of Nolan Hillhurst, questions are arising about the circumstances surrounding his untimely demise. Officially, Hillhurst died of a heart attack in his home, a tragedy attributed to years of rumored anabolic steroid and recreational drug abuse. However, several aspects of his death have sparked controversy and speculation.

Sources reveal that police reports from the scene of Hillhurst's death have been sealed, fueling rumors and whispers within the industry. Unlike many celebrity deaths, Hillhurst did not have an open-casket wake, and his body was quickly cremated. These unusual decisions have led some to wonder what the legendary actor's family might be hiding.

Further complicating matters is the fact that Hillhurst's wife, Miranda Sterling, was not present at the time of his death. Sterling has remained largely silent on the details, asking for privacy. Yet, insiders hint at underlying tensions in the marriage, suggesting that all may not have been as perfect as it seemed.

While no official accusations have been made, the combination of these elements has led some to question whether foul play could have been involved. The tragic death of their pet cat, Snowball, found crushed under Hillhurst's body, adds a poignant and tragic layer to the mystery.

As the entertainment world grapples with these revelations, fans and friends of Hillhurst are left to ponder the truth behind the curtain of Hollywood's glitz and glamour.

Ava was shocked by the article's insinuations. She couldn't believe anyone would suspect Miranda of being involved in her husband's death. The thought seemed preposterous, almost cruel. She went to close the article but lingered on a photo attached to it. In the picture, Nolan and Miranda were smiling. Miranda held a fluffy white cat, its fur immaculate and eyes bright.

Ava stared intently at the cat, her mind drifting back to the eerie mewing she had heard the other night and the white blur she caught out of the corner of her eye during their initial tour. This cat was also white, and that seemed like too much of a coincidence.

The sound of the eerie meowing, hissing, and growling echoed in her head, sending a chill down her spine. She couldn't shake the feeling that the house, or something within it, was trying to tell her something. The cat's image stayed with her, a haunting reminder of the unsettling events that seemed to be unfolding around her.

15

That night, Ava and Chase were sitting in the living room, watching an action movie Chase had picked out. Adding to Ava's growing concern, the film starred none other than Nolan Hillhurst himself, and Chase had been very into it from the beginning.

Ava, on the other hand, had been far less enthusiastic. She didn't dislike action films per se—she had even starred in a few herself—but Nolan Hillhurst's action films were a different breed. They were all explosions, wooden acting, and paper-thin plots. There was nothing engaging about them unless you were a thirteen-year-old boy. And since Chase had discovered Nolan at that age, it was understandable why he would be so enthralled.

Ava, however, didn't have that nostalgic attachment to these films. Watching them now with adult eyes and sensibilities, she saw them for what they were. She had told Chase in the past that these movies weren't her cup of tea, and he had always been good about not forcing them on her. But tonight, that consideration seemed to have flown out the window. He had walked into the room and put the movie on without even asking her what she wanted to see. He'd then settled in with a huge smile on his face. One meaty, muscular arm draped over her almost possessively.

Ava had tried to shift more than once to get more comfortable against him. But when she moved, his strong arm would restrict around her, pulling her in as though he were worried she was going to try to escape. She felt, not for the first time, like a prisoner in this room. It brought back sour memories of when he had moved to block her from leaving the gym that morning.

For the first time in Ava's life, she had felt completely trapped in one place. It had terrified and deeply unsettled her. She had hoped it was just a one-time thing, a single anomaly, a drop in the ocean of their relationship. But it seemed as though Chase was only becoming bolder in his desire to keep his wife by his side. Now, instead of just blocking her way, he'd taken to physically restraining her under the guise of affection.

When the first film had ended, before she could suggest they watch something else, he had put another one on. It was like there was a massive Nolan Hillhurst marathon going on, and she hadn't agreed to attend.

Ava sighed inwardly, glancing up at Chase. He was so engrossed in the movie, his eyes glued to the screen with a childlike fascination. She had humored Chase a few times over the years and watched these films with him. But he had simply been watching as a fan. He'd smile at fun parts and explain certain bits of trivia to her. But for the most part, he would just watch it normally. But now, there was something in his face as he watched Nolan on the screen.

It was more than just the admiration of a dedicated fan. As weird as it seemed, Ava thought it seemed almost like…pride. It was as if, for some reason, Chase was taking pride in the performance of the long-dead action star. It was strange, to say the least. Ava wondered if, perhaps after living in the man's former home and spending his day working out in his gym, Chase had developed some kind of emotional connection to Nolan that went beyond just fandom or admiration.

Adding to the growing unease Ava was feeling, Chase was drinking quite a bit. He had a bottle of vodka on the floor that he kept picking up and refilling his glass with. And he was drinking it straight. Chase had never been a heavy drinker. His father had been an abusive alcoholic, and Chase had always sworn he would never repeat those horrible mistakes. But there he was, downing glass after glass of straight vodka.

Ava had tried to tell him that maybe he'd had enough, but she was either ignored or bluntly told to be quiet. By now, the alcohol seemed to be leaking out of every pore, and he stank like a distillery.

Ava shifted uncomfortably in her seat, trying to focus on the movie but finding it impossible. Her mind kept drifting back to the articles she had read earlier. It was impossible to see Nolan Hillhurst up there stumbling his way through wooden dialogue and one-liners without imagining the vengeful, angry, abusive drug addict described in those articles she had read. It turned her stomach. She found herself glaring at the screen more often than not, her nose crinkling with disgust at the pig of a man.

And what would she do if Chase truly was following in his idol's footsteps? What would she do if the man she loved, the man she had dedicated herself to, was following the path of an abusive addict who tormented the ones he loved and died at forty-five?

The idea of Chase taking performance-enhancing drugs like anabolic steroids still lingered in her mind, but she didn't dare bring it up. There were so many dangers to taking those drugs. Off the top of her head, Ava knew it weakened the heart muscles and could even cause the heart itself to become enlarged. An enlarged heart could only continue on for so long until it just stopped beating one day.

There were also several side effects to watch out for, not the least of which were shrinking genitals, impotence, and erectile dysfunction.

"Isn't this great?" Chase slurred, pulling her closer in a tight, almost desperate, entrapping embrace. "Nolan was the best. No one could do action like him. He was more than just an action hero. The guy was a freaking artist. He brought a real artistry to the craft, a real elegance to every performance."

Ava forced a smile. "Yeah, it's... something," she said.

Chase had never talked about Nolan like that before. Whenever he'd mention him, he'd just say that he was "the man" or "a total badass." What was with all this talk of artistry? It wasn't like they were watching *Macbeth* at the Globe Theatre. It was a bad action movie, and the guy couldn't act his way out of a paper bag. What was Chase seeing that she wasn't?

Of course, Chase didn't seem to notice her lack of enthusiasm. He was entirely too engrossed in what he apparently believed to be the height of sophisticated cinematic art. Ava rolled her eyes as Nolan jumped a speedboat into the air to take out a helicopter. It wasn't exactly high cinema worthy of Scorsese.

Her husband took another swig of vodka, his eyes never leaving the screen. Ava glanced at the clock. It was getting late. She was tired, but she didn't want to leave Chase alone in this state. Not that she thought she even could if she tried with the way he was holding on to her. She sighed again, trying to focus on the movie.

As the film dragged on, Ava's thoughts wandered. She remembered the last two days and how she had tiptoed around Chase, trying to avoid any conflict. His overbearing, demanding, and demeaning personality was becoming more pronounced each day.

Then, of course, there was the hole in the wall that had mysteriously vanished. He had insisted there had been no hole, that she had imagined the entire thing. But that was impossible. Ava knew what was real and what wasn't. But it wasn't possible that he had somehow patched the hole and repainted it in such a short amount of time. If he had, there would have at least been wet paint on the wall. But there had been nothing. It only added to the eerie feeling that something was very wrong in this house.

Ava glanced at Chase again, watching as he laughed at a particularly over-the-top explosion on the screen. His joy seemed so misplaced, so disconnected from the man she knew. She wanted to reach out to him, to ask him what was wrong, but the fear of another outburst held her back.

Ava looked down at her hands, wringing them nervously. She needed to find a way to break through to Chase, to bring back the man she loved. But how?

The Nolan Hillhurst marathon continued, and with each passing minute, Ava felt more trapped, more isolated than ever before. The movie played on, the sound of explosions filling the room, but all Ava could hear was the echo of her own thoughts and the chilling mewing that haunted her from the other night.

The irony of the situation wasn't lost on Ava whatsoever. The reason they had moved was because Chase had believed she had monopolized their former home. He had called it her palace and said he felt like he lived in her purse on more than one occasion.

She'd seen his point and made sacrifices, giving up her dream home to make a new life with her husband. She'd tried to meet him halfway, even selecting a home she knew he would love, a home that connected with his passions and career.

But it felt as though Chase wasn't interested in compromise anymore. He just wanted everything done his way, according to his rules. It was alarming, to say the least, and Ava was starting to feel like a stranger in her own home at the best of times and a prisoner in it at the worst.

If Chase really was using steroids, she wasn't sure what she'd do. Should she confront him about it? Call him out? Get rid of his supply? She wasn't sure how she could safely breach the subject without putting herself in danger. She didn't believe Chase would ever hit her knowingly. It would have been the most out-of-character move for her historically gentle and kind husband, something she felt that even the influence of drugs could never make happen.

But she also knew that one of the major side effects of anabolic steroid abuse was explosions of rage. Perhaps Nolan had also been a gentle soul at one time, and the drugs he'd used to maintain his physique had driven him to his more destructive tendencies.

But not Chase. Not her Chase. It wasn't possible. It couldn't be.

Then Ava glanced at the bruises on her arms, which were still faintly visible. There was a time she had never thought even that was possible. Her thoughts drifted to Miranda, wondering if she had watched this same transformation occur before her marriage had turned violent. Had she denied it the way Ava was now? Telling herself that she had nothing to fear? That it was never even a possibility?

And what then had it felt like the day Nolan had proven her wrong? Ava didn't even want to think about it.

She wondered if she was just in that same denial. What if that was what awaited her as well? It was a terrifying thought, one that felt inescapable as Chase's presence loomed so large beside her. At one time, she'd felt protected and shielded by his size and strength. Now, for the first time, she saw it as a threat.

Chase laughed loudly at another explosion on the screen, jolting Ava out of her thoughts. She looked at him, the man she had loved so deeply, now almost unrecognizable. His muscles, once a symbol of his dedication and hard work, now seemed menacing. The bottle of vodka on the floor was nearly empty, and his glass was never far from his hand. Ava's eyes drifted to the bottle, and she wondered how much longer this could go on.

"Chase," she said softly, trying to get his attention. "Maybe we should call it a night. It's getting late."

"What's the matter?" he replied, not taking his eyes off the screen. "Can't handle a few more movies?"

"It's not that," Ava said, choosing her words carefully. "You've been drinking a lot, and I think you need to get some rest."

Chase finally looked at her, his expression hardening. "I'm fine, Ava. Just relax."

Ava felt a pang of frustration and fear. She was pushing on some dangerous ground here, and she had to tread very carefully. "I just think you should take it easy," she said gently, floating the idea of possibly slowing down. "You've been working out a lot and drinking this much isn't good for you. I mean, it's all empty calories, right? You don't want it eating into your gains."

Chase's grip on his glass tightened, and for a moment, Ava thought he might lash out. But then he sighed and leaned back, staring at the screen. "Fine," he said, shaking his head in annoyance. "We'll call it a night after this one."

Ava nodded, relieved. She turned her attention back to the movie, though her mind was far from the action scenes playing out in front of her. She couldn't stop thinking about the man sitting next to her and the dark path he seemed to be on.

As the credits finally rolled, Chase turned off the TV and stood up, swaying slightly. Ava stood up as well, ready to help him to bed if needed. But he brushed her off, heading toward the kitchen.

"Where are you going?" Ava asked, her voice trembling slightly.

"Just need another drink," Chase muttered.

Ava watched him go, a sinking feeling in her stomach. She knew she couldn't go on like this, living in fear and uncertainty. She needed to do something, to find a way to reach Chase and pull him back from the brink. But how?

After a moment to gather her strength and bravery, Ava took a deep breath and followed him into the kitchen. She had to try, for both their sakes.

"Chase," she said, her voice firmer this time. "Please. Let's just go to bed."

He turned to look at her, his eyes glassy from the alcohol. For a moment, she thought she saw a flicker of the man she loved, the man who had always been there for her. But then it was gone, replaced by a blank, unfeeling stare.

"Fine," he said, setting the bottle down with a heavy thud. "Let's go."

They walked to the bedroom in silence, the tension between them palpable. As they lay down, Ava stared at the ceiling, her mind racing. She needed a plan, a way to help Chase and save their marriage. She needed to find the strength to face whatever was happening in their home, no matter how terrifying it might be.

But to help, she needed to know for sure what was happening here. If he was using drugs, she would need to find them first, to have tangible evidence to place in front of him that he couldn't possibly deny.

Despite wanting to sleep and despite being incredibly tired, sleep seemed nearly impossible for Ava. She tossed and turned for a bit as Chase snored beside her, completely unconscious and in a deep, deep sleep.

He had never snored before, and Ava chalked it up to just another ridiculous new thing he'd developed that she didn't like. She looked at his arms as he lay there, vaguely able to make out their definition in the dim moonlight filtering in through the window.

They seemed somehow bigger than normal. They had grown quite a bit in the short time they had been in this house. That also gave credence to her belief that he might be using anabolic steroids. Muscles didn't grow that much in such a short time.

Ava finally told herself that enough was enough. She was going to find proof of what was going on and confront him with it so that he couldn't deny it for a second longer. She was going to get her husband back. He was the love of her life, and he was worth fighting for. Even if the one she would have to fight against to save him was him. Ava quietly slipped out of bed, putting on her slippers and robe before creeping out into the hall.

Once more, the house seemed strangely twisted and almost demonic in the dark, as though the fabric of reality itself was warping through the hallway. Telling herself that it was just her imagination, Ava made it to the bottom of the stairs.

She knew that if Chase was keeping any kind of substance from her, there was only one place he would be able to hide it. Only one place in the whole house where he could be sure that she wouldn't look. That was the gym. She remembered the way he'd reacted when she had been in the gym last night. He was angry with her, as though she were trespassing in a room in the house they both owned together.

As Ava made her way toward the back of the house, something stopped her in her tracks.

The hole in the wall was back.

The very same hole Chase had created earlier with his enraged boulder of a fist was once again sitting there in the middle of the wall for all to see. She gasped and backed up, hand covering her heart as she weighed the meaning of this.

How was it back? There was no way it could be back. The wall had been intact when they went to bed, and Chase hadn't left her sight all night. Shaking her head, Ava backed away from the wall, turning and fleeing from it like it was some kind of monster.

The implications spun through her head at a million miles per hour. Ava was so engrossed in these chilling thoughts that she hadn't realized the gym doors were right in front of her.

She stopped in front of them and took a deep breath before entering. "One thing at a time," she told herself, trying to steady her breathing. There was nothing she could do about the hole in the wall right now, regardless of how impossible it seemed. The main goal she had to focus on right now was getting into the gym and finding whatever it was Chase was hiding from her in there.

She slid the door open and stepped inside, closing it behind her once more, if only to add an extra barrier between her and the resurgent hole in the wall. It was dark in the gym, but she could see her outline moving in the large mirrors. She began to creep through, looking in and around all the equipment for any place where Chase might hide drugs. She searched high and low, using her phone's light to guide her, but found nothing. Ava felt relieved at first, but that quickly turned into a cold, prickling dread.

Because if it wasn't drugs, if he wasn't taking steroids, then what the hell was happening here?

A sound split through the darkness, causing her to jump. It was the yowl of a cat, insistent and terrified. Ava noticed something in the mirror dash quickly through the dark room, a sudden blur of whiteness. But when she looked, there was nothing.

"What the hell are you doing in here?" a deep voice boomed out at her.

She screamed and turned around, coming face to chest with Chase, who was standing there in his shorts and no shirt, glowering down at her with a smoldering fury she'd never seen before.

What was even more insane and terrifying was that she hadn't seen him come up behind her in the mirror. How was that possible? How was any of this possible?

"I was just curious about the equipment in here," she stammered, hoping he was still drunk enough to believe her.

But Chase's eyes bore into hers with crystal clarity. He was focused and intent. Somehow, even after all he'd had to drink, Chase was stone-cold sober. "You're lying," he said flatly.

"I couldn't sleep, so I just wanted to see what was so great about this space," Ava said, switching gears and stumbling over her words. She took two steps back into the room, and he cleared the space between them with one long stride. "I mean, you're always spending so much time in here. I wanted to see if I could…you know, use it with you! It might be fun to work out together, babe!" She was trying to keep her voice steady, but there was no hiding the quaking quiver that shook her words.

"You're lying!" Chase screamed, his voice suddenly deeper and distorted, as though unnaturally modulated in some otherworldly way. As he screamed, his eyes shifted, turning midnight black and vanishing into the shadows.

Ava screamed in horror as the mirrors in the gym suddenly shattered in a spray of broken glass. Chase grabbed her by the arm and, with the effort one might use to shoo away a fly, flung her through the air and out the door. Ava slid along the floor, her hip and side aching in the wake of the horror. Chase was strong… but he wasn't that strong! No one was *that* strong! This was something else, something unnatural and horrifying.

His black eyes settled onto her, and in that deep, distorted voice, he called out to her. "Get your ass back in here and clean up this mess," he demanded, his voice seemingly coming from all directions at once. It was as though the entire house was speaking in that horrific tone.

Ava shook her head frantically. "This isn't you, Chase," she said, scooting back away from him on the floor as he slowly walked out of the gym like a horror movie monster. "Baby, it's not you!"

Chase laughed at her, the distortion in his voice turning that new laugh of his into an insane cackle that bounced off every wall of the mansion. "Chase is far better off now than he ever was before," the voice said, and Ava's heart sank.

Chase was talking about himself in the third person. It was as if she was somehow right…and this wasn't her Chase standing in front of her.

"Now, you need to learn your damn place and shut up about things you don't understand."

Chase took a step toward her. He was strong, but Ava was faster. She scrambled to her feet and ran for the foyer as though her life depended on it. She had no idea what it was chasing her, what that thing was that was wearing her husband like some kind of mask, but it wasn't natural. It wasn't human. It couldn't be.

He came after her, but he was bulky and slow. Ava was able to scramble beyond his reach and make a break for the exit.

Without so much as a look back, Ava grabbed her keys, ripped open the door, and ran out onto the porch. Chase stopped at the threshold of the house as though he couldn't physically walk through the doorway.

He stood there in a rage and screamed out into the night. His bellow was so powerful and filled with such otherworldly malice that it actually made the ground beneath her shake. Ava fell onto her hands and knees in the driveway and turned to see Chase standing in the doorway, blackened eyes wide with a wild rage. His lips were pulled back in a snarl, baring not the perfectly straight white teeth she had known so well for so long but the feral, sharpened fangs of some kind of beast.

Ava had no words for what she was seeing or experiencing. It was impossible, and yet it was happening right in front of her face.

"Get back here!" Chase bellowed. "Get back here now!"

But it was clear to Ava now that he was, for some reason, unable to walk through the doorway. The more she thought about it, Chase hadn't actually left the house at all since they'd moved in.

Not looking a gift horse in the mouth, Ava got to her feet, ran to her car, climbed in, and, with shaking fingers, started the engine. Still clad in her robe and slippers, Ava Monroe sped off into the night as Chase's unnaturally loud and distorted voice screamed after her from the doorway. The force of his voice shook the vehicle, and Ava nearly veered off the pavement onto the grass.

However, she was able to gain control of the car and floored it through the opened gate, putting the house and the monster that had been wearing the face of her love behind her.

As Ava drove through the night, her mind was a hurricane of terror and confusion. She had to find help. Someone had to understand what was happening to her husband and their home. Surely, someone could explain it to her and ultimately help her.

But for now, all she could do was drive and hope she could escape the nightmare her life had become.

16

Lenny sat at home in his robe with a glass of scotch, settling into his comfy chair to watch TV at the end of a long day. He thought about everything that had happened that day, including a very tense conversation with Miranda.

She'd, of course, asked him about progress with auditions and the roles that she had her eye on. And unfortunately, Lenny hadn't been able to sugarcoat things anymore. She'd been incensed, calling him incompetent. They'd gotten into a huge argument, with Lenny having to remind her of the extreme lengths he'd always gone to, to help her when she needed it the most. But Miranda hadn't wanted to hear it. She had kicked Lenny out of her house in a fit of tears.

"You're not doing your job, Lenny!" Miranda had screamed at him, her face flushed with anger. "I haven't landed a single decent role! You said this was going to be my comeback! You said it was going to work!"

"Miranda, I'm doing everything I can," Lenny had replied, struggling to keep his voice calm. "But you have to understand, it's a competitive market. There are younger actresses, new faces—"

"I don't want to hear excuses!" she interrupted, her voice shaking with frustration. "You've always managed to get me the best before. What's changed?"

Lenny sighed, running a hand through his hair. "It's not that simple," he said simply with a shrug. "Times have changed, Miranda. The industry has changed. But I'm still fighting for you every day."

"Fighting for me?" Miranda's voice was dripping with sarcasm. "It doesn't feel like it. It feels like you've given up on me."

"That's not true," Lenny said firmly. "I've been with you through thick and thin. Remember five years ago? Who stood by you and got you back on your feet? I did."

Miranda's eyes welled up with tears, but her anger didn't wane. "I don't need a reminder of my past, Lenny," she spat at him. "I drink to forget it! What I need is for you to fix this."

"I'm trying, Miranda," he sighed, shaking his head. "But you have to give me something to work with. Maybe we should consider some different types of roles—"

"Different types of roles?" she scoffed. "You mean step down from leading lady to what? Supporting roles? Cameos? I'm not ready to be put out to pasture, Lenny!"

"That's not what I meant," he tried to explain, but it was too late. The damage was done.

"Get out," Miranda said coldly. "Just get out of my house!"

Lenny had stood there for a moment, a mix of frustration and sadness churning inside him. "Miranda, you know I'm on your side," he said. "This isn't easy for either of us."

"Out," she repeated, tears streaming down her face now. "I need you to leave."

He had left, feeling more defeated than he had in years.

The argument replayed in his mind as he sat in his comfy

chair, trying to shake off the day's events. He had a genuine fondness for Miranda, a real personal connection from years of continued association. He knew it was just Miranda's insecurities bleeding through, and it wouldn't lead to any kind of forced separation between them.

Lenny told himself that everything would be fine, just as it had always been before.

As soon as he raised his glass to his lips for the first time, the bell from his home's gate buzzed. Confused as to who might be paying him a visit so late at night, he took out his phone and checked the feed from the camera.

Lenny was shocked to find Ava in her car, looking into the camera and calling out to him with a crazed desperation.

"Lenny!" she practically screamed into the box. "Lenny! Are you there? I need help! I need help right now!"

He activated the intercom immediately. He could see through the feed that her hair was disheveled, her eyes were wide, and there were tear streaks running down her cheeks. There was also the unmistakable sound of tense panic in her voice.

"Ava, what's wrong?" he asked again, his concern growing.

"Just open the damn gate, Lenny!" she yelled, her voice cracking as though she were trying to get inside the safety of the gate before something pounced on her from the shadows.

He quickly complied, opening the gate as she drove in. Lenny stood up, setting his glass down and running a hand through his hair. He was still in his robe, but the urgency in Ava's voice had left no room for hesitation. He hurried to the front door, opening it just as Ava's car screeched to a halt in his driveway.

Lenny held the door open for Ava, who rushed inside, still in her own bathrobe and slippers. He was shocked at her disheveled state and the wild look in her eyes.

"Ava, what on earth happened to you?" he asked. Lenny's

eyes were wide as he gestured toward the starlet incredulously. "Are you all right? Are you hurt?

Ava's eyes were wide, and her breath was coming out in ragged gasps. Her hands shook uncontrollably as she tried in vain to say something, anything. But it seemed as though blind panic had somehow robbed her of her voice. Without a word, she reached over and grabbed the scotch from his hand, taking a long drink of it. Ava then coughed violently at the burning sensation it left behind, tears streaming down her cheeks with renewed intensity.

Lenny noticed the bruises on her arm that looked suspiciously like finger marks. His heart sank as he started to piece together what might have happened. He couldn't hide the snarl of fury that began to spread across his face.

That son of a bitch… He'd end his career. He'd have him beaten within an inch of his life. And maybe he'd even take that inch as well. There was no hell dark enough for a man who would raise his hand to a woman.

But Chase could wait. There was a horrified and traumatized girl in front of him right now who needed his help. Lenny gently took the scotch from her hand and looked into the eyes of his biggest client.

"Ava, you need water right now, not alcohol," he said firmly. He guided her to the couch and sat her down, then hurried to the kitchen to fetch a glass of water.

When he returned, Ava was trembling. He held out the glass for her, and she took it with both hands.

"Don't drink it too fast," he said, urging her to take a sip.

Ava brought the glass up with her shaking hands and took a few careful sips. Once it seemed as though she was breathing normally again and Lenny was fairly certain she wasn't going into shock, he decided to try to get to the bottom of this situation. However, experience told him there was only one logical explanation.

"Ava, tell me what happened," he said slowly. Trying to be as gentle as he could under the circumstances. "Did Chase hit you?" He kept his voice soft as he sat down beside her.

Ava shook her head, but the tears kept coming. "It wasn't just Chase," she said, her voice barely above a whisper. "Something is wrong with him, Lenny. Something... not natural. It's not Chase. It's not my Chase."

Lenny had heard this kind of thing before. When a spouse turned violent, the victim of their aggression would try to say that it wasn't them, that it was someone else. Their minds just couldn't piece together at the moment how someone could go from supposedly loving them to striking them. It had to be a different person. But it wasn't.

"What do you mean?" Lenny asked, frowning as he tried to make sense of her words. "Just start from the beginning."

"He's been acting strange ever since we moved into that house," Ava began, her voice trembling. "He's been obsessed with Nolan's gym, spending hours in there, and when he's not in the gym, he's... different. Angrier. More aggressive. Tonight, he threw me across the room like I was nothing."

Lenny's eyes widened in shock. "Threw you?" he asked. "You mean he pushed you down? The bastard!"

"No, Lenny, I mean, he threw me with a shrug of his arm," she insisted. "He threw me twenty feet across the room like I was nothing! He's strong, Lenny, but no one is that strong!"

"Ava, that's...," Lenny was trying to be gentle with the clearly traumatized starlet. "Hun, that's not possible."

"It is!" she insisted, turning to him so violently and with such insistence that she spilled the water she'd been drinking on his robe. She hadn't even noticed, though, in her rush to get this story out. "He grabbed me, and...and his eyes... Lenny, his eyes turned black. Completely black. And his voice, it wasn't his voice. It was deeper, distorted. He told me to 'know my place.' He's never talked to me like that before!"

Lenny's mind raced. He didn't know how to respond. He couldn't feed into this delirium. But she seemed so certain. That level of certainty was painting a much clearer picture for Lenny now. He understood what was likely going on here all too well. He took a deep breath and looked into her eyes.

"Ava, what you're saying...," he said, keeping his tone gentle. "It's impossible. Are you and Chase taking any kind of drugs? If you have a substance problem, you need to tell me. We can get you into treatment quietly so the press never finds out."

Ava shook her head vehemently. Her teeth were gritted in frustration. "I'm not on anything, Lenny," she insisted. "I never touch that crap. You know that! I thought maybe Chase was taking steroids, but this is something different, man. Something terrifying."

Lenny still couldn't believe what he was hearing, but he didn't want to dismiss her fears outright. If he did, she might leave and get behind the wheel. He still fully believed she was high as a kite, and the only thing to do in this situation was to let her sleep it off.

"Okay, okay," he said, trying to sound soothing. "You can stay in one of my guest rooms tonight. We'll figure all this out tomorrow, I promise."

Ava's relief was palpable as she reached out and hugged her agent, crying into his chest. "Thank you, Lenny," she sobbed. "Thank you so much."

"It's the least I can do," Lenny said softly, wrapping his arms around her and patting her on the back. After a moment, Lenny helped Ava to her feet and led her to the guest room. He then helped her into bed and tucked her in. "Just...try to get some rest, Ava," he said. "We'll sort all of this out in the morning."

She nodded, her eyes filled with gratitude. "Thank you,

Lenny," she said again, sniffling and wiping a tear from her eye. "I don't know what I'd do without you."

"Just rest," he said, patting her shoulder gently. "We'll figure this out."

As he closed the door behind him, Lenny shook his head in confusion. He wasn't sure how to respond to all this. She was clearly delusional, and despite her protests, he was convinced she had to be on something.

Once she was in bed, Lenny sat down and flipped through his phone. If, in the morning, she still insisted on sticking to this delusion, then he knew someone he could call. He just hoped it didn't come to that.

17

The next morning, Lenny woke after a fitful night of sleep. He was beyond worried about Ava and the nonsense she'd been spouting the night before in her drug-addled delirium.

He was just glad she had come to him and hadn't gone somewhere public or, God forbid, on social media to rant and rave in her bathrobe about demonic strength and black, glowing eyes.

It was clear to Lenny that she and Chase had likely gotten into some pretty hardcore drugs, probably laced with something bad. It wasn't unheard of for bad trips to take a violent or even tragic turn in this town. Honestly, it was a miracle Ava had managed to drive all the way there without crashing.

Lenny could already imagine the headlines labeling her as the latest in a long line of troubled starlets. She'd be the next Lindsay Lohan or Britney Spears. The entire tabloid media would have a field day eating her alive, and soon enough, the roles would begin to dry up as studios wouldn't want to take part in the drama.

Lenny knew he needed to do everything in his power to fix this problem fast before it became a disaster for them both.

As he groggily reached for his phone, it rang. He saw that it was Miranda calling and sent it to voicemail. He didn't have the time or energy to talk to her now and possibly get screamed at again. He knew that the issue with Ava was likely going to take up most of his day. He had already called his assistant, saying he was taking a personal day.

Ava appeared in the hallway, still wearing her robe and slippers, while wiping at her eyes. Lenny greeted her warmly.

"Good morning, Ava," he said with a kind smile. "How are you feeling?"

She shrugged, her eyes downcast. "I didn't get much sleep," she admitted, bringing her arms up to hug her sides. She was still shaking, still clearly traumatized by the aftereffects of whatever drug was working its way out of her system.

"Come on," Lenny said, leading her to the kitchen. "Let's get you some coffee." He poured a cup and handed it to her.

"Thanks," Ava murmured, wrapping her hands around the mug as if it were a lifeline.

Lenny sat across from her, studying her face carefully. They were going to have to level with each other now, but Lenny knew that he'd have to do so carefully. He'd had many such conversations with clients in the past as personal demons bulldozed their lives and careers.

"Ava," he said slowly, gently, "I need you to tell me exactly what happened last night. Can you remember more clearly now?"

Ava looked up at him, her eyes filled with frustration. "I told you everything last night, Lenny," Ava said with a frustrated growl. "Chase has been acting strange ever since we moved into that house. Last night, he...he threw me across the room like I was nothing. His eyes turned black and started glowing. And his voice... It wasn't his voice. It was deeper, distorted."

"Ava," Lenny said, cutting into her narrative in an attempt to steer her back to reality. "Are you sure you and Chase weren't taking anything? Any drugs or substances that could have caused—"

"No!" Ava's voice rose, her grip tightening on the mug. "I told you. I'm not on anything, Lenny! I never touch that crap! You know that."

"Sweetheart, I've met many people in your position who never touched that crap who end up in recovery or worse," Lenny said. "You have to understand how this all sounds."

"I know," she said, shaking her head and looking down into her coffee. "I know it sounds crazy. Even I thought I was going crazy. I mean, at the worst, I thought maybe Chase was taking steroids or something. But I was wrong, and this is something different. It's something...unnatural and terrifying."

Lenny sighed, rubbing his temples. "Ava, what you're saying... It just doesn't make sense," he said. His frustration was mounting, but he was trying to hold on to what little patience he had left. "There has to be a logical explanation for what you saw, and the most logical explanation was that you saw something under the influence. Is it possible that you took something without knowing? Do you think he drugged you?"

"What?" Ava exclaimed; her voice was trembling with anger. "You think I'm lying? You think I'm crazy?"

"I don't think you're crazy," Lenny said quickly. "I just think...maybe it was a hallucination. Maybe you were stressed and—"

"Don't patronize me, Lenny," Ava snapped, standing up so abruptly that the chair she sat in nearly toppled. "I know what I saw. If you don't believe me, then I'll find someone who will."

"Ava, wait," Lenny said, holding up his hands in a placating gesture. "I'm sorry. Look, I'm not the best person to talk to about this kind of stuff. But I do know someone who might be able to help."

Ava stopped, her eyes narrowing. "Who?" she asked. It was clear that she was suspicious of him now. She probably thought he was going to try to lead her into a rehab center.

"How familiar are you with Jacob Shepherd?" Lenny asked, watching her reaction carefully. "He specializes in…this kind of thing."

Ava's eyes widened at the mention of the name. "Jacob Shepherd?" she asked, instantly recognizing the very famous name of a very famous man. "The *Shepherding Souls* guy? With the TV show? The guy who deals with…supernatural stuff?"

"Yes," Lenny confirmed. "If you're adamant that this is what happened, I can't think of anyone else who would be better to talk to. If anyone can help you with this, it's him."

18

Ava sat alone at a table in a swanky restaurant. She glanced down at her phone to check the time.

The starlet was dressed in new clothes that Lenny's assistant had procured for her earlier in the day. Now, she was waiting for the arrival of Jacob Shepherd, the famous psychic medium.

She knew a bit about the man. Although she had never watched his hit television show, *Shepherding Souls*. On the show, he would give members of the audience messages from their deceased loved ones.

She also remembered reading something about Shepherd in the news about a month ago. A young actress had died at one of his house parties. It was a real tragedy, but there wasn't a lot of follow-up on it. It was all chalked up to some bad drugs, but now Ava found herself wondering. Lenny had, after all, thought she had been on drugs.

Honestly, she wished she had been. That might have made it easier to accept. But she knew that what she'd seen was all too real, all too terrifying.

Shepherd's show had never interested Ava because it was

never a subject she had been particularly intrigued by. She hadn't believed in occult nonsense before now. The Hollywood star had never even considered the possibility that spirits lingered on earth and delivered messages to the living.

Honestly, it was absurd to even consider.

But there was no other explanation for last night. What she had seen, what she had experienced, had been nothing short of otherworldly. She wished there could be some rational explanation for what had transpired, but she had turned over the experience in her mind time and time again.

It was beyond terrifying, beyond explanation. Chase's voice, his eyes, his unnatural strength—it had all been like something out of a fantasy story. But it was all too real, and she had the bruises to prove it.

It was 2:15 now, which meant Shepherd was fifteen minutes late.

That didn't surprise her. Hollywood types were always fashionably late. It was something about the Hollywood culture she had never liked or adopted. As she stared at her phone, it started buzzing. Chase's name and face popped up on the screen. She gasped and dropped the phone as though he might leap off the screen and attack her directly. This was the seventy-fourth call she had received from him since leaving the house last night. She had been surprised by the fact that he hadn't pursued her when she had run to her car, but she was thankful he hadn't.

What was keeping him in the house? It had seemed as though he'd been physically unable to exit. But how could that be possible? She clicked the red button on her phone screen to send his call to voicemail.

A server approached and brought her an unsweetened iced tea. Ava thanked the man and took a sip, wondering how her life had gotten to this point.

It was then that a tall man with dark hair and light-blue

eyes entered the establishment and approached her with a steady, almost ethereal gait. He was dressed in an immaculate suit jacket and pants with a black turtleneck underneath. His hair was styled with precision, looking effortless yet requiring so much effort at the same time.

He greeted her with a soft, almost detached voice and no noticeable shift in his expression, introducing himself as who she already knew him to be. "Jacob Shepherd," he said simply, extending a hand.

Ava stood nervously and shook his hand. "Hello, Mr. Shepherd," she said simply. "I'm Ava. Please, won't you join me?"

"Please," he said as they both sat down, "call me Jacob. Now, Ava, why did you want to see me today?"

Ava bit her lip nervously, casting a look behind her as though someone might be listening in. The last thing she needed was for her account of last night's horror show to make it into the press. Lenny was right in that she'd become the laughingstock of the industry.

"What did Lenny tell you?" she asked, hoping she might be able to avoid discussing the specifics in public.

"He just said that you needed some of my unique perspective," Jacob replied, his voice calm and measured.

Ava took a deep breath. She cursed mentally, wishing Lenny had given him something, anything, to prep the medium about her situation so she wouldn't have to relive it yet again.

"Last night," she began, her voice trembling at the memory, "Something…something happened. Something…that was just…terrifying."

Jacob leaned back in his chair, his expression still neutral. "What happened?" he asked, studying her with eyes that seemed to pierce their way through her, as though he could see deep into her soul.

She wasn't entirely sure she liked that feeling.

"My husband, Chase...," she said, once more casting her gaze around the room in the hope that no one was close enough to catch wind of what she was about to say. "He...well, he changed. It started with little things. Like he was angrier, more possessive of me in a way he'd never been before. Then last night, everything kinda came to a head and... I don't know how to... I mean... His eyes turned black, Jacob. And...his voice got deeper, distorted. And then he... I mean, he threw me across the room like I was a rag doll."

Jacob's eyebrows raised slightly, the first emotional response he'd given her during their encounter. "And you're sure this wasn't some kind of hallucination?" Shepherd asked her, much in the same way Lenny had.

She wanted to groan in frustration at the repeated accusation, but she couldn't truly fault Jacob for asking.

"Perhaps brought on by stress or something you might have ingested?"

"No," Ava said firmly. "I'm not on anything. I've never touched drugs. And I know what I saw. This was real. I have the bruises to prove it."

Jacob nodded slowly. He sat back in his chair thoughtfully, as though he were absorbing her words. "Tell me more about what happened," he said.

Ava took another deep breath, trying to steady herself. "It started a few days ago," she said. "We moved into a new house. It was the house that used to belong to Nolan Hillhurst, the action star."

"I'm familiar," Shepherd said nonchalantly.

"Right," Ava said with a nod. "Well, Chase became obsessed with Nolan Hillhurst's gym. He was spending hours in there, working out like a madman. He started acting strangely, more aggressively. He punched a hole in the wall, and then, an hour later, it was gone. But then, last night, it was back again. On top of that, I've been hearing these weird sounds like there's a cat somewhere in the house, and... Well, last night, he completely lost it.

"I thought he might've been taking steroids or something, so I was looking around in the gym. He found me and... I mean, he freaked out, and that's when his eyes turned black, like completely black. And his voice... I mean, it wasn't his voice. It was deeper, almost demonic. Like something you'd hear in the exorcist. Then he threw me across the room with one hand like I weighed nothing."

Jacob leaned forward, his interest clearly piqued. "And you think there's something... supernatural at play here?" he asked.

"I mean, wouldn't you?" she asked, her hands upturned as though she were literally grasping at anything she could reach to explain all of this. "I don't know. I never believed in that stuff. But there's no other explanation. It was like he was... possessed."

Jacob's eyes narrowed, and he gave her a nod of understanding. "Possessed, you say?" he asked.

"I know it sounds crazy," Ava said quickly, "but—"

"You don't sound crazy at all, Ava," Jacob interrupted, his voice suddenly much more engaged. "In fact, I think, based on the information you're giving me here, that you might be right."

Ava blinked, a mix of relief and fear washing over her. She wanted to cry and hug the man at the same time. She was relieved that someone believed her, but at the same time, horrified that this phenomenon was actually possible.

"You believe me?" she asked, her voice dripping with hope.

Jacob nodded. "I've encountered similar cases before," he said. "It's rare, but it happens. Tell me, has Chase been acting differently in any other ways?"

Ava nodded, her mind racing. "Yes. He's been more

controlling, more demanding," she said. "It was like there was this…darkness in him that I've never seen before."

Jacob took a deep breath, leaning back in his chair yet again. "It sounds like you might be dealing with a possession," he said. "And a particularly nasty one at that. It's not something to take lightly, Ava. This could be very dangerous for both of you."

Ava's eyes widened, the hopelessness of her situation evident. "What can I do?" she asked, tears glistening in her eyes. "How can I help him? How can I get him back?"

"We'll figure it out," Jacob said, his voice firm and reassuring. "But first, I need to know everything. Every detail, no matter how small."

Ava nodded and started to go through every detail she could remember, going over every minute issue that had sprung up from the moment they had walked into that house for the first time. Jacob never interrupted her. He simply sat there, still as the grave, listening as she recounted every dark and terrifying anomaly that had taken root in her life.

After hearing everything Ava had to say, Jacob's expression grew more serious.

"Do you know if anyone has ever died in the house?" Jacob asked simply.

Ava nodded again. "Yes," she said, swallowing hard to try to keep her voice from shaking. "Nolan Hillhurst himself passed away there. He had a heart attack."

Shepherd nodded thoughtfully. "Sometimes, displaced spirits set up shop in the place of their death," he said. "Especially if that place was somewhere they were connected to in life, like, say, their home."

Ava's eyes widened. "You mean Nolan's spirit could still be in the house?" she asked, her hands coming up to her mouth in disbelief.

"It's possible," Shepherd said. "And if he had a strong attachment to the place, it's even more likely."

Ava hesitated, a question forming in her mind that she was almost afraid to ask. "How is it possible for spirits to actually possess someone?"

Shepherd looked uncomfortable, as if reliving a painful memory. "It's very possible," he admitted. "But both the spirit and the host have to be willing for the bond to take place."

Ava shook her head defiantly. "No," she said, pressing her lips into a thin line. "Chase would never agree to let any ghost set up shop in his body, even if it was Nolan Hillhurst."

"Most times, the host doesn't even realize they're agreeing to it," Shepherd explained. "It's a subconscious thing, like responding to a thought the spirit places in their head or in a dream. Even agreeing with a thought that the spirit whispers into their mind can be enough gray area for a possession to occur."

Ava's eyes filled with desperation. She imagined Chase trapped within his own mind, a prisoner of some horrifying spirit that was driving his body, using him for whatever sinister deeds it wanted. And someone like Nolan, a notorious egomaniac and violent man with a history of abusing women, would likely try to recapture his former glory with a fresh young body like Chase's.

"Is there anything you can do to help?" Ava asked, desperation in her voice. She looked at Shepherd now as though he were a white knight on a hill, the only one who might be able to help her get her husband back.

Shepherd sighed and shook his head, causing Ava's heart to deflate with horror. "Unfortunately, possession is way out of my league," Shepherd said, looking down at the table as though weighing options in his mind. He looked back up at her with another deep exhalation. "Mediums all have different abilities, you see. Some can hear spirits, while others can see them. Some can even communicate with them in dreams. But some are so powerful that they can actually touch spirits and exert control over them. These select few can become exorcists, and they help people dealing with instances of possession."

Ava looked bewildered, unsure of what to do with this information. "Well," she said, shaking her head, "how do I find an exorcist?"

Shepherd leaned back in his chair, his expression grave. "I happen to know the best there is in the exorcism game," he said, though he didn't sound happy about it.

Despite Shepherd's apparent misgivings, Ava's eyes lit up with hope. There was someone out there who could help her get Chase back, and she had a living, breathing connection to that person sitting right in front of her.

"Can you get me in contact with this person?" she asked, wringing her fingers together hopefully.

Shepherd nodded but again seemed uncomfortable with the idea. "You need to understand that this man is the very best there is at what he does," Shepherd said. "I mean, he's world-class. There's legitimately no one better."

Ava frowned, confused at his countenance while delivering this news. "That sounds like a good thing, Jacob," she said with a confused shake of her head. "But you don't seem very comfortable with it."

Shepherd sighed, bringing one hand up to massage the bridge of his nose gently with two fingers. He instantly looked stressed. "I can put you in contact with him, for sure," he said slowly. "But…you just have to prepare yourself. His personality is…a bit of an acquired taste. He's…eccentric, to say the least."

Ava raised an eyebrow. "What do you mean?" she asked.

Shepherd hesitated, as if trying to find delicate words that didn't seem to exist. Finally, he just shrugged and shook his head. "To be blunt, he's an asshole," he said simply. "But there's no one better."

Ava took a deep breath, steeling herself. She could deal with an asshole. She'd been dealing with them all her life. If it meant getting Chase back, she'd work with anyone who could offer any amount of help.

"What's his name?" she asked.

Shepherd's eyes met hers, his voice steady. "Michael Merlyn."

19

Michael Merlyn wandered through the dimly lit aisles of the San Francisco Public Library, muttering under his breath at the sorry state of the place.

This library, like many others around the world, had once been a beacon of knowledge and community. Now, it seemed more like a forgotten relic of times long ago. Aisles that were supposed to be bustling with eager readers seeking the power of knowledge sat mostly empty, save for a few homeless individuals seeking refuge from the streets.

He walked along the bookshelves, running a finger over the dusty spines of old books, grimacing at the residue it left on his finger. He wiped the dust off on his long black coat, shaking his head in dismay.

"Libraries, going the way of the dodo," he muttered to himself in a clipped London accent. "What do you bloody expect at a time when knowledge and porn are literally at everyone's fingertips?"

Merlyn reached into his pocket and pulled out his phone, squinting at the screen. There were four text messages from

Kate, his former police detective partner, who now worked with him as part of his paranormal investigation agency.

Michael, where are you?

Micheal...

Are you leaving me on read?

Dammit, Merlyn, Victoria and I are in New Mexico. When the hell are you getting here?

Michael smirked at the insistent texts. The angrier she got, the longer he was going to make her wait. That was how it had worked with the two of them since the day they had met in a small town in Texas. Which also happened to be the night she had arrested Michael for a wild bar fight.

As he went to put his phone back in his pocket, it suddenly roared to life in his hand, blaring the British anthem of "God Save the Queen" at full volume. Michael hadn't lived in England since he was a small boy. He had no loyalty to the crown or his native country. He just thought the song went perfectly with his accent, like an accessory to an outfit.

On the screen, he saw a photo of Kate, her blond hair askew and her mouth twisted in a snarl of annoyance. He had snapped that particular picture of her one afternoon by asking her if she was getting fat and then hitting the shutter button the moment she looked up. It had been her contact photo ever since.

The short-haired female librarian at the reference desk flashed him a dirty look as he answered the phone.

"Detective," he greeted his supposed friend and partner with feigned warmth. "How are you on this fine day? How's the land of enchantment? I was just about to head your way."

"Cut the crap, Merlyn," Kate snapped. "Where the hell have you been? You were supposed to meet us in Albuquerque three days ago."

"Time sure flies when you're having fun," he said, forcing a chuckle.

"Look, I know you said you needed a little break, but we all agreed it was time to get back to it," Kate said. Her tone softened slightly, which Michael hated.

He much preferred it when she was annoyed and yelling at him. It was so much easier to deal with than this mushy, understanding nonsense.

"If you're still a little shaken up after that last case in LA, I get it. But there are people out there who still need our help. So, it's time to come meet with us. Then we can all move on together."

"Shaken up?" Michael laughed, a sound that was more bitter than amused. "I'm simply enjoying all California has to offer. There's a lovely selection of boarded-up shops, homeless tent cities, and litter, the likes of which I've never seen."

"Merlyn, when should we expect you?" Kate asked, her frustration evident. "Hold on."

He could hear her jostling with the phone.

"Mikey, it's me," a voice he instantly recognized as his foster sister, Victoria, said into the phone. She was the third member of their little team. She was their resident computer ace and tech wizard. "I know you like pissing off Kate, but can you please let me know when you're getting here?"

"Ugh, that's bad form tagging you in, sis," he said with a scoff. "Tell the detective I'll be there in a day, maybe two." He heard Victoria relay the message and then some jostling with the phone again.

"So, two days?" Kate asked, trying to confirm.

"Absolutely, Detective," he replied simply. "I mean, three if I happen to pass a really good flea market. Or maybe four since they just opened a twenty-four-hour gas station down the road, and I really want to check that out."

"Get here as soon as you can," Kate grumbled. "We already have a case lined up."

"I'm practically on my way," he replied with mock enthusiasm. He felt a tap on his shoulder and turned to see the librarian standing there, fuming with anger. "I need to go," he told Kate. "Something annoying just popped up." He hung up before Kate could respond.

"Sir, this is a library," the librarian said, her tone icy.

"Is that so?" Michael feigned surprise. "No wonder no one's shown up to take my drink order."

"Keep it down. You're disturbing the other patrons," she hissed.

Michael looked around, scoffing. "Are you referring to the homeless man sleeping by the window? Or the homeless woman trying to shower in the restroom sink?"

"Quiet down, or I'll have you removed," she warned, her eyes narrowing.

"I've been thrown out of worse dumps," he replied, running a finger along the dusty books again. "Actually, never mind that."

He turned away from her, slipping his phone back into his coat pocket. The librarian walked away, muttering something under her breath. Michael sighed, glancing around the library one last time.

He had come here on a whim, his unique talents often telling him where he was needed in the form of a feeling that he might be needed in a particular direction. He had entered the library, knowing he was searching for something. He just wasn't sure what. Perhaps the feeling that had brought him in there wasn't something otherworldly after all. Maybe he just needed a place to think, a momentary escape from the chaos of his crazy life.

Michael continued to wander among the books, passing the homeless man asleep under the window.

The man jerked awake and pointed at Michael, eyes wide with wonder. "The power of Christ compels you, sir!" he shouted.

Michael laughed, a hollow sound in the quiet library. "You have no idea, mate," he said, shaking his head as he moved on. His fingers trailed along the dusty shelves, leaving streaks of clean wood in their wake. He wiped the dust off on his long black coat once more, grimacing.

The man's words inadvertently brought memories flooding into his mind. He thought about his past, coming up as a Catholic priest, becoming an exorcist, and then getting excommunicated for taking extraordinary steps to save a soul the Church hadn't agreed with. His methods had been unconventional, invoking deities from various pagan faiths. It had ultimately saved the life of the person who needed his help, but it also had led to his excommunication.

The Church had labeled him a heretic, but he knew he had done what was necessary. Since then, he'd considered himself something of a freelance exorcist, traveling the world and righting the spiritual wrongs that slipped through the cracks of normal society. He had no idea how many people he'd helped over the years. He'd stopped counting long ago.

It wasn't a game, after all. There was no need to keep score.

Michael's thoughts drifted to what Kate had said about their last job, and he wondered if there was a speck of truth to her words.

Their last case had been a whopper. He remembered standing face to face with another medium of equal power, a demented psychopathic killer who was able to match him blow for blow. Michael had nearly been beaten to death in the process.

The only reason he'd survived at all, and he would never actually admit this to anyone outside of his own head, was because of Jacob Shepherd. Michael hated it, but had it not been for Shepherd, he would have died, along with many others.

Despite the fact that the man was a damn charlatan, he'd

come through for them in the end. Shepherd was a phony, a fraud with no actual psychic power. Michael had been utterly disgusted by him from the start, but he had formed a begrudging respect for the phony bastard after the whole saving his life thing.

The homeless man from before approached him again, this time grabbing him by the wrist. "Christ will be your ally," the man said, pressing something into Michael's hand.

Instantly, Michael felt a scorching burn along his palm and screamed in pain, dropping the object and recoiling back into a bookshelf. The man stared at him in disbelief. Michael looked down at what the man had given him. It was a small wooden cross. A crucifix. The man stared at Michael in disbelief, looking from the cross to Michael's smoking hand.

He pointed a disbelieving finger at Michael and started shouting. "He's the devil!" the old man shrieked. "The devil!"

Michael shrugged. It wasn't the first time someone had called him that.

He quickly turned and hurried away from the raving homeless man as the librarian approached with a scornful look on her face. Michael felt his cheeks grow hot and a pressure build in his chest and mind. He stopped for a moment, closing his eyes as he said a quick prayer in Latin to Saint Michael, the Archangel, who pushed the invasive presence within him back down.

Michael Merlyn was more than just an exorcist. He was also possessed. But the spirit within him had no actual power over him. Michael had been able to keep the demented soul chained within his heart to prevent it from getting out into the world.

The deranged soul in question was that of Jeremiah Kassidy, a serial killer who went by the name of the Bayou Butcher. When Michael had encountered Kassidy embedded in the soul of a young boy, he'd finally met his match. The only way to save a young boy was to take the unclean spirit into himself, where he could trap and contain him forever.

Michael had vowed to be the murderer's prison for as long as he could. But because of that, holy relics like crosses and holy water burned him as they would any other possessed individual. It wasn't all bad, though. He was gifted with unnatural strength and speed that allowed him to go punch for punch with just about any possessed person.

He just had to be careful at all times, lest he lose control and allow Kassidy to take over completely. It was a nonstop struggle that dominated his life and made his personal mission to help people a lot more difficult.

Michael felt the thrashing of the spirit die down as he focused inward, content that Kassidy was once more subdued and back where he belonged.

Opening his eyes, Michael saw the librarian shooing the homeless man out of the building. The bum was still hollering and pointing at Michael, calling him the devil made human flesh. With that, he decided that he likely needed to get going too as soon as possible.

But then he noticed something. There was a young woman sitting at a table by the window, hugging her torso and looking out into the world sadly. Michael quickly realized why he had felt a need to come in here.

He took a deep breath and slowly approached the woman. He flashed her a kind smile. "Mind if I take a seat?" he asked.

She looked up at him in surprise but said nothing.

He pulled out the chair and sat down. "It seems like you've been here a while," he said gently.

The woman simply nodded.

"Do you think it might be time to move on?" he asked.

She shook her head, looking back out the window.

Michael followed her gaze. "I understand," he said with a slow nod. "You know, sometimes it's hard to leave, to move on, to accept things as they are. It's something I've struggled with as well. But there are some things a person can't change. Like the fact that you're dead."

The woman looked up at him silently and shook her head.

Michael nodded patiently. "I know it sucks," he said in commiseration. "But it's the truth. You don't belong in this world anymore. There's a whole world where you do belong, though, waiting for you on the other side."

She shook her head again. This time, she looked afraid.

"I wish I could tell you it's all sunshine and rainbows over there, love," Michael said dryly. "But I don't wanna lie to you. I've got no bloody clue what's on the other side of the veil. However, I've touched it more than once, and I know there is something good out there. I've felt the warmth of it in my heart."

The woman tried to speak, but no sound came out.

"You won't be able to speak," Michael said softly. "You won't be able to be a part of this world, no matter how long you stay. You'll just be alone, and eventually, your sense of self will slip away as you become bitter and resentful. At that point, you might decide to take up shop in a living host. And once that happens, you'd have to deal with someone like me. And those confrontations can become…unpleasant."

She paused and seemed to be considering what he was saying for a long moment.

"It's natural to be afraid," he said, trying to be patient and compassionate. These were two attributes that had never been his strong suits. "Moving on to something new is scary. But it's a step you need to take for yourself."

She looked up at him sadly and gave a slow nod of admission.

Michael smiled at her, relieved that she was agreeing to go voluntarily. "I'm glad you agree," he said. "Do you need a little boost to cross over?"

She nodded again.

Michael reached out and touched her hand. "Good things are waiting for you," he said. "You're about to get a second chance in a world with no worries, no cares, and most importantly, no twenty-four-hour news networks."

He gave the girl a playful wink as she vanished. Once she was gone, Michael's phone rang loudly again. He expected it to be Kate but saw, to his great annoyance, that it was Jacob Shepherd calling. Michael made a face and considered letting the call go to voicemail. However, the man had saved his life, and he supposed he owed him a favor.

Surely, answering his phone call would suffice in that regard… Michael hit the accept button and raised the phone to his ear.

"You have reached Sexy Centenarians, the dating service for men who have a fancy for women over the age of one hundred," he answered.

"Cut the crap," Shepherd said, already sounding exasperated.

"Well, hello to you, too, my favorite fanciful phony," Michael replied with a wry smile. "What do you want?"

"Can you come back to LA?" Shepherd asked, getting right to the point.

Michael blinked in surprise. "Why would I ever want to do that?" Michael replied, his nose crinkling in disgust. "I didn't even want to go there the first bloody time you tricked me into walking into that den of crap."

"I have a case for you," Shepherd explained. "We've got a clear possession and a terrified wife."

"Well, why not use all your phenomenal psychic powers to help?" Michael asked sarcastically.

"Dammit, Michael," Shepherd said, his ire growing the longer this conversation droned on. "Should I tell the crying young woman that you won't be helping her?"

Michael looked over and saw the librarian approaching him, walking with an angry purpose. He thought about Kate and Victoria waiting for him in New Mexico and decided they could wait a little longer.

"Tell her help is on the way, mate," Michael said before hanging up.

The librarian had reached him and opened her mouth, likely to scold him or to kick him out of the building once and for all. But before she could speak, Michael silenced her with a raised hand.

"Sod off," he said simply, watching as her eyes tripled in size. "I'm already leaving."

He blew past her and out the front door, taking a deep breath. He texted Kate, saying a case came up, no need to worry, and that he'd be back soon. He didn't wait for a response before slipping the phone into his pocket. He was sure one was coming in all caps that he could read later.

Michael approached his motorcycle parked outside the library building and threw one leg over it. "LA, here I come," he said, revving up the engine and hitting the open road.

20

Chase listened to the phone ringing in his ear yet again, only to be greeted with the sound of an automated voice telling him that he had reached a voicemail box.

He snarled in anger, pulling the phone away and resisting the urge to crush it in his fist. However, he knew that if he wanted to, he could easily. He could fold it up like tinfoil and throw it so hard it would embed itself in the wall. That was how strong he felt since coming to live in this place. It was like this house had somehow reinvigorated his drive to succeed and refilled the confidence he had lost in himself.

But now, as always, Ava was trying to take that away from him. She was being selfish and trying to make everything about herself and her feelings once again. Chase wasn't putting up with it this time. She had a lot of nerve sneaking into his gym last night and then trying to make her mousey little excuses.

She had looked so small last night, so minuscule in his world of power and strength. She should be happy that he was coming into his own, happy that he was happy. But of course, she wasn't. She couldn't be. It enraged him beyond belief. The anger he felt was so powerful it was almost like a tangible thing he could hold in his hands.

She never should've snuck around, never should have lied, never should have challenged him or run off. He told himself that he should go after her. He should just drive out to wherever she was and bring her home. And if she didn't want to come along... Well, they could cross that bridge when they came to it. But he wasn't going to take no for an answer. Not this time. Not ever again.

He stormed out of the gym and threw open the front door, exposing himself to the afternoon light. He went to take a step outside into the world and stopped, wincing as he tried to lift his foot and take a step out into the light of day. He wasn't alarmed by his seeming inability to take that first step. If anything, he was curious. This should have been a simple thing. One step out the door and out into the world where somewhere out there, his woman was waiting for him to bring her home.

But he didn't move. Not a single inch. Something inside him was practically screaming in his mind, telling Chase that he shouldn't go. Some deep instinct spreading out from his heart whispered into his mind that going after her was something a weak man would do. It reminded him of the need to be strong, saying she was only trying to make him come after her because it would make him weak.

Chase wasn't weak. Not anymore and not ever again. From now on, there was only forward momentum in his life. He would only get stronger. Every moment in his life from here on out would simultaneously be the strongest he'd ever been and the weakest he would ever be again.

There would be gains every single day, massive strides toward perfect power, drawing ever closer to the very peak of human perfection.

She wasn't going to take that from him. No one ever was again.

Resigning himself to remain where he was, Chase slammed the door and stormed back inside. Though he was steadfast in his decision to stay there, he was still incensed at Ava's selfish decision to leave, to try to take everything from him that he'd worked so tirelessly for.

Pacing the foyer, he tried to calm himself. His mind buzzed with thoughts of power, strength, and control. He wanted to dominate everything around him, to bend the world to his will. He knew he could do it, especially now with his newfound strength.

Chase shook his head, trying to clear his thoughts. He needed to focus. Ava would come back. She always did, and she always would. But when she came back, there would be consequences for her actions. There would be prices she had to pay for denying him and testing the limits of his patience. She'd taken advantage of his leniency, of his benevolence. He'd been willing to let her flit about the house as she wished while he worked tirelessly in the gym to better himself.

And this was how she thanked him for it. This was her response to his quest for perfection.

Chase knew he just needed to be patient. She would realize her mistake soon enough and return to him, ready to accept his authority. And he would show her the true meaning of that word the very moment she walked back into his life.

Taking a deep breath that did nothing to quell the inferno of his ever-burning rage, he walked back to the gym. He knew a workout would put his mind at ease. It was the place where he felt the most in control, and control was what he sorely needed right now.

The equipment, his equipment, gleamed in the artificial light. It was a testament to his dedication and hard work. Chase walked over to the weights, picking up a dumbbell and curling it effortlessly. The muscles in his arms bulged with each movement, and he relished the sensation of power coursing through his veins.

But even as he worked out, his thoughts kept returning to Ava. He couldn't shake the feeling of betrayal, the anger that simmered just beneath the surface. He needed to channel that anger, to use it to fuel his drive. He moved to the bench press, loading the bar with an impressive amount of weight. As he lifted, he imagined Ava's face, her fearful expression as she had looked up at him last night. The thought fueled his rage, and he pressed the weight up with a grunt, his muscles straining with effort.

"Why couldn't she just understand?" he muttered to himself. "Why couldn't she see that this is what I need? What *we* need?"

He slammed the bar back onto the rack, the weights clanging loudly. Chase then sat up, breathing heavily and wiping the sweat from his forehead.

The gym felt stifling, the air thick with tension and humidity. Lifting wasn't doing the trick this time. He needed to get his hands on something and inflict damage. He needed a release, something to take his mind off things.

Chase looked around, his eyes falling on the heavy bag in the corner. He walked over to it, wrapping his hands with the tape that hung nearby.

As he started to punch the bag, he imagined it was all the obstacles in his life, all the things that had held him back. Each punch was a release of his frustration, his anger. Anger at Ava, anger at the film industry. Both had turned their backs on him. But he was going to reclaim both, to show both that they had been oh, so very wrong.

The bag swayed with the force of his blows, the sound of his fists hitting the leather echoing through the gym.

"Why couldn't she just support me?" he shouted, landing a

particularly hard punch that sent the bag swinging wildly. "Why couldn't she just be happy for me?"

His punches grew more erratic, his movements more desperate. He was losing control, the anger consuming him. Finally, the huge man stopped, panting heavily, and leaned against the bag, his forehead resting on the cool leather. Chase then closed his eyes, trying to calm his racing heart.

"She'll come back," he whispered to himself. "She always does."

But even as he said the words, doubt crept in. What if she didn't come back? What if she was really gone? The thought sent a chill down his spine. He couldn't lose her. Not now. Not when he was so close to achieving everything he had ever wanted.

He pushed away from the bag with a disgusted grunt of anger. He would wait for now. He would give her time to come to her senses. And when she came back, when she shuffled her feet back into this home, their home, his home, then she would have to make it up to him. There would be a penance to pay for every moment of anguish she had caused with her absence. And this time, he wouldn't make the same mistakes. He wouldn't let her leave ever again.

Chase picked up the phone and called her again. Once more, there was no answer, nothing on the other side. He grunted in frustration and punched the wall, putting another hole in the house with ease. He stared at the hole, at what his strength had created. That was the strength she was running from.

He almost felt bad for Ava, for her simple mind. How could she run from power like that? That power would keep them safe for the rest of their lives. He would be the envy of every man on Earth. And if Ava couldn't see that just yet... Well, they had time. He would make her see it, eventually.

Chase's phone buzzed in his hand, breaking his thoughts.

He saw that a Google Alert had popped up for the keyword Ava Monroe, which he always followed. His eyes widened as he saw the headline:

Trouble in Paradise? Ava Monroe Spotted with Psychic Medium Jacob Shepherd!

By Gossip Guru Gemma

Ava Monroe, the beloved starlet of Hollywood, was spotted earlier today at a swanky LA restaurant with none other than renowned psychic medium Jacob Shepherd. Eyewitnesses say Monroe looked visibly upset, and Shepherd seemed to be offering her comfort.

"She looked really distraught," said one onlooker. "Jacob was holding her hand and talking to her softly. She was definitely seeking comfort."

Another source added, "Ava seemed pretty lost in thought. She was barely touching her food. It looked like more than just a friendly lunch."

Could there be trouble brewing in Monroe's marriage to action star Chase Parker? Speculation is rife that Monroe might be seeking solace elsewhere else, especially given that Shepherd is far more famous and well-known than Parker. Could this be a case of trading up?

Shepherd, known for his hit TV show "Shepherding Souls," where he connects audience members with their deceased loved ones, has been a household name for years. His recent controversies, including the tragic death of a young actress at one of his house parties, have only heightened his notoriety.

Meanwhile, Chase, once a rising star in the action movie scene, has seen his career stall in recent years. Critics have noted his reliance on the same old muscle-bound roles, which haven't evolved with the changing times in Hollywood. Some wonder if Ava Monroe, whose star continues to rise, is outgrowing her husband both professionally and personally.

The article also included a photo of Ava and Jacob Shepherd sitting in the restaurant together. She was looking down at the table, and he seemed to be reaching over and putting his hand on hers. The image was enough to send Chase into a blind rage.

Chase exploded in fury, screaming as he crushed the phone in his fist and tossed it off to the side. The image of Jacob Shepherd touching his wife had burned itself into his mind now, and he was seeing nothing but red. The powerful rage made him feel even stronger than he already had, and something within him seemed to rise and fill him with more power, more anger, more drive to do what had to be done.

He wanted to rip Shepherd apart, to make him pay for even thinking he could comfort Ava. The fact that he thought he could dare to touch her when she belonged to Chase and Chase alone was maddening. How could someone be so mind-numbingly arrogant and stupid? Jacob Shepherd was going to learn quickly that no one took what belonged to Chase Parker.

He ran to the door again and threw it open. He felt stronger now, and the idea of going out no longer seemed off-putting. He charged through the threshold, making a beeline for his car. He got into the driver's seat and sped off into the afternoon with one thought on his mind.

He was going to find the man who had put his hands on his wife and make him pay. Then, he would bring her back home, where she belonged.

As Chase drove, his mind continued to race with thoughts of Ava and Shepherd. How dare she turn to another man? And how dare Shepherd think he could be her comfort? The anger bubbled over inside him, driving him to push the accelerator harder, weaving recklessly through traffic.

Every moment they had shared in the last few weeks seemed to flash before his eyes. The moments of passion, the arguments, the feeling of her slipping away from him. It was all Ava's fault. She was the one who had changed, who had started this downward spiral. She needed to understand that she couldn't just walk away from him, from their life together.

The anger within him surged, and Chase felt a strange energy coursing through his veins, amplifying his rage and emboldening his thoughts. He barely noticed the honking cars and the blaring horns as he sped through intersections, his focus solely on finding Jacob Shepherd and making him pay.

As he drove, the image from the article burned in his mind. Ava, looking so vulnerable, with Jacob's hand on hers. The thought of her seeking comfort from another man, especially someone like Shepherd, drove him to the brink of madness. How could she betray him like that?

He tightened his grip on the steering wheel, his knuckles turning white. The cityscape blurred around him as his vision narrowed to a tunnel focused on one goal.

Total retribution.

He would show Shepherd what happened when someone messed with his Chase Parker. And he would make sure Ava always understood that she belonged to him and no one else.

21

Ava sat nervously in Lenny's living room, her fingers tapping rhythmically against her knee. She was supposed to meet Michael Merlyn, the man Shepherd had told her about, there soon.

Shepherd had left for the night, joking that he was going to enjoy going to bed early since his daughter was away at camp for the next several weeks.

That meant the only safe place for her to meet with Merlyn privately was here. She assumed Lenny wouldn't have a problem with hosting the meeting. He'd always been so supportive of anything she'd wanted before. She had assumed that he would tell her that his home was her home for as long as she needed and that she could use the space in any way she needed.

She had apparently assumed wrong.

Lenny paced back and forth in the foyer, clearly upset with her decision to hold the meeting in his private residence. He was muttering to himself and shaking his head, his mouth twisted into an irritated snarl.

"I can't believe Shepherd is sending some...con artists to

my home," he raged, one hand up to his mouth as though contemplating how his old friend could have done something so reckless without checking with him first. "This is insane. Legitimately insane!"

"Jacob is trying to help," Ava replied, trying to keep her voice calm. "And I'm the one who invited Mr. Merlyn here." She understood Lenny's skepticism, but she also knew they needed all the help they could get.

"Well, that was irresponsible of you," Lenny said, rounding on her with a red face flushed with anger. "This is my home, my private residence, and you don't even know this person you're inviting through my front door!"

As much as she wanted to argue, Ava could certainly see Lenny's point. "I'm sorry, Lenny," was all she could think to say. "But Jacob says he is the best in the world at dealing with problems like this."

"Oh, Jacob says, eh?" Lenny snapped back, his agitation only growing by the second. "Jacob is just full of great ideas, isn't he?"

"You're the one who sent me to him," Ava pointed out, placing her hands on her hips.

"Yes, but this isn't what he was supposed to do!" Lenny hissed, though a second later, his face fell as though he'd walked into a trap.

Ava frowned, taken aback. "What was he supposed to do then?" Ava asked, tilting her head in confusion.

Lenny's face turned red with anger. "I figured he'd just say some mumbo jumbo to make you feel better!" he said suddenly.

Ava's eyes widened, and she stood up, her voice rising. "Mumbo jumbo?" she asked, completely shocked and appalled by his reaction. "Do you still think I'm making all this up? Do you think I want to be going through this?"

Lenny threw his hands up in frustration. "It's all insane,

Ava," he spat, shaking his head as though he couldn't stand even another second of this issue. "Spirits, possessions—none of this is real!"

Before Ava could respond, their argument was interrupted by a sudden buzzing from the intercom. Lenny roughly pulled out his phone and pressed a button.

"What?" he barked into the intercom. "Who is it?"

"Pizza delivery," a clipped British accent replied.

Lenny looked confused, but Ava remembered what Jacob had said about Merlyn's personality.

"That's him," she said. "That's the man we're waiting for."

Lenny's face turned redder. "There's still time to turn him away and get you into treatment," he said, his finger hovering over the button on his phone screen that would open the gate.

"For the last time, I'm not on anything!" Ava insisted, her frustration mounting.

"Fine," Lenny said, pressing the button. "But you're responsible for anything this…person does while in my home!"

"I understand that, Lenny," Ava said with a nod. She thought that was only fair.

A few moments of uncomfortable silence later, there was a knock at the door. Ava took a deep breath and went to answer it.

She opened the door to find a tall, thin man in a floor-length black coat with long black hair that fell around his face. In his mouth, he held a lit cigarette, which he took a quick drag of before blowing out the smoke. The man, who could only be Michael Merlyn, stood there with a casual smile on his face as he ashed his cigarette and flicked it back into the driveway. Without waiting for an invitation, he sauntered into the expansive home and looked around Lenny's foyer.

He turned to Ava with a small nod. "Evening, love," he said to her before turning to Lenny. "Mate."

Lenny's face hardened, looking past Merlyn out into his

driveway. "Take care of your business and leave, sir," he said roughly. "And when you do, make sure you pick up that cigarette butt!"

Michael looked at Lenny before turning back to Ava with his eyebrows raised. "If this is the husband, love, I'm sorry to say he's not possessed," Michael said dryly. "He's likely naturally this grumpy and gross-looking."

Lenny's anger flared, but Ava quickly intervened.

"He's not my husband," she said quickly, though she believed Michael might have been joking with her. "He's my agent."

Michael pretended to mishear and gave her a playful wink. "Oh, I see. Doesn't look Asian to me, love," he said dryly. "And I think it's bad form to claim another person as yours."

"Oh…I didn't mean," Ava stammered, trying to correct him, but Michael gave her another smile and a wink.

"Only kidding, love," he said with another smile and a twinkle in his eye. Ava let out a small, embarrassed laugh, her cheeks flushing.

Lenny, however, was not amused. "Show some respect, dammit," He marked at the snarky Brit. "Do you know who this is?"

Ava suddenly felt very awkward as a direct result of that comment. She didn't think she deserved to be treated like royalty just because she appeared in movies.

Michael looked at Ava, then back at Lenny. "Pretty blonde lady with a possessed husband, from what I was told," he said simply, and she blushed again, even more.

Lenny's face was also turning red but for a far different reason. "It's Ava Monroe!" he shouted, gesturing at her with both hands. "*The* Ava Monroe."

Michael gasped and turned back to Ava, taking out a pair of square black glasses and placing them on his face. He tilted his head slightly as he studied her. Ava shifted uncomfortably under his gaze "Get out!" Michael said, squinting through the lenses. "For real? Are you really *the* Ava Monroe?"

Ava nodded, her embarrassment noticeable to anyone who might've seen her in that moment. "Yes, I am," she said, her voice small and meek.

Michael turned back to Lenny with his face scrunched up. "Who the bloody hell is Ava Monroe?" he asked, with a tilt to his head.

Lenny's eyes bulged with rage, and Ava thought he might blow a gasket. Honestly, it was kind of refreshing that Michael seemingly had no idea who she was. It was a nice change of pace from the way people usually interacted with her.

"You idiot!" Lenny practically screamed, gesturing at his client as though she were some exquisite work of art in the Louvre. "She's the hottest actress in Hollywood!"

Michael turned back to Ava, adjusting his glasses to look out over her. His gaze traveled up and down her body. Eventually, he shrugged. "Pretty girl, but calling her the hottest actress in Hollywood is subjective, isn't it, mate?" Michael added, turning back to Lenny. "That's more a matter of taste, right? I mean me, personally, I like a lass with a bit more meat on her bones."

"Get the hell out of my house," Lenny screamed, pointing at the door as his anger boiled over its limit. "How dare you come in here and disrespect my client like that!"

Ava didn't feel disrespected. It was honestly a breath of fresh air to have someone in her immediate orbit who wasn't falling over themselves to fawn at her like she was some fragile antiquity or oddity. But Lenny was being Lenny. He was always fiercely defensive of his clients.

Of course, Ava knew what he was actually so fiercely defensive about. His money.

Michael's expression turned to mock realization, his eyebrows up as though a lightbulb had just clicked on over his head. "Oh, *agent*, not Asian," he said with an exaggerated groan, bopping himself on the forehead with the heel of his hand. "Aye, that makes more sense. And I feel better now about calling you a prat since I won't be canceled for it."

"You didn't call me a prat," Lenny said, blinking in surprise.

"I didn't?" Michael said in astonishment. "Huh…Must've just thought it. All right then, you're a prat."

Ava actually laughed at that, and Michael turned to her, smiling.

"Ah, you've got a sense of humor," he said. "I like that. We'll get on fine while we're dropkicking the forces of darkness out of your hubby."

Lenny was vibrating now, and Ava thought she might be able to fry an egg on his forehead.

Ava composed herself quickly and looked from Lenny to Michael, wanting to avoid any further scene at all costs. It would probably be a lot more productive if she got Michael out of Lenny's general area.

"Maybe we should go out by the pool to talk," Ava said with a helpful smile and a nod toward the yard. "Then you and I can talk privately."

Lenny's face darkened as he stepped up, putting himself physically between Michael and Ava. "I'm not letting this con man out of my sight while he's on my property," Lenny said with a growl. "And I'm certainly not letting him go anywhere alone with you, Ava."

"Wonderful," Michael said, standing on tiptoe to look over Lenny's head at Ava. He then walked around the fuming agent to stand directly in front of her. "To the pool we go, love. We'll be besties soon enough."

Lenny was about to speak again, but Ava intervened. She held up a hand as though ready to physically hold him back and gave her longtime agent a pleading look.

"I'll keep an eye on things," Ava said sincerely, nodding toward Michael. "We'll stay outside. I'm serious about this."

"Fine," Lenny said after a moment of silent, grumbly contemplation.

She was relieved he'd finally agreed, albeit reluctantly. Now, she would be able to talk one on one with him without the constant interruptions.

She quickly led Michael through the house and out the back door, walking with him along the ornate patio and manicured lawn until they came to Lenny's oversized pool, beyond which was a fence and sitting area that looked out over the surrounding landscape.

Michael gave a low whistle as they walked around the side of the huge swimming hole.

"Nice pool," he said, gesturing at the clear blue water. "Is Louie in there overcompensating for something, you think?"

Ava snorted and laughed again. "His name is Lenny," she said, offering a gentle correction to her would-be savior.

Michael shrugged. "Doesn't really matter, now does it?" he asked, sitting down at the pool bar while motioning for Ava to join him. "All right, love. Give me the rundown."

Ava took a deep breath. It was time yet again to dive back into this story, and it wasn't getting any easier telling people about it. At least with Michael, she was certain she wasn't going to be judged for saying that her husband was possessed by the angry spirit of his idol.

"It started when we moved into a new house," she said.

"Aye, if I had a nickel for every story I'd heard that starts with those fateful words," Michael said, giving her a reassuring nod.

"I'm sure," Ava said with a nervous laugh. "So, like, at first, it was just little things. Chase, my husband, was acting kinda clingy and possessive. But at the same time, he was spending a lot of time in the home gym. Then, the other night, he…he just kinda changed."

Michael listened intently, his eyes never leaving hers. "Changed how?" he asked gently. There was no longer a gentle twinkle of amusement in his eyes. Now, they were just soft and kind and, above all else, understanding and patient.

Ava's voice trembled as she started to recount the more fantastical elements of her story. "Well, like, I started hearing a cat in the house, but I couldn't find it," she said, sniffling and holding back tears. "And he got mad that I wouldn't stop looking for it, and he punched a hole in the wall. And, like, that's totally unlike him and everything, um, but then, it vanished. The hole, I mean. It was just…kinda gone. And when I asked him about it, he swore he never even made the hole in the first place. But then it reappeared later. I thought I was going crazy."

Michael's expression remained calm. "You're not going crazy, love," he reassured her. "These things happen. What was your husband doing when the hole came back?"

"He was asleep," Ava said. "He had just drunk like an entire bottle of vodka, which, again, is not like him at all. And he was passed out in bed."

"That makes sense," Michael said with a nod. "The spirit is manipulating reality around you. But with the host body asleep coupled with the alcohol, it lost its grip on the illusion for a moment."

"R-really?" she asked, her voice breathy with relief. Finally, someone was giving her some kind of real honest-to-goodness answers to why all of this was happening around her.

"Aye," he said with another nod. "Now, tell me a bit about this cat of yours."

Ava continued, her voice breaking every few words as she tried to speed through the story. "Well, I kept hearing a cat meowing," she said simply. "But it's not our cat. We don't have a cat. And I could never find it. But I heard it a few times, and I think I saw it twice. Once out of the corner of my eye and another time in a mirror. I just figured maybe a feral cat had gotten inside."

"And did the cat typically make itself known to you when Chase was present?" Michael asked again.

The fact that he was asking questions was such a huge relief to Ava. He believed her, and he was listening to her. He was taking in her information and giving her actual honest-to-goodness answers.

"A few times, yeah," Ava said. "Like one time I heard it hiss when Chase was around, and another time it growled."

"You've got more than one ghost, then," Michael said simply.

"Really?" Ava asked, her eyebrows raised in shock.

"You've got a person who sounds like a bigger prat than your pal, Louie, in there," Michael said. "And then you have an animal spirit. And it sounds like the cat is on your side. I don't know for sure, but the hiss and the growl seem a bit like a warning to me."

"That would make sense," Ava said, suddenly remembering a key point. "And when Nolan, the guy who lived in the house before, when he died, he was holding a cat and it got smushed in the fall."

"And there you go," Michael said with another understanding nod. "Clear creation event coupled with a vendetta against the opposing spirit. Classic. So, what happened with your husband? How'd it all come to a head?"

Ava was so relieved to hear something concrete about the cat that she almost forgot what happened next. But then the memory came flooding back, and she felt cold inside all over again.

"Well, Chase, he… I mean his eyes… They… They weren't

his eyes," she said, trying not to stammer and failing miserably. "They actually...turned black. And his voice, it was all distorted, and it sounded like it was coming out of the walls. Then he threw me across the room like I was nothing, and I..." Emotion choked her in that moment as she relived that horrifying event one time too many. She started to cry softly into her hands.

Michael placed a reassuring hand on her shoulder. "It's all right, love," he said simply. "You're not alone in this anymore. I'm here now, and we'll figure this out. You mentioned a bloke named Nolan died in the house?"

Ava nodded. "Yeah, Nolan," she said with a sniffle and a frantic nod. "Nolan Hillhurst. The action movie star."

"Oh, see, now him I've heard of," Michael said, and Ava tried not to take it personally that he hadn't heard of her. "What happened to him? Someone killed him, I assume? A murder most foul?"

But Ava shook her head. "No," she said simply, wondering why on earth Michael would assume such a thing. "He had a heart attack. Apparently, he was abusing anabolic steroids. He just had a heart attack in the house and fell on the cat when he died."

Michael raised an eyebrow, his lips pursed in thought. He actually shook his head slowly. "That actually doesn't track," Michael said thoughtfully. "A heart attack usually isn't enough to cause a spirit to linger. It's a fairly natural death, even if it's premature. Plus, this spirit not only lingered but it's also pissed off and already inhabiting a human host after just five years. Typically, it takes a lot longer than that to whip a gentle spirit into enough of a frenzy for them to try that. It's far more likely with a violent or sudden death."

Ava hesitated, thinking back to the tabloid article she'd read. The last thing she wanted was to spread unfounded rumors. Especially rumors that pointed toward someone she considered a friend. But she also didn't want to leave anything unsaid with Chase's life on the line.

"So, there were some rumors," she said slowly, carefully. "That maybe his death wasn't what was reported."

"Ah, now we're getting somewhere," Michael said.

"I mean, I read an article suggesting foul play," Ava said before feeling the sudden need to clarify her statement. "But it was just a tabloid."

Michael's eyes narrowed. "Tabloids sometimes hit closer to the truth than we like to admit," he said slowly. "But I'm sure I don't have to tell you that, love. Now, show me the article."

Ava pulled out her phone and found the article, handing it to Michael. He skimmed through it, then looked up at her.

"What about the wife?" he asked. The question she was absolutely dreading.

Ava swallowed hard before answering. "Miranda?" Ava asked, as though the thought hadn't even occurred to her. "Well, she was devastated by Nolan's death."

"Mmm, I'll bet she was," Michael hummed. "Conveniently away when it happened, too? That's something worth looking into."

She watched him take a small notepad out of his pocket with a pencil attached and scribbled something down. She thought it was so interesting to see someone using a notebook in today's electronic era of notebook apps. But Ava shook her head. She wished she could grab the notebook from his hands and scribble over whatever it was he wrote.

"Miranda isn't capable of that," Ava said quickly, trying to divert his attention from this train of thought.

"Oh, people are capable of a lot more than what they show, love," Michael sighed. "These situations reveal the worst in them. It's a harsh reality of life, and I wish you didn't have to learn it. But wishing doesn't make the world work, and we need to consider all possibilities."

Ava glanced nervously back toward the house, half expecting to see Lenny standing beside them, gawking in horror at what Michael was insinuating.

"You shouldn't say that here," Ava said, lowering her voice. "Miranda is also one of Lenny's clients. He didn't like you saying that you hadn't heard of me before. I can't imagine what he'd say if he heard that."

"Ah, right then," Michael said as he stood up. "I suppose we should move this party elsewhere, shouldn't we? How about Shepherd's mansion?"

Ava blinked in surprise at the casual nature of that statement. He spoke of Jacob's house as though it were his, as though he could just waltz in there whenever he wanted. That surprised Ava because, judging by the way Jacob had spoken of Michael, it didn't seem as though he liked him very much.

"Did Jacob say that's all right?" she asked, trying to prod at the subject gently.

Michael shrugged with a wry smile. He reached up to brush a strand of dark hair out of his face. "Don't know, don't care," he said flippantly, already starting to walk away from her. Ava quickly stood and followed at his heels. "Shepherd called me in, so the least he could do is offer up his house for us to do a little digging. After all, the phony ponce owes me one."

Ava considered this for a moment, not knowing what Michael meant by phony. But she decided she needed to trust the man. Where he went, she would have to go if she wanted to get Chase back.

"All right," Ava said, nodding as she continued to trail behind.

"Great," Michael said, smiling back over his shoulder. "Let's go."

As they walked back through the house, Ava couldn't help but glance nervously at Lenny. He was fuming, clearly unhappy with the situation, but he didn't say anything further. She was all but certain that he was uncomfortable with her leaving alone with the man, completely unsupervised, but Ava wasn't about to argue with her agent like he was her dad.

Michael, on the other hand, seemed entirely unbothered by Lenny's anger. He walked with a confident stride, giving Lenny a little wave as his long black coat billowed behind him.

Ava gave Lenny a look as if to ask for his trust and understanding in that moment. Lenny rolled his eyes and literally threw his hands in the air, as though he were finally relenting and telling her to just go off and do whatever it was she had to do.

She gave him a smile of thanks, but Michael was already halfway out the door. She followed close behind, jogging up in front of Michael to lead him into the driveway where her car was parked.

She saw that he had apparently arrived on a motorcycle and thought her luxury vehicle would be a more pleasant experience for the two of them.

"I'll drive," she offered, opening the door for him as though she were a valet.

Michael nodded appreciatively. "Thanks, love," he said as he slipped into the passenger seat. "It's been a while since I had the luxury of being chauffeured around. But don't expect a bloody tip."

Ava smiled and closed the door as she ran around to the other side, opened her door, and climbed into the driver's seat. She started the engine, and they pulled out of the driveway wordlessly.

As they drove through the city, Ava took in everything Michael had told her. All his explanations were plausible. They all made sense if one opened their mind up to the possibility of the impossible.

She glanced over at Michael from time to time, trying to

gauge his reaction to everything she'd told him. But he was unreadable. He just sat there silently, bopping his head to the radio every once in a while.

"You all right?" he asked without turning to face her. Clearly, he'd been able to feel her eyes on him.

"Yes, sorry, I just still can't believe this is all real life," Ava said with an exasperated sigh.

"That's another of those phrases I hear a lot," he replied. "But don't worry. You're not alone in it anymore. You're not crazy. And you did the right thing for your husband by calling me. This isn't something you can just handle on your own."

Ava nodded, feeling the stinging burn of tears welling up in her eyes once more. But she blinked them away. She wasn't going to help Chase by crying over him again. The only way she'd be able to help him now was to be strong.

"I just want Chase back," Ava said simply. "I want the real Chase. Not…whatever that was."

"We'll get to the bottom of this," Michael assured her. "And we'll get your husband back. I promise."

22

Michael tapped his fingers on his leg in time with the radio's beat. Ava, driving, glanced over and marveled at his composure. How could he possibly be so relaxed in a situation like this? She finally broke the silence.

"Why are you so calm? Don't things like this scare you?"

Michael chuckled, his eyes twinkling with amusement. "I've been interacting with ghosts since I was a lad," he said casually, adjusting his seat to lean back, as though for dramatic effect. "Faced off against violent, deranged spirits on six continents. If a penguin ever gets possessed, I'll be able to get all seven. It takes a lot to scare me these days."

"When was the last time you were scared?" Ava asked, genuinely curious.

Michael's expression turned serious for a brief moment, as though he were replaying some horrifying memory through his mind. "The last time I walked into Jacob Shepherd's house," he said finally.

Ava's curiosity piqued. "What happened?" she asked, though she almost didn't want to know.

Michael shook his head, though smirking, before letting out a weary smile. "Sorry, love," he said. "I don't give particulars on cases. It's bad form. But it was a pretty big deal, and ultimately, the good guys won."

Ava stewed on his words, wondering what could have been more terrifying than what she'd experienced in her own house. She thought back to Chase's eyes, the shattering glass, the screeching cat. All of it was pure terror.

She had felt, for the first time in her life, like she was going to die. Her hands started shaking on the wheel as she recalled those events.

Michael noticed right away. "What's wrong?" he asked, adjusting his seat again to sit up straight.

Ava tried to brush it off and gave a short, humorless laugh. "It's nothing," she replied.

Michael made a buzzing noise like the hint heard on a game show. "Wrong," he said. "Try again, love."

She sighed, gripping the steering wheel tighter. It was clear he wasn't going to just let it go. "I was just thinking about what happened in the house," she said. "How...scared I was, especially compared to you."

Michael nodded, understanding her plight. "Just because I'm not scared doesn't mean you can't be," he said. "I'm an old pro at this, but you're a newbie. It's your first brush with the occult. So, if you ask me, your reaction is justified. And even though I don't give particulars on cases, you're already doing a lot better than most."

"Really?" she asked. "Other people fell apart worse than me?"

"I had a bloke poop his pants once," he said simply. "So, yeah."

Ava laughed and hoped that wasn't mean of her. "Seriously?" she asked, wondering if Michael was just trying to make her feel better.

"God's honest truth, love," he said with a wry grin. "Ghost popped up, and…there it went. Just filled his trousers up right then and there."

"Oh, that's brutal," Ava said, shaking her head in disgust while grimacing.

"No, what was brutal were the jokes I lit him up with after," Michael said with a laugh. "By the time I left, his pride was more soiled than those knickers."

Ava laughed again in spite of herself. "It's just weird for me," Ava admitted after another moment.

Michael didn't respond so she just continued.

"I play these characters in movies, right? These badass girl bosses, who smirk their way through fear and rise against enemies so much bigger and stronger than they are. But when faced with a legit struggle in reality, all I could do was cower and run."

Michael leaned back, chewing on the inside of his mouth in thought. "Look," he said slowly. "Real life and movies are very different. If you had tried to smirk and girl boss your way through that encounter, the spirit would have snapped you like a twig."

Ava shuddered, trying to suppress the terrifying image. "Why was he so strong?" she asked, thinking of the ease with which he had tossed her across the room.

"When a spirit sets up shop in a person, their speed and strength are increased to supernatural levels," Michael explained. "It's one of the many things that makes them so dangerous. It's like demon strength."

"How do you fight back against something like that?" Ava asked, looking at Michael's lean frame. "You're not a big man."

Michael nodded, a knowing smile on his lips. "It doesn't come to fisticuffs often," he said with a shrug. "Usually, I can exert my will on a spirit and stop them in their tracks. But before we can exorcise this spirit, I need to learn more.

Knowledge is power, and I'm going to need as much power as I can get."

Ava pondered his words but noticed the qualifier he'd used. Often. That meant, occasionally, things did get physical. "What do you do when it does come to a fight?" Ava asked.

Michael shifted in his seat, giving her a wink. "In those instances, I have a few tricks up my sleeves," he said and seemed content to leave it at that.

"What do you mean by that?" Ava pressed, unwilling to take that for an answer.

"A magician never reveals his secrets," Michael replied with a sly grin.

She simply shook her head at the non-answer.

"But let me ask you, love, when you ran, did Chase actually follow you outside the house?"

"No," she said quickly, remembering how strange that had been but how grateful she'd been for it.

"From the time he started acting odd, did he leave the house at any point in time?" he pressed further.

"Not at all," Ava said quickly, having already noticed that herself when replaying these events in her head earlier.

"That's actually a good sign," he said with a smirk.

"How so?" Ava asked, hungry for any kind of good news.

"Well, the spirit is set up in the house," Michael said. "If Chase were to leave the house, it would have to control him from a distance. A piece of the spirit would be in Chase while the rest of it stayed in the house. But if the connection between host and spirit isn't strong enough yet, the ghost will typically do everything in its power to keep the host inside until it has more control."

"So, you're saying that Nolan doesn't have full control of Chase yet?" Ava asked. She felt the weight of the world partially lift from her shoulders when Michael nodded.

"Now, I need to know a little more about your husband

before I can help him," Michael said. "So, tell me about Chase. What was he like before all this?"

Ava's eyes softened, and she stared out at the road ahead. "He was a wonderful, caring man," she said, her voice soft and nostalgic for those days of normalcy before her life had turned into a horror show. "I don't think I ever appreciated what I had back then, you know? I was so focused on my own career. I didn't care enough about what was going on in his life, in his career. It was deteriorating so fast, and I never gave too much thought to how he felt about it. I was always just moving on to the next project."

"What does Chase do?" Michael asked.

"He's an action movie star," Ava replied, her voice tinged with regret.

Michael sat up straighter, surprise evident on his face. "Wait, are you talking about Chase Parker?" he asked, suddenly more interested than ever.

Ava was taken aback by this sudden jolt and nodded. "Yes," she said cautiously, not sure what Michael was about to say.

Michael's eyes widened with excitement. "Well, how about that?" Michael exclaimed, slapping a palm down on his knee. "Chase bloody Parker. I love his movies!"

That certainly hadn't been what she'd been expecting, and Ava couldn't help but laugh, despite the situation. "How have you heard of Chase but not me?" she asked, genuinely curious. That wasn't something she'd encountered before.

Michael shrugged and gave her an apologetic look. "Listen, my line of work requires a lot of brainpower," he said, and she could hear a weariness in his voice that she hadn't noticed before. "When I sit down to relax, in those rare moments that present themselves, I prefer to veg out in front of something that doesn't require much thought."

Ava laughed again, this time with genuine amusement. "All right, that makes sense," she replied, thinking it was an apt description of the kinds of films Chase had starred in. "I understand that."

Michael's easygoing nature was a comfort to her. Shepherd had described him as an asshole, but Ava genuinely enjoyed his company. She could certainly see how the saucy Brit might rub some the wrong way. But right now, Michael Merlyn was just what she needed in more ways than one.

Of course, she needed an ally who could help her retrieve Chase from the grip of a sinister spirit. But she also needed someone to ground her and act as a small light in the darkness that had enveloped her life. As they drove on, Ava felt a glimmer of hope that maybe, just maybe, things could get better.

"Take a left up here," Michael said, pointing to a narrow side street.

Ava complied, turning the car onto the indicated path. Before long, Shepherd's massive home appeared in front of them. Ava's eyes widened as she took in the sprawling mansion. It was huge and luxurious looking. A modern style but with a more rustic charm. She liked it a lot.

But her attention was then quickly drawn to the open gate in front of them. "That's strange," she murmured, pulling into the driveway and glancing at the cars parked there.

"What are you looking at?" Michael asked as she killed the engine.

"One of Shepherd's cars is exactly like Chase's," she said, pointing at a big black Corvette.

Michael shrugged. "No accounting for taste," he said, making a disgusted face.

Ava nodded and gave a small chuckle. For a moment, the sight of that car had really unnerved her for some reason. Michael undid his seatbelt and opened the door, but she remained in the driver's seat, her fingers gripping the steering wheel.

Michael looked back at her, and his brow furrowed in concern. "You all right, love?" he asked.

Ava shook her head, biting her lip to hold back tears. "I dunno," she said honestly. "I just...I'm scared."

Michael nodded patiently, walking over to open her door and holding out his hand. She took it, climbing out of the car.

"It's natural to be scared right now," he said. "But we're safe here. No one knows you're here, and that spirit isn't strong enough yet to leave the house."

Ava nodded again. She knew Michael was speaking the logical truth. "I just hate that we're doing this," she said. "I hate that we *have* to do this. I hate hiding away from him like I'm on the lam or something."

Michael squeezed her hand reassuringly. "We're not hiding away from Chase," Michael said, looking directly into her eyes. "We're creating distance between you and that spirit while coming up with a plan to save Chase."

She took a deep breath, trying to calm her nerves. "That's a better way of looking at it," she admitted, sniffling and allowing a long tear to fall from her eye and travel down the side of her cheek.

"Just stay close to me, and I'll keep you safe," Michael said. His voice was steady and reassuring, which was exactly what Ava needed right now.

They approached Shepherd's door together, but their progress halted abruptly when they saw—at the same time—that the door was open, hanging off its hinges. Ava's heart pounded in her chest as fear washed over her. Michael's expression also turned grim as his eyes darted all over the area.

"Stay behind me," he instructed, coming to stand between Ava and the doorway. "If I tell you to run, you run. Got it?"

She nodded, unable to speak. The terror was manifesting physically now in her shaking hands and pounding heart.

Michael walked inside cautiously, calling out into the vast open home. "Shepherd!" he yelled, his voice bouncing off the walls and ceiling.

"Michael!" Jacob screamed out from somewhere in the house. The echo made it impossible to pinpoint where he was, but the unmistakable sound of pain and strain was laced around his cry. "Michael, run!"

Michael spotted Shepherd before she did. Ava turned to see him lying on the floor in the lounge just off the foyer. He was bleeding and bruised as a huge, hulking man crouched over him.

Ava's breath caught in her throat as the man's head snapped up. It was Chase. Ava screamed and fell back, landing in a seated position on the polished floor. Michael tried to put himself between her and her possessed husband, but it was like Chase didn't even see him as his black, glowing eyes locked onto her.

"Chase, what are you doing?" she cried out, horrified, thinking that he may have done serious harm to Shepherd. He could have killed them had they not arrived fast enough.

"Oh, bugger…," Michael muttered under his breath.

Chase's eyes were wild with fury as he took a step toward Michael and Ava. "I knew I'd find you here," he said, his deep, distorted voice pushing out through his lips, impossibly loud. "You've been here all this time, cheating on me with this phony." Chase gestured disdainfully down at Shepherd, who continued to writhe on the floor in a pool of his own blood.

Ava looked up at Michael, tears streaming freely down her cheeks with her voice trembling. "Michael," she gasped, nearly choking on the word. "How is this possible?"

Michael's eyes narrowed, and his lips pulled back in an expression that mirrored a snarling wolf. "Remember when I said a spirit can't leave their place of power until they're stronger?" he said down to her, and she could only nod in response. "Well…he got stronger."

Chase's eyes locked on Michael now, as if seeing him in the room for the first time. "Who the hell is this?" Chase hissed, pointing a finger at the thin exorcist. He looked even bigger now than he had when she had fled their home.

His muscles had nearly doubled in size since then. It was completely impossible, and yet Ava no longer doubted her senses, given what she now knew. "This another guy you're cheating on me with? You damn whore!"

"Watch your mouth, mate," Michael snapped back at him, the spirit's eyes snapping from Ava to look at him fully.

"He's here to help you, Chase!" Ava screamed, hoping to get through to him somehow.

"I don't need help," Chase growled. "We've never been better."

"We?" Michael asked, his head cocked in surprise. He didn't look happy. The exorcist quickly raised a hand, as though he could stop Chase from charging with a single arm. "You should listen to the lady, mate."

Chase's eyes flicked between Michael and Shepherd. When he spoke again, his voice was a deep, distorted echo. "You're the real deal, aren't you?" he chuckled, looking at Michael now with a note of trepidation. "Not at all like this one." He gestured rudely down at Shepherd, who was still writhing at Chase's feet.

Ava wasn't sure why Chase was hesitating. He seemed almost intimidated by Michael's presence. "What does he mean?" Ava asked up at Michael.

"Spirits can sense mediums," he replied with a confident smirk on his face. "They recognize them instantly. The stronger the medium, the more powerful the sensation. And right now, your hubby here is getting a big whiff of exactly what I am and what I can do."

He said that loudly enough that Chase could hear him. Ava realized Michael was trying to intimidate the huge spirit. What truly surprised her, though, was that it seemed to be working. Chase wasn't charging. He wasn't swinging. He actually took a half step back.

Those unnatural black eyes were drinking in something completely unseen in Michael, something Ava could only venture a guess at. But it wasn't long before Chase's arrogant smile returned to his lips, and he looked back down at his wife.

"Did you bring this twiggy little Brit here to kill us?" he demanded, a snarl of accusation in his words.

"No," Ava said quickly, aghast that he would even say such a thing. She knew that what was speaking to her now wasn't fully her husband, but she still felt the need to explain herself, as though Chase was still somewhere in there and could hear her. "He's here to help you!"

Chase's lip curled in disdain. "We don't need any help. We're taking you back home where you belong."

Ava was confused. Who was Chase talking about? Why did he keep referring to himself as we and us? Could he be referring to himself and the spirit of Nolan Hillhurst?

Ava didn't have time to think about it any further. Chase was already trying to take a step toward her, but Michael shifted to stand in his way once more.

"That's not going to happen, mate," Michael said simply.

Chase's eyes glowed with that same unholy light, brighter and more powerful than she'd seen up to that point. "You'll need more than that to stop us," Chase growled at him.

Michael tilted his head and held up his hand once more. "I am addressing the entity inside," he said in a commanding tone that seemed worthy of attention and awe. His voice echoed through the house as though it carried within it some kind of divine authority.

But Chase smiled at him in response, shaking his head. "There is no entity inside, priest," he sneered down at Michael. "There is only us."

"Shit," Michael said suddenly as Chase charged at him.

Chase swung at Michael with all his unnatural strength, but Michael, to Ava's complete astonishment, blocked the blow with one arm, stopping Chase in his tracks. There was a loud bang, and a small gust of wind displaced the air, causing Ava to gasp.

Michael smirked at Chase, who was staring down at him wide-eyed.

"What the hell are you?" Chase asked Merlyn.

"Someone who's got more tricks than you could ever know, lad," Michael replied. He punched Chase in the chest with his free fist, taking the Goliath off his feet and sending him sliding across the floor.

Ava gaped in utter shock, her mouth hanging open as Michael turned back to her.

"Ava, run!" he shouted.

She remembered what he had said before coming in here, what she had agreed to. If Michael said run, she was to run without question. But Ava was too terrified to move, too rooted to the spot as the fight erupted. And Michael didn't have time to push the issue. Chase had risen from the floor and was charging at him again.

Michael ran back at him, and the two men clashed in the center of Shepherd's sitting room. Their thunderous blows sent shockwaves reverberating through the foyer that washed over Ava's still body.

Michael was agile, which allowed him to avoid Chase's clubbing blows, each of which seemed to fall with the intent to disable or, to Ava's horror, kill. Michael landed a powerful kick to Chase's midsection, sending the possessed giant crashing into a wall.

"You know, for two blokes who spent your lives making action movies, you fight like a pansy," Michael said with a wink. "You're pretty predictable. I figured since the two of you are so united and all that, at least one of you might try to surprise me."

Chase roared, lunging at Michael. "Shut up, you smug bastard!" he screamed, his bellow shaking the floor beneath Ava.

Michael dodged as Chase swung again, but he was just a hair too slow. Chase connected with a powerful, meaty fist into the center of Michael's chest that sent him spinning through the air. Ava screamed in horror as her supposed savior smashed into the floor.

Chase pursued Michael's prone body, but the spry Brit was ready for it. He kicked up from the ground, doubling Chase over and rising into a crouch where he tackled his larger opponent into one of Shepherd's bookshelves. The polished wood splintered, with heavy, bound books falling from the shelves and bouncing off the two men as they continued their battle.

Ava noticed Shepherd now, completely still. She hoped he was unconscious, but he was too far away from her to be certain. If Chase had killed him, there would be nothing that could break Ava's guilt and horror.

Michael gritted his teeth, dodging another punch. "Big, bad ghost man, eh?" Michael said, waving his fingers around to mock Chase. "I've seen scarier things in haunted houses at amusement parks, mate."

Chase's eyes blazed, and he roared in abject fury. He sounded like a beast of the forest issuing a territorial challenge. "You haven't seen anything yet!" he cried out, swinging again.

Chase's next punch came fast. Clearly, it was far faster than Michael had anticipated. It caught him off guard, landing squarely on his jaw. Michael staggered back, dazed. Chase took that opportunity to deliver a powerful blow to Michael's head, which sent him crashing to the ground.

Michael hit the floor hard and didn't move again. Ava looked on in horror as Chase continued to approach his downed foe, a look of feral victory in his predatory eyes.

"Michael!" Ava screamed as Chase raised one huge boot to stomp on the British exorcist's head. "Wait!" she screamed at the top of her lungs, summoning the strength to rise to her feet.

Chase stopped and looked at her, his snarl remaining as his head tilted in question.

"Don't kill them," Ava begged, tears freely streaming down her face. "Please, just…I'll go with you, all right? I'll go with you, and I won't leave again. Just please don't kill them."

Michael was starting to stir and twitch, but Ava likened the movement to the spasm of a bug smashed on the bottom of a shoe. This was the only way. She was terrified, but she knew that was what needed to happen.

"Fine," Chase said in a growl, rushing away from Michael and toward her. He snatched her off the floor with one arm and slung Ava over his shoulder. "Time to head home…my love."

Chase ran out the door with Ava, leaving Shepherd's home behind them as he made a beeline for the car. Ava fought the urge to scream in horror as she said a silent prayer to whatever deity might be watching over this house that Jacob and Michael would somehow be all right.

23

Three hours later, Michael sat in a stiff hospital chair, bandages covering his face as he groaned in pain. The rhythmic beeping of hospital machines surrounded him, and every one of them made his already aching head pulsate with a fresh stab of agony.

Across the room, Jacob Shepherd lay in a bed, his face a mess of bruises and lacerations. Exactly how he'd been since Michael had regained consciousness and called 9-1-1.

Shepherd coughed gently, which drew Michael's attention. He wasn't sure how banged up the false medium was, but the fact that he was coming to so quickly was a good sign.

"Morning, Sleeping Beauty," Michael said sarcastically, a smirk pulling at his lips.

Shepherd groaned louder, his hand instinctively reaching for his face.

Michael pointed to the morphine drip beside him. "Morphine's right there, mate," he said. "Might want to make friends with it."

Shepherd's hand shakily found the button, and he pressed it, sighing in relief as the pain ebbed. "What...happened?" he asked, his voice strained. "Where are we? Why are…why the hell are you here? Where's Ava?"

Michael leaned back in his chair, his demeanor nonchalant despite the fact that deep in his heart of hearts, he felt anything but. "Ava's incredibly possessed husband showed up at your house," Michael said matter-of-factly, as though he were describing a sporting event and not a climactic battle that had nearly spelled the end of them both. "He beat you within an inch of your life, then fought with me and kicked my ever-loving ass. Then he took his wife and buggered off."

Shepherd's eyes widened in confusion and pain. He shook his head, as though something in Michael's story didn't make any sense. "How did Chase manage to get the better of you?" he asked, looking Michael up and down. "Why didn't you just start the exorcism right there?"

"I tried," Michael said, with more than a hint of the annoyance he felt wrapped around his words. His expression darkened slightly as he remembered what had happened. "This case is a lot more complicated than it seems."

Jacob struggled to sit up a bit more, wincing as he moved. "How so?" he asked.

"We'll get to that in a moment," Michael said, holding up a finger. "First question: was anyone else in the house when Chase came calling?"

Shepherd shook his head slowly. "No, I was alone," he said wearily, though he certainly sounded thankful for that fact. "Grace is away at camp for the week."

Michael let out a sigh of his own at that. "As lucky breaks go, that's a fairly big one," he remarked.

Shepherd nodded, clearly troubled by the thought of what might have happened if Grace had been there.

Michael tapped his fingers on the armrest of his chair. "Second question: how the hell did Chase know there was a connection between you and Ava?" Michael asked, sitting forward, eyes narrowing in an accusatory manner.

Shepherd's face twisted in frustration as he groaned. "It's my fault," he admitted after a moment.

"Not surprised," Michael said, not missing a beat. "How exactly did you screw this up so royally, Shepherd?"

Jacob took a deep breath and blew it out entirely. "When Lenny contacted me about meeting with Ava Monroe, I thought it was going to be the standard cold read," Shepherd began, his voice heavy with guilt. "You know, tell her what she wants to hear about a dead relative or something."

Michael's eyes narrowed in pure contempt. "You mean scam her," he said, making it well known that he still had no love for Shepherd's brand of false theatrics.

Shepherd winced at the bluntness but nodded. "Yeah, well, I called my publicist about it," he said. "He thought it'd be a good idea for me to be photographed with an actress on that level."

Michael groaned, the pieces falling into place. "Did you alert the media?" he asked, shaking his head. He already knew the infuriating answer to this question.

Shepherd sighed deeply and nodded. "My publicist let it slip to a few gossip sites," he said. "We thought it would be good PR."

Michael's frustration bubbled over, his teeth gnashing together as he slammed a hand down on the armrest of his chair. "You bloody, putrid idiot!" he exclaimed. "So, of course, Chase must've seen it! And the shock and rage of that moment probably gave old Nolan the boost he needed to gain more control and build up his strength enough to pay you a little house call. Ugh, you rip-roaring ponce!"

Shepherd's face flushed with anger and embarrassment. "It's not like I planned for any of this to happen!" he barked back, getting defensive but also clearly knowing deep inside how badly he had screwed up.

Michael shook his head, struggling to keep his composure. "You never do, do you?" Michael asked with a slow, scornful shake of his head. "You just bumble around, thinking about the next photo op, and now look where it's landed us both."

"Oh, don't act like you're innocent in all of this," Shepherd sniped back, clearly grasping at straws now to try to save some of his bruised ego. "If you hadn't been so wrapped up in your little hero complex, maybe you would have been there sooner and stopped Chase before he did all this!"

Michael's eyes flashed with dangerous anger. The desire to hit Jacob Shepherd wasn't a new one for Michael, but it was more intense than usual at this moment.

"My hero complex?" he scoffed. "I'm the one out there fighting real threats while you play pretend with your cold readings and fake séances!"

Shepherd's face contorted in a combination of pain and fury, the heat of the moment getting to him.

Michael stood up, the pain in his side a reminder of the beating he had taken. It wouldn't last, though. He thankfully healed fast. It was just another side effect of his dark passenger. He'd never been thankful for Kassidy's presence within him, but right now, in this scenario, it certainly didn't suck.

"At least I'm trying to make a difference," Michael spat. "I'm out there on the street fighting the fight where it needs to be fought. I'm not just padding my bank account with lies!"

Shepherd pressed the morphine button again, his body trembling with a mix of pain and anger. "You think you're so much better, don't you?" he said, his voice quivering as the drugs made their way into his system. "But you still need people like me. Without the fame, without my money financing your operation, how would you help anyone? Who would call you when things get bad?"

Michael leaned over the bed, his voice low and intense. "I never asked you for anything, mate," he snarled. "You offered and worked through my partner. You went over my head. And yes, no one knows my name like they know yours. I'm not selling books and marketing products, but I keep people safe from the likes of that thing that's taken over Chase."

"And I help how I can," Shepherd retorted, and this time, Michael just let the comment hang in the air, unanswered.

He wasn't necessarily wrong here. Shepherd was a huge part of the reason he'd seen such success over the last year. His money helped keep Michael moving from town to town in search of the next unexplainable phenomenon.

The room fell into a tense silence. The beeping of machines was the only sound between them as both men stewed in their own substantial egos.

It was Shepherd who finally broke it. A fact that Michael was proud of.

"So," Jacob said, his voice softer and apologetic without actually apologizing.

Michael was fine with that.

"What's the plan?"

Michael sighed, his anger fading as well. He'd been trying to piece together a plan for the last few hours while waiting for Shepherd to recover. "First, we need to figure out exactly what we're dealing with," Michael said. "This isn't just a simple possession. There's something else going on here."

"What do you mean?" he asked.

"When I pushed my will at Chase, he shrugged it off," Michael said. "He was also referring to himself as *we*."

"What does that mean?" Shepherd asked, bewildered.

"For an exorcism to work, you need to be able to isolate the spirit," he explained. "Then you urge the victim to help tear themselves away from the spirit little by little."

"Right," Shepherd said. He certainly already knew that much.

"But what's happening here if you have a victim who unconsciously gave himself over so completely that there's no separation between the two for me to grab onto."

"Holy hell," Shepherd said, blinking in surprise.

"Yup," Michael nodded. "That means we need to find a way to pry one away from the other just a little bit. The slightest separation and I can get in there and do my thing."

Shepherd nodded, his face still twisted in pain. "And what about Ava?" he asked. "Do you think she's safe?"

"Most likely for now," Michael said firmly. "I was in and out at the time, but it seemed like she went with him willingly, probably to save our skins. So, I guess we owe her one there."

"Seriously," Shepherd replied.

"But as long as she plays ball with him, I don't think he'll harm her," Michael said thoughtfully.

"You don't *think?*" Shepherd asked, clearly believing that wasn't enough.

"There's nothing else I can bloody well do now," he said. "The most I could do if I went in there now with no information is have another go at throwing hands, and you saw how well that went."

Shepherd closed his eyes, the morphine finally taking the edge off his pain. "All right, then," he said softly. "Let's figure this out."

Michael sighed, leaning forward to tap his fingers on the bed rail. "Nolan Hillhurst," Michael said. "Tell me everything you know about the wife. How can I get in touch with her?"

"Miranda Sterling?" he asked thoughtfully. "I've never met her personally. But I know that she and Ava share the same agent, Lenny. The guy who put me in contact with Ava to begin with."

Michael's eyes lit up. That was a start. "Lenny it is then," he said. "That little oaf is our doorway to advance this case."

With a determined look, Michael patted Jacob's leg, causing him to wince. "Stay put," Michael said with a wink and a small measure of satisfaction. "I'll be right back."

Shepherd nodded and tried in vain to push the morphine button again. Michael turned and walked toward the door with a flick of his coat. Nolan had made this fight personal for him now. And Michael was looking forward to drop-kicking that muscle-bound moron back to the hell where he belonged.

24

$\mathcal{A}$va sat on the couch in the TV room. Her TV room. The one in her house, her home. Though it certainly didn't feel like that now.

She could feel the pulsation of her heart pounding in her chest as Chase's massive arm draped over her. She could feel the unnatural strength in his muscles now. It was a strength that held her in a way that was both affectionate and possessive.

She knew that even if she tried to get away from him, she'd never succeed. Ava had to play ball. She had to buy time. She needed to go along with whatever Nolan or Chase or whatever she could call him wanted for the time being. That was the only way to survive until help arrived or she had an opportunity to get away.

They were watching another Nolan Hillhurst movie, and Chase was clearly enthralled by it. It was the same situation they had been in just a few days ago, but this time it felt more sinister. Chase was acting like he hadn't just beaten two men nearly to death in front of her and essentially kidnapped her, imprisoning her in their shared home.

The triumphant action movie music from the TV felt jarringly out of place.

"Chase," Ava tried to say, but he ignored her.

He simply kept his eyes glued to the screen.

"Chase," she said again, more insistent this time.

But again, he ignored her. Desperation and frustration made her grind her teeth. Why wasn't he answering her? Then Ava had a horrible thought. What if the person beside her was no longer Chase?

"Nolan," she called out, her voice trembling. She recoiled in horror as Chase's head snapped unnaturally toward her.

His eyes were dark and empty as they drank in the sight of her pressed against him. "Yes and no," the deep, unnatural voice replied. "We are something completely new."

Ava's heart pounded faster. At least he was acknowledging her now. She wanted to keep him talking to learn more about what was going on. Every time Michael had explained some new element of how this unseen world of the occult worked, it had set her mind at ease. Ignorance was the enemy here.

"What do you mean by *we?*" she asked, her voice meek and small.

"Nolan and Chase have combined to create something new," he said. "Something better, something that's going to take Hollywood by storm and redefine the action genre."

Ava shook her head, her eyes wide with fear. "Chase would never go along with something like that," she insisted. "Not my Chase."

The voice laughed, a chilling sound that made her skin crawl. "Chase does whatever I tell him to do," the creature beside her said. "He was so desperate to find success, so desperate to be Nolan Hillhurst, that he opened the door to become this. Now he's getting what he always wanted, and you shouldn't be standing in the way of that. You should be celebrating it. Not whoring around with other men and bringing in Nancy boy Brit exorcists to try to take this away from him."

Ava's hands clenched into fists. "I'm not trying to take anything from Chase," she insisted. "I'm trying to save him."

"Chase doesn't need saving. He needs me," Nolan's voice hissed, sounding so eerily different from Chase's.

Ava noted that in that moment when challenged, it seemed as though Nolan's personality was the one who started to shine through. "I'm making Chase more than he ever was before."

Tears welled up in Ava's eyes. "You're destroying him," she said, her voice no more than a whisper. "This isn't what he wanted. He wanted to be successful, but not like this."

Nolan's laugh echoed through the room. "Success is success, Ava," he replied. "And Chase is stronger, faster, and more powerful than he ever was. He's becoming the legend he always wanted to be."

Ava's mind raced, trying to find a way to reach Chase and pull him out of this nightmare. "Chase, if you can hear me, you have to fight this," she said with urgency. Consequences be damned. She needed to reach her husband. "You have to fight him. This isn't you. This isn't who you are."

For a moment, there was silence, and Ava thought she saw a flicker of recognition in Chase's eyes. But then it was gone, replaced by Nolan's cold, dark gaze.

"Chase is gone, Ava," the voice said. "Accept it and move on."

"No," Ava whispered, her voice breaking. "I won't accept it. I won't give up on him."

Nolan's grip on her tightened, making her wince in pain. "You don't have a choice."

Ava's mind raced. She had to find a way to break through to Chase. There had to be a way to make him fight back. She couldn't lose him to this monster. Not like this. She took a deep breath, trying to steady her nerves.

"Chase, if you can hear me, I love you," she pleaded. "I know you're still in there somewhere. Please, baby, fight this. Fight him. Come back to me."

The room was silent, the only sound that of the TV. Ava held her breath, hoping for a miracle. She saw another shift in Chase's eyes, the dark energy flickering like an old lightbulb for just an instant, but it was quickly extinguished.

"You're wasting your time, girl," Nolan spat down at her. His voice was venomous with contempt. "Chase belongs to me now."

Ava's heart sank, but she refused to give up. She had to find a way to save him, no matter what it took. She would not let Nolan win. Not now, not ever. Ava took a deep breath, steeling herself as she looked up at the man, who was now a twisted amalgamation of her husband and Nolan Hillhurst.

"What do you want with me, then?" she asked suddenly. "I'm Chase's wife, not yours. If you're going to take over, then why keep me here?"

Nolan's voice, using Chase's vocal cords, was cold and unfeeling. "You're here because we want you here," Nolan replied. "And you're going to stay. You took a vow of marriage to Chase, and you're going to honor it. That means being here with us, cooking, cleaning, and performing your duties as a wife in the bedroom whenever we want it."

Ava's stomach churned as the implications of his words settled over her. The horror of her situation intensified as Nolan continued.

"Enough of this acting garbage," he spat. "Your career is over. You don't need anything beyond what you have right here in this house."

Her mind reeled, struggling to comprehend the vastness of what he was demanding. Nolan's arm, with Chase's unnatural strength, tightened around her, nearly crushing her against him. The oppressive weight of his hold left her feeling more trapped than ever.

"You won't be able to run off as easily as last time," Nolan said. "No matter where you go, we'll follow you and bring you back here, where you belong."

"What about Miranda?" Ava suddenly asked out of pure desperation. "Don't you care about your wife at all?"

Nolan's expression darkened, and his grip on her became even more painful. He grabbed her and threw her to the ground with a force that left her breathless. "Miranda is a traitor who left me," he said slowly.

She could feel him glowering down at her, though she lacked the conviction to look up and meet his gaze.

"She deserves every bad thing that could ever happen to her. And once I'm back on top, I'll make sure that's what happens."

Nolan stood to loom over Ava as she cowered on the floor. "If you ever start to act like Miranda, I won't make the same mistakes I made last time," he said. The edge of his threat was more than implied. "I'll do something I should have done back then." With a snarl, he ripped the massive TV off the wall and threw it down beside her. The screen exploded, and tiny shards of glass and plastic went flying about the room.

Ava screamed, covering her head as tiny fragments pelted her skin. The room fell silent except for her sobs and ragged breathing.

The physical aspects of her panic consumed her. Ava's heart raced, her chest tightened, and her hands shook uncontrollably.

"Clean that crap up and then start on dinner," Nolan commanded before walking out of the room toward the gym.

Ava lay on the floor, staring at the door and contemplating a desperate run for freedom. But deep down, she knew it would be useless. Even if she made it outside, Nolan would find her. He could leave the house and follow her wherever she went. She was trapped now, trapped in this house and in a life she didn't want.

But she had noticed one thing. When Nolan had threatened her, he was no longer saying we or us. He was saying I and me. That told her something important. Chase was still in there, still fighting. He wasn't going to let that monster hurt her, and when Nolan had threatened to, Chase had fought back.

It was a small consolation, but Ava was going to have to take whatever she could get at that point.

As she lay there amid the devastation, Ava was startled by a gentle mew and a purr. She jumped when she felt something furry brush against her leg. Looking down, she saw nothing. That might have, at one time, alarmed her, but now that she understood its meaning, she took a measure of comfort in it. The presence of Miranda's cat, Snowball, seemed to surround her now. It was as though the spirit of the feline was trying to protect and comfort her in her lowest moment.

Ava took a deep breath and calmed down, realizing she had an ally in this house, even if she couldn't see him. Snowball's presence and Chase's momentary resistance gave her a small glimmer of hope. She also knew she had allies out there. She hoped Michael and Jacob were all right and that they weren't going to just give up on her.

The thought of Michael and Jacob brought a sliver of strength back to her. She knew she had to survive this. Ava had to find a way to endure until they could come to her aid.

She forced herself to stand, ignoring the pain from the cuts and bruises along her arms and legs. She then bit her lips, exhaled deeply, and began to clean up the shattered remnants of the TV. She would need to do as Nolan commanded for now. But only for now. She had to stay safe and bide her time.

That meant no more questions, no more arguments. Just hold the line until Michael unleashed whatever he was brewing somewhere out there.

As she cleaned, Ava thought of Michael's words. He had said that he would help her, that he wouldn't give up. He'd promised they were going to save Chase together.

She had to believe that. She had to believe that they would find a way to break Nolan's hold on her husband and bring normalcy and love back into their lives. Ava clung to that hope as she finished cleaning and made her way to the kitchen to start on dinner. Each step felt like an eternity, but she knew she couldn't let Nolan break her spirit.

She would never let him win.

25

Michael stepped out of a cab as the sun dipped below the horizon, casting long shadows across Lenny's expansive driveway. He approached the intercom and pressed the button, the metal cold against his fingertips. A crackle of static preceded Lenny's irritated voice.

"What the hell are you doing here?" he exclaimed, his voice oozing with utter contempt. "And where's Ava?" He sounded suspicious now, and Michael knew he needed to tread carefully.

Michael turned his face slightly, trying to hide the bruises marring his features. He'd been able to remove the bandages, but most of the marks left behind from his grand scuffle in Shepherd's home were still dotted along his face. He took a deep breath before responding.

"Ava's at home with Chase," Michael said, and technically, he was telling the truth, so he gave himself some bonus points. "I just came to collect my motorcycle, if you'd be so kind."

"It's about damn time," Lenny snapped. "I was going to have the damn thing towed if it stayed here any longer."

Michael rolled his eyes, fighting back a retort. He just needed the idiot to open the gate and let him in so he could do what had to be done for Ava's sake.

"Just buzz me in," he said quickly before adding, with some difficulty, "please. I'll collect the bike and be on my way."

There was a brief pause filled with the hum of the intercom. But eventually, the gate before him buzzed open.

Michael walked up the driveway. The crunch of the pavement under his boots was the only sound in the evening quiet. He stopped beside his motorcycle, taking a moment to inspect it. He could feel Lenny's eyes on him, watching from one of the windows. He turned his head, catching a glimpse of a curtain twitching as the Hollywood agent ducked out of sight.

With a resigned sigh, Michael approached the front door and knocked.

"What the hell do you want now?" Lenny's voice barked from inside, the irritation even seeping through the thick wooden door.

"My helmet's missing," Michael replied evenly, his voice calm despite the growing tension. "I came in with it, and it's an expensive one."

"You didn't come in the house with a helmet," Lenny shot back. "Get off my property before I call the cops."

"If you steal that helmet, I'll call the cops myself, mate," Michael retorted. "And I'll dial up the local gossip bloggers before I do. I'm sure your clients would love to see squad cars out front with their lights flashing."

There was a moment of prolonged silence as Michael waited to see if his gamble was going to pay off. Then the door cracked open, revealing Lenny's scowling face.

"There's no helmet in here," he said, glaring into Michael's eyes.

Michael seized the opportunity, shoving the door open

with a force that sent Lenny sliding across the polished floor. He stepped inside, closing and locking the door behind him, the click of the lock resonating ominously.

"You're insane!" Lenny screamed in fear, scooting back on his rear, away from the intruder. "I'll sue you for this!" He eventually managed to scramble to his feet.

Michael noted dueling instances of anger and fear quaking how jowls. "Do as you like," Michael said, his voice cold and unwavering. "But do it after you tell me everything there is to know about Nolan Hillhurst and his blushing bride, Miranda Sterling."

Lenny's face twisted in horror. "Where's Ava?" he asked, the color draining from his cheeks. "Is she all right?"

"She's where I said she is," Michael replied simply. "She's home with Chase. But that's not a good thing, mate. She's in a lot of danger right now. And the sooner you tell me what I need to know, the sooner we can help her."

Lenny's defiance crumbled. He looked away, his shoulders slumping. "I don't know anything about Miranda and Nolan," he said, though Michael knew a lie when he heard one. "Why does it matter now? The man's been dead five years!"

Michael stepped closer, his eyes boring into Lenny's. "Well, mate, if you don't know anything, then I need to talk to Miranda immediately."

Lenny's eyes widened in shock. "Absolutely not," he scoffed, backing away from Michael as though he could somehow jump into an escape pod and rocket away. "Miranda won't talk about anything concerning that pig."

Michael narrowed his eyes, picking up on the bitterness in Lenny's voice. "Why call him a pig, Lenny?" he asked, an eyebrow raised in question. "What exactly did Nolan do to his wife?"

Lenny hesitated, but Michael's intense gaze bore into him,

showing him that there was no escaping this. Not now or ever. Lenny sighed and shook his head, his posture slouching in defeat.

"Nolan treated Miranda like she was his property," he said bitterly, as if the simple act of recalling the memory was enough to leave a disgusting taste in his mouth. "He was abusive in just about every way a person can abuse another person. She was trapped in that marriage and in that house. It's traumatic for her, and she won't want to talk about it."

Michael leaned in, his tone softening slightly. He needed to take a different approach here, and he had a good idea of what might work on this man. "If Miranda doesn't talk to me, Lenny, you're going to lose your moneymaker," Michael said, keeping his voice tight to show that he wasn't bluffing. "Ava Monroe must bring in significantly more money than Miranda."

"Is that some kind of threat?" Lenny asked, his eyes alight with fury. "Did you do something to her?"

"No, mate, I'm trying to bloody help her," Michael said. "Everything you just said about Nolan and Miranda can be applied right now to Ava's situation. Now, unless you want this situation to take a far worse and infinitely more tragic turn, I suggest you take me to Miranda right bloody now."

Lenny looked shocked at Michael's accounting of the situation. Faced with this choice, his resolve ultimately faltered. The agent's expression was conflicted, but he seemed resigned to do what had to be done.

"Fine," he finally relented with a heavy sigh. "I'll take you to Miranda."

Michael nodded, stepping back to give Lenny some space. "There you go," he said, slapping the older man on the back. "Proud of you, mate. Now, let's move quickly, if you don't mind."

As they made their way out of the house, Michael couldn't

help but feel a swell of sympathy for Miranda after what he'd just heard. If Nolan had been as monstrous as Lenny had suggested, then it was no wonder she'd want to distance herself from any memories of him.

And if, as he suspected, she was somehow responsible for his death, Michael couldn't say he blamed her all that much for taking matters into her own hands to gain her independence. It was certainly frontier justice if he ever saw it, but Michael wasn't a by-the-book kind of guy. Some people just deserved death. And after his painful encounter with Nolan at Shepherd's mansion, he was starting to believe he might have been one of them.

They walked briskly to Lenny's car, and the tension between them was evident as they traded sidelong glares at one another. They were working together for the moment, solely for Ava's sake. But it was clear to Michael that Lenny wouldn't be adding him to his Christmas card list anytime soon.

Lenny fumbled with the keys, his hands shaking slightly as he unlocked the door and climbed into the driver's seat. "You better be right about this," he muttered, though it seemed he was speaking more to himself than to Michael.

Michael slid into the passenger seat, watching as Lenny started the engine. "We don't have time for doubts, Lenny," Michael said. "Ava doesn't have the time. Just drive."

The car pulled out of the driveway, headlights cutting through the growing darkness. The silence inside the car was heavy. It was filled with unspoken fears and questions. Michael glanced at Lenny, noting the tight set of his jaw and the worry lines etched deeply into his face.

Lenny's hands gripped the steering wheel tightly, his knuckles white. "How did we get into this mess?" he muttered, almost to himself.

Michael sighed, leaning back in his seat. "Sometimes, life

throws you a curveball, mate," he said simply. It was the only wisdom he could think to offer at the moment, and it basically boiled down to "shit happens." He felt he should give a little more, though. "The important thing is how you handle it."

Lenny shot him a skeptical look. His lip curled with cultivated distaste. "Easy for you to say," he replied. "You're not the one who has to explain this to Miranda."

Michael chuckled humorlessly. "Trust me, mate," Michael said, cycling through a multitude of awkward memories from cases long since closed. "I've had to explain worse."

They drove in silence for a few more minutes, the cityscape giving way to quieter suburban streets. The houses here were large, set back from the road, with manicured lawns and towering trees. Lenny finally turned into a gated driveway.

"This is it," Lenny said. He still seemed committed to their mission, but his voice was tight with apprehension.

Michael nodded in acknowledgment. With every second that passed, he imagined Ava trapped in that house and what she might be enduring.

"Let's get this over with," Michael said, hoping to make his grand return to the battlefield sooner rather than later.

Michael could see the mansion off in the distance through the barred gate. The grandeur of the place was highlighted perfectly by the soft glow of the outdoor lights. If Michael were the kind of person who appreciated opulence, he might have been impressed by it.

Lenny rolled his window down and pressed the buzzer button on the gate. Michael noticed that his finger lingered for a moment before pulling away. He was scared. Michael wasn't sure whether he was scared for Miranda, Ava, or himself. He told himself it was likely some winning cocktail of all three.

After a few tense seconds, an irritated voice crackled through the intercom. "Lenny, what do you want? It's late," Miranda said, her tone clearly annoyed.

Lenny cleared his throat, trying to sound calm. "Miranda," he said, succeeding in keeping the specter of uncertainty and anxiety from shaking his words. "I need to see you right away. It's important."

There was a pause, followed by a weary sigh. "Why, Lenny?" she asked, clearly irritated at this intrusion. "What's so important that it couldn't wait until morning?"

Lenny exchanged a glance with Michael, who gave him a nod. "Please, Miranda," he said again. "I wouldn't be here if it wasn't important."

Michael assumed that if Lenny told her why they were there, she'd never grant them access. The fact that he was trying this hard to get in showed that he was committed to helping his client.

Miranda let out another sigh. But this was a sigh of resignation rather than irritation. "Fine, come in," she said.

The gate buzzed open, and Lenny drove up the long driveway, parking near the front entrance.

"This better really be to help Ava," Lenny muttered as the two of them climbed out of the car. "Because bringing up all this trauma for Miranda is not going to end well for either of us."

Michael shot him a reassuring look. "I'll be delicate," he said. "I promise."

The front door opened, and Miranda appeared, her expression shifting from curiosity to confusion as she saw Michael. "Lenny, who the hell is this?" she asked.

"Someone here to talk to you about your chode of a dead husband," Michael blurted out, stepping forward into the doorway.

Lenny gasped, and Miranda's face darkened with anger. "This was delicate?" Lenny exclaimed in horror, to which Michael simply shrugged.

"Not my specialty," he admitted.

"What the hell do you mean?" Miranda asked. Her nostrils were flared with anger as her eyes moved from one annoyance at her door to the other.

Lenny quickly interjected, trying to take control of the situation and speak to Miranda in a way he likely knew worked on her. "Miri, there's been some weird things happening with Ava and Chase," Lenny said, taking a deep breath before proceeding. "This man is a private investigator Ava hired to look into it."

As far as generalizations went, Michael thought that was a decent one. He wasn't shocked that Lenny didn't lead with talk of ghosts and haunted homes. It was clear to Michael that he still didn't even believe it himself.

Miranda eyed them both suspiciously. "I have no comment on my husband," she said simply. Her voice was utterly devoid of emotion. "His loss was a great personal tragedy that I don't want to relive."

Michael glanced at Lenny, who looked desperate. He raised his eyebrows at the shorter man, essentially telling him that if he didn't make this happen soon, Michael was going to try his hand again.

"Please, Miri," Lenny said, his eyes pleading with his client. "Please, just hear him out. It's for Ava."

Miranda looked at Lenny for a long moment. Then she turned a narrowing glare in Michael's direction. "Did something happen with Miranda and Chase?" she asked, as though she might have known something already. It was almost as if she had been suspecting that the couple might've been having troubles.

"Aye," Michael responded. "And you might be able to help us make sure that what happened to you doesn't happen to anyone else."

"What happened to me?" she asked, her eyes wide as she fixed Lenny with a torching glare.

He seemed to shrink beneath it and offered her an apologetic look. There was a long moment of tension before Miranda sighed and stepped aside.

"Fine, come in. But you have ten minutes. Make them count."

"I'll make the most of every second, love," Michael replied.

Miranda led the two men to a sitting room, where they took seats in plush chairs. The room was elegant, but the tension passing between the three of them seemed to drown out the decor. Miranda sat across from Michael and Lenny, her gaze icy.

"All right," she said, pointing a red manicured nail at Michael. "Start talking."

Michael leaned forward, cutting right to the heart of the matter. "Was your marriage a happy one?" he asked bluntly.

Miranda's eyes narrowed. "How is that relevant to anything happening with Ava and her husband?" she asked with a growing scowl.

"Humor me," Michael said. "Answer the question."

Miranda took a deep breath. Michael knew this moment well. The moment in which someone steadied themselves to bring words into this world they didn't want to share.

"My husband was a good man," Miranda said, apparently deciding that it was easier to lie. Michael thought that she had wasted a perfectly good, deep, resigned breath. "He was a kind, gentle giant who loved me dearly."

Michael glanced at Lenny, who looked visibly uncomfortable. Miranda's eyes darted between them suspiciously.

"Lenny here spins a far different tale, love," Michael said calmly. "One of controlling actions and abuse that you were desperate to get away from. Trauma of the highest order."

Miranda's eyes blazed with rage. "Those ten minutes you just turned to three," she snapped.

Michael, however, didn't flinch. "I believe Ava might be going through something similar right now," he said, laying his cards on the table. "Something eerily similar, actually. I'm trying to understand the mindset of what pushes a man to that place."

Miranda looked at Lenny, who gave a hesitant nod. When she spoke next, it was through gritted teeth. "There were definite tensions in our marriage," she admitted.

Michael nodded encouragingly, but it seemed as though Miranda believed she was done. "Can you be more specific?" Michael asked, encouraging more from her.

"Nolan was a very controlling man who viewed me more as personal property than a partner," she finally said, leaning her neck back as though trying to angle her face away from those horrible words.

Michael's expression remained neutral. "Did you ever push back against that?" he asked simply.

"I tried," Miranda admitted. She cast her gaze down and away. "I was always threatening to leave. And eventually, he got violent over it."

Michael's voice softened. "That must have been very hard on you," he said, easing his approach with this far more delicate topic.

"It was," Miranda said, her voice barely above a whisper. The three minutes she'd penalized him with had come and gone by now, but she didn't seem to be holding him to it. "I always thought Nolan's possessiveness was part of some kind of…insecurity he had."

Michael leaned in. Now, they were getting somewhere. "What was he insecure about?" he asked.

Miranda hesitated, then sighed, as though asking herself why she should bother keeping the secrets of a long-dead abuser. "Long-term steroid use might grow the muscles, but it shrinks other things on a man's body," she said bitterly.

Michael nodded in understanding. "Performance issues, then?" he asked.

Miranda's eyes flickered with pained memories. "Yes," she admitted. "When he couldn't perform his…husbandly duties, he'd get so angry. And, of course, it was never his fault. It could never be his fault. And the only other person he could take it out on was me."

"Were you trying to have a child?" Michael asked gently. He wasn't sure how he knew, but somehow, he had an inkling that this was where some of the resentment was coming from.

Miranda's eyes filled with unshed tears. "We did try," she admitted. "But the drugs lowered Nolan's sperm count to the point of infertility. When I suggested a sperm donor and IVF…well, let's just say that was a temper tantrum I'll always remember."

She ran her fingers absent-mindedly over her jaw, and Michael didn't need a psych degree to realize what must have happened.

"He trashed the whole house," she said. "He even broke some irreplaceable family heirlooms from both sides. That was the last straw for me. I left for my mother's the next day."

Michael's eyes softened. His heart went out to this poor woman for what she'd endured. He actually found himself hoping that she had actually murdered this bastard. If anyone deserved to, it was her.

"Why didn't he stop you from leaving?" he asked.

Miranda's voice wavered as she recalled her escape that

night, and Michael felt himself pulled into her tale. "I put two Valium in his food that night," she said with a shrug. "It put him out like a light. I drugged him and then snuck out. I don't feel bad about it. I had to do it. If I hadn't, there wouldn't have been any escape. I was so terrified that I only took whatever I could carry in my arms. I even left my cat behind. And, of course, he blew my phone up and tried to find me at my mother's house, but I made it clear that we were done. *I* was done. A few days later, I got a call from Lenny saying he'd died of a heart attack."

Michael internally noted that he thought she was holding something back but decided not to press it. He turned to Lenny. "You were the one who found him?" Michael asked.

Lenny looked pale. "Nolan hadn't been heard from in days," he said, his voice low and gravelly. "I knew Miranda had left, so I went to check up on him and found him there."

Miranda's voice was strained. Michael could see her hands were shaking. She looked back up at him with glassy eyes glistening with tears.

"Is that enough for you to leave now?" she asked. She no longer sounded irritated or angry. She didn't even sound sad. She just sounded tired.

Michael nodded, standing up. "It is," he said with a grateful half-smile. "I'm sorry for bothering you."

Michael made his way to the door, opting not to even look back. He genuinely hated having to dig all of this up for this poor woman, but he didn't see any other way to navigate this horror and get the information he wanted. The fastest solution was always to go right to the source, no matter how painful that might be.

"Wait," Miranda called out.

Michael stopped and turned back to her.

She was standing now, one hand over her heart as she looked at him. "Is Ava all right?"

Michael looked at her and sucked his teeth for a long moment. She had been mostly honest with him, so he felt he owed her the same.

"I don't know," he said with a shake of his head. "But I'll do my best to help her."

26

Ava was running down a long, dark hallway in Hillhurst Manor as the walls started warping and closing in around her. She could hear her heart pounding in her ears. It was a frantic rhythm that matched her desperate footsteps.

"Chase!" she screamed. Her voice echoed back at her off the narrow walls. "Chase, where are you?"

But there was no response. The only sound was her own breathing, ragged and terrified. She turned a corner, and her feet slipped on the slick floor. Looking up, she found herself in another endless hallway, just as dark and claustrophobic as the last.

Panic clawed at her chest as she realized she was getting nowhere. It was as if the house itself was trying to trap her. It was a living monster that sought to keep her running in circles forever.

She turned another corner and came to a dead stop. There, at the end of the hallway, stood Chase. Relief flooded and softened her panic, and she started to run toward him.

"Chase!" she exclaimed in joy, her voice echoing in the endless hallway. "Thank God, I found you!"

But as she drew closer, she saw that something was wrong. His face was twisted in a grotesque grin, his eyes black and soulless. He reached out to her, but she recoiled in horror. Ava had realized too late that this wasn't her Chase. It was still Nolan, always Nolan. And he was wearing Chase's body like a suit.

"No!" she screamed, backing away. "Get away from me!"

Nolan's laugh echoed through the hallway, a deep, guttural sound that sent chills down her spine. "You can't run from me, Ava," he said. His distorted parody of Chase's voice was mocking her as she resisted him. "I'm everywhere."

She turned and ran, her breath coming in short, painful gasps. The walls started to close in even tighter, and she could feel Nolan's presence behind her. He was looming like a shadow, bathing her in darkness.

Finally, Ava burst through a door and found herself in a dimly lit room. It was filled with old, dusty furniture, and the air was thick with the smell of decay. Ava stumbled to the center of the room and was instantly wretched by the vile odor. She held her arm up over her nose and mouth in order to stop herself from vomiting.

Her eyes darted around for an escape. It was then that Ava saw a familiar figure in the corner, and her heart leaped. "Chase?" she whispered, her voice trembling with audacious hope.

The figure turned, and for a moment, she thought it was him. But as it stepped into the light, she saw that it was Nolan again, his grin even wider and more menacing.

"Did you really think you could get away?" he taunted, advancing at her with his hands raised like the talons of a bird of prey that was going to swoop down and take her away.

Ava backed away, her hands shaking with legitimate terror.

"This isn't real," she whispered to herself. "This is just a nightmare. You're not real!"

But it felt real. The fear, the desperation—it was all too vivid.

Nolan lunged at her, and she screamed, turning to flee. She ran down another hallway, her surroundings warping and twisting like the mirror of a funhouse. It was difficult to run under the shifting floor, and doors appeared and disappeared all around her. The walls pulsed in and out as though they were bleeding, and there was a faint red glow like the heart of the devil himself, just visible through a few cracks in the paint.

She was trapped in a living nightmare. And now there was no way out.

She found another door and threw it open, stumbling into a room that looked like a twisted version of their living room. The furniture was warped and melted, the walls oozing a dark, viscous substance. She saw Chase again, sitting in an armchair, his back to her.

"Chase, please," she begged. Tears streamed down her face as she hoped against hope that, on this third try, it might actually be her Chase. "Baby, please, we have to get out of here."

But when he turned around, his face was a horrific mask of rotting flesh and empty eye sockets. Ava screamed and fell back, scrambling away from the ghastly, crumbling corpse of the man she loved. She could hear Nolan's laugh echoing through the room now. It seemed to come from everywhere and nowhere at the same time.

"You'll never escape me," his voice whispered in her ear, so close that she could feel his breath tickle her earlobe. She turned, expecting to see him there, leering just behind her. But there was nothing and no one, save for the shifting hellscape of this horrible room.

"You're mine, Ava," the voice said again, once more blowing into her ear like a hot breeze. "You're mine, forever."

She felt a cold hand on her shoulder and turned to see Nolan standing over her now. Only he no longer looked like Chase. He looked like himself now, the way she had seen him in those horrible movies.

Nolan's own eyes burned even brighter with malevolent glee. She tried to scream, but no sound came out. He leaned in close, his breath hot and foul against her skin.

"You're mine," he repeated, his voice a sinister whisper.

Ava's vision blurred as she felt herself being pulled into the darkness. She was falling, spinning, her mind a whirlwind of fear and confusion. She reached out, grasping for something, anything to hold on to. But there was nothing.

She landed with a jolt, the impact knocking the breath from her lungs. She was in another room now, this one a nightmarish horror-show version of their bedroom. The bed was a twisted, skeletal frame, the sheets stained with dark, ominous blotches of blood. She saw Chase lying there, his body so lifeless and cold. He seemed so far from her now, so removed from their life together.

"Chase!" she cried, rushing to his side. She shook him, but he didn't respond. She sobbed harder. "Baby, please, wake up!"

But as she looked closer, she realized it wasn't Chase. It was Nolan, his face a grotesque mask of death twisted into a riotous grin. He sat up suddenly, grabbing her by the wrist. His touch was ice cold, and she felt a wave of nausea wash over her.

"You can't save him," Nolan hissed, his grip tightening. "He's already mine."

Ava yanked her arm free, somehow breaking through his frozen grip. She stumbled back away from the bed and turned to run yet again.

She reached the door and flung it open, only to find herself in the kitchen. She could see Chase standing by the windows, his figure blurry and indistinct.

"Chase?" she called out, her voice desperate. She couldn't bear to lose him again. She couldn't bear to run to him, to call for him, only to be greeted with Nolan's deteriorating demonic visage.

But when he turned to her this time, it was him. It was actually him. It was her Chase, looking at her with his eyes and his face contorted in fear.

"Ava, run!" he shouted. "Get out of here!"

But she couldn't run away from him now. Not after she had worked so hard to find him. Ava ran to him, but no matter how fast she moved, he seemed to stay just out of reach.

"Chase!" she screamed again, her voice breaking. "Please!"

They held out their arms to one another, their fingertips coming so tantalizingly close. Ava knew that if she could just reach him, just touch him, they'd be able to pull themselves out of this nightmare.

Suddenly, the walls around her began to close in, the ceiling lowering. They were trapped, the space growing smaller and smaller, threatening to crush them into nothingness.

Ava could feel her panic rising, her breath coming in short, frantic gasps. She reached out to Chase, but he vanished, dissolving into the darkness as the shadows pulled him away.

"No!" she screamed, her voice echoing in the confined space. "Please, no!"

The walls closed in around her so close now that they restricted her movements. But they didn't stop there. He kept squeezing her, crushing her, suffocating her. She could hear Nolan's laughter, a cruel, mocking sound that filled her mind.

"You can't escape me," his voice whispered. "You'll never escape."

Ava woke with a start, her heart pounding in her chest as she sat bolt upright in bed. She tried to scream, tried to let a blood-curdling exclamation of her horror explode out of her throat. But no sound escaped. And when she realized where she actually was, she was thankful for it.

Ava was in bed, the familiar surroundings of their bedroom a stark contrast to the nightmare she had just endured. She took a deep breath, trying to calm herself. It was just a dream, she told herself. Just a terrible, terrible dream.

But as she turned her head, she froze. Standing at the foot of the bed, bathed in the pale moonlight filtering through the window, was Chase. Or rather, it was Nolan in Chase's body, watching her silently. His eyes were dark, empty voids that felt as though they were dissecting her and peering at her insides.

Ava's breath caught in her throat, her heart pounding so hard she thought it might burst. She wanted to scream, to run, but she was paralyzed with fear. Nolan's lips curled into a chilling smile, and he tilted his head, watching her with a predator's gaze.

She could feel the cold sweat on her skin, her hands trembling as she clutched the sheets. She knew she wouldn't be getting back to sleep that night.

27

Michael Merlyn rode his motorcycle through the dimly lit streets of Los Angeles. The engine's roar was a comforting constant amidst his swirling thoughts and careful planning. The city's perpetual hum was nothing more than a distant echo now. It had been completely overshadowed by the unsettling case he was entangled in.

He'd thought this would be an easy win. A layup that he desperately needed after the last Shepherd situation. But all he'd found here was horror. And he was determined to see that horror defeated and driven back into the depths where it belonged.

He often got a sense of satisfaction from tossing deranged spirits across the veil that separated the material world from the next. But this one? He was really going to enjoy this one.

He'd faced countless spirits and exorcised malevolent forces so powerful and insidious that they could have called themselves demons. In fact, many of them had. But this situation gnawed at him differently. Nolan Hillhurst's spirit had a grip on Chase that defied the usual rules of possession.

Michael's mind replayed recent events as he tried to turn

the situation over and over in his head to come up with the perfect battle plan.

He could recall the brutal fight with Nolan back at Shepherd's mansion with unsettling clarity. He recalled every thundering punch, every time the floor rose up to meet him. He could still practically taste the blood in his mouth as he tried and failed to put the threat down with nothing but his own two hands.

The raw, unnatural strength Nolan had displayed wasn't your typical strength-boosted possession. If it was, he would have, more than likely, been able to stop him then and there. But Nolan's spirit exhibited unprecedented power and a level of control over Chase that Michael's usual methods couldn't counteract.

Chase's apparent willingness to surrender himself to Nolan, at least initially, had created a bond so strong that traditional exorcism techniques were rendered less than ineffective. But there was no other way. There was no alternative method for getting a spirit out of a living host. It was, as he'd said to Shepherd in the hospital. He had to cause the two to split from one another, even just a little bit. Once he could establish a foothold, Nolan was all but done for.

The hospital loomed ahead. Michael hated hospitals but found himself frequenting them more often than most people outside the medical profession. His work often came with some dangerous territory, and unfortunately, people got hurt.

But for now, the hospital would have to serve as his temporary base of operations, a war room from which he planned out his attack and bounced ideas off the one ally he had in this entire mess.

Michael pulled into the parking lot and cut the engine. He sat in silence for a moment, gathering his thoughts. He had to be strategic, finding a way to exploit any weakness in Nolan's hold over Chase.

Inside the hospital, the sharp smell of disinfectant greeted him, a reminder of his own injuries. He navigated the corridors, nodding at curious nurses and doctors. Room 314 was where Shepherd was recovering. Michael could hear the faint beeping of machines and the murmur of hospital staff as he approached.

Shepherd was awake, propped up on his bed and being attended to by a nurse. His face was still a mosaic of bruises and cuts, exactly how Michael had left him just a few short hours ago. His eyes lit up with relief as Michael entered, and that quickly shifted to curiosity as his head tilted.

"Is it sponge bath time, then, love?" Michael asked with a wry smile. "If you don't mind, I'll take over from here. I think he'd be more comfortable with me doing it, if you know what I mean."

The nurse seemed unsure of whether she should laugh or ask Michael to leave. She looked back at Jacob awkwardly, and he gave her a gentle smile and a nod.

"It's all right, nurse," he said. "He's a fr— Well, he's something of an acquaintance."

"Oh, all right," the nurse replied, giving Michael a more pleasant smile this time as she moved out of the room.

Once she was gone, Michael moved to close the door so he and Jacob could talk about all the things that went bump in the night uninterrupted.

"So, how'd it go with Miranda?" Shepherd asked, cutting right to the point. "What did you find out from her?"

"I'm fine, thanks, Shepherd," Michael replied, crossing his arms over his chest. "Thanks for asking."

"Come on, Michael," Shepherd said impatiently. "Ava's waiting for us. What do we have?"

Michael leaned forward, his expression intense. "Miranda confirmed that Nolan was abusive, controlling, and had a serious steroid problem," he said with a sigh, still not able to get the look in her eyes out of his mind. "It was apparently pretty brutal. The drugs made him violent and paranoid. It also had a few other side effects that he was kinda testy about." Michael held in pinky finger out and let it sag there limply. "If you get what I mean, Shepherd."

"Yes," Jacob said with a roll of his eyes. "Noted. Moving on."

"All right," Michael replied, clapping his hands together. "She also mentioned that they'd been trying to have a child. But apparently, Nolan's drug use made it impossible. When she suggested a sperm donor, he went nuts, and she hinted that there was some major violence. That was when she left him."

Shepherd's face remained thoughtful through Michael's recounting of the tale. He stroked his chin as he tried to put all the pieces in place.

"So, he had a lot of unresolved anger and frustration," Shepherd said. "And it sounds like a staggering amount of insecurity for just about everything in his life."

"Exactly," Michael said. "And if he felt betrayed by Miranda, his spirit might have latched onto those emotions. That would only give it more power after life. His desire to prove that he's a quote-unquote real man might be what's keeping him around. Though I'm not ruling out a murder here. Ava had mentioned an article she read about potential foul play in Nolan's death. That's an angle I need to explore further."

Shepherd's eyes narrowed as he bit his lower lip in thought. "Do you think Miranda could have had something to do with it?" he asked. Michael shrugged in response.

"It's possible," he said. "There's definitely a motive, and honestly, I wouldn't blame her if she had."

"Michael, it's murder," Shepherd admonished. "It's not something that's ever justified."

"Sorry, I forgot you're going for your exorcism merit badge

this week, Mister Boy Scout," Michael said with a mock salute and a roll of his eyes. "But if Nolan was as dangerous as she described, it's possible that Miranda might not have seen any other way out. But we need to confirm it. The more we know about Nolan's death and his relationship with Miranda, the better chance we have of breaking Nolan's hold on Chase."

Shepherd sighed, leaning back against the pillows. "And what about Chase?" he asked simply. "What do we know about him?"

Michael thought for a moment. Outside of what Ava had told him earlier, he hadn't done much digging on Chase. "All right," he said, rubbing his hands together. "Chase is an action movie star who has been out of work for a while. From what Ava said, he was a wonderful, caring man before this. But his career was on a downward spiral. He looked up to Nolan. Idolized him, even. It's likely that his desperation to succeed made him more vulnerable to Nolan's influence."

"So, Nolan preyed on Chase's insecurities," Shepherd said, nodding. "That makes sense. He used Chase's admiration and desperation to gain control."

"Exactly," Michael said. "It's easy enough to just implant that thought in his head. Ask if he wants to be Nolan Hillhurst, and the moment he responds in an overwhelmingly positive way to that one stray thought, boom. Instant possession."

"It's terrifying that that's all it takes," Shepherd said.

Michael could only nod in agreement. "But we need more than that," Michael said. "I feel like I need just a little more ammunition against Nolan. I mean, don't get me wrong. Going in there and making baby dick jokes at him does sound like my idea of a good time, but I think I'll need a little extra. I need to find a way to weaken Nolan's influence, to give Chase the strength to fight back."

Shepherd frowned, deep in thought. "What if we could

show Chase the truth about Nolan?" he offered. "Expose the reality of who Nolan was, rather than the idealized version Chase has in his head?"

Michael shrugged at that. "At this point, Nolan has thrown his wife across the room in front of him," Michael said. "I feel like Chase has already seen more than enough. But if Nolan has his claws in deep enough, he might not be able to get away on his own. And if that's the case, then Nolan would be holding on very tight to maintain that level of bond. Which means a little distraction could help Chase create some distance."

"That's assuming you're right about this," Shepherd said.

"Mate, I'm always right about this stuff," Michael replied with a wink. "Thought you'd learned that by now."

"So, how do you want to distract him?" Shepherd asked, too exasperated to push back on that.

"I'll do what I do best, mate," Michael replied. "I'm gonna piss him off."

"Merlyn, I think we've finally found the case you were born for," Shepherd said with a slow, disapproving shake of his head.

"I just need a little more ammunition," Michael said. "Because I mean, I pissed him off in your house, but for this, I need to get him really pissed off. Like, can't see straight levels of anger. It's going to have to be my quipping masterpiece."

"I can't believe this is the plan," Shepherd said from his bed.

"We just need to dig deeper into Nolan's past," Michael said. "Find out more about his relationship with Miranda, the circumstances of his death, and anything else that might help us paint a clearer picture. And we need to get Ava out of there. She's in danger as long as Nolan has control over Chase."

Shepherd nodded. Michael was surprised to see his expression so resolute. He seemed to have really taken a personal stake in this case as well. Michael respected that, but he wasn't about to tell the celebrity medium that.

"All right," Jacob said. "I'll help however I can. We'll find a way to break Nolan's hold and save Ava."

"You've done all you can from that bed, mate," Michael said.

"I haven't done anything," Jacob protested. "I just laid here and listened to you talk."

"Exactly," Michael replied. "I always perform better with an audience. Thank you very much and be sure to tip your waitress. Don't try the veal."

"Ugh," Shepherd said, massaging his forehead with his fingertips. "As long as it helps Ava."

"It will," Michael said as he turned toward the door without so much as a farewell to his partner in this case. It hadn't been intentional, though. Not this time, anyway. Michael's mind was just racing with possibilities that he felt the need to chase right away.

Sometime later, Michael arrived at the small hotel where he'd rented a room for the duration of this job. He parked his motorcycle out front and headed inside. The lobby was quiet, with only a few guests milling about. Michael then made his way to his room, unlocking the door and stepping into the dimly lit space. He tossed his jacket onto a chair and collapsed onto the bed, staring up at the ceiling.

He reached for his phone and dialed a number, waiting as it rang.

On the fifth ring, Kate answered. "Hello?" she asked, her voice groggy with sleep.

"Detective," Michael said, in a tone that was far too cheery even in the best of circumstances. "It has been too long."

"Michael, it's late," Kate groaned. "What's going on?"

"This is a booty call," he said quickly.

"Hanging up," Kate replied.

"Wait, Detective," he exclaimed, sitting up on the bed. "You've seen through my clever ruse. Yes, I know it's late, and I'm quite sorry to wake you from your beauty sleep. But I find myself in a position with this case I'm on where I need your help."

"With the simple possession case you mentioned to us days ago?" Kate asked, more awake now and certainly more annoyed. "I thought you said it was gonna be an easy one."

"Detective, I know you, of all people, love to relish in those oh-so-rare moments when I'm wrong," he said. "So, I'm giving you your moment now. But get over it quickly because I'm dealing with a case that's more complicated than usual. I need you and V to dig into Nolan Hillhurst's past for me."

"The action movie meathead?" Kate asked, clearly bewildered. "Why?"

"He's the spirit I'm chasing on this one," Michael said simply.

"Are you kidding me?" Kate exclaimed in annoyance. "You go on a job alone and you're dealing with celebrity ghosts while we're running from air conditioning to air conditioning in the middle of New Mexico?"

"They say it's the land of enchantment, Detective," Michael said defensively. "It can't be all that bad."

"Remember, you said that when you eventually get here," she grumbled.

"All right, all right," Michael said, realizing they needed to move this conversation along. "I need dirt on this man. A lot of his time should center around his career and his relationship with his wife, Miranda Sterling. Give me anything you find surrounding the circumstances of his death as well. I need *anything* you can find, Detective, no matter how small."

Kate sighed. "All right," she said. "I'll see what I can do. What are you looking for specifically?"

"Anything that can paint a clearer picture of who Nolan

Hillhurst really was," Michael replied. "I have a good idea of who this cretin was and what made him tick, but I need a little more."

"I'll get on it first thing in the morning," Kate said.

"Actually, I was hoping you'd put V on it," he said. "She is the researcher, after all."

"Well then, why did you call me?" Kate exclaimed, her voice still dragging with weariness. "You shoulda just called her."

"Detective, it's late," Michael said. "I didn't want to wake her."

"I hate you," she said into the phone and sounded like she meant it.

"I look forward to getting the full report ASAP, Detective," he replied, as though he hadn't heard her.

"Hey, Michael," Kate said, stopping him before he was about to hang up. "Just be careful. This sounds like it's getting dangerous, and you don't have us there for backup."

"It is," Michael said, betraying a hint of the weariness in his voice that he'd been hiding throughout this conversation. "But there's a very nice girl who's in a very tight spot, and right now, I'm all she has."

There was silence on the other end of the line for a moment. Michael knew Kate was having one of those very rare moments when she actually had some respect for him. He decided to let her hold onto it this time.

"All right," she said. "I'll call you as soon as we have something. Stay safe."

"Wear sunscreen," Michael said back as Kate hung up the phone in his ear.

28

Michael woke up in his hotel room, blinking against the morning light that seeped in through the thin curtains. He reached for his phone on the bedside table, squinting at the screen as he unlocked it. A new email notification caught his eye. It was from Victoria. She had compiled a list of information on Nolan Hillhurst.

"That was fast," Michael said with a nod.

He sat up, rubbing the sleep from his eyes, and opened the email. He scanned the contents of the information she had gathered, but Michael told himself that it was high past time that he actually called her to discuss these findings. Michael tapped her number and waited as the phone rang.

"Morning, Mikey," Victoria's voice came through, warm and familiar.

"Morning, sis," Michael replied, a smile tugging at his lips. "Looks like you've been busy."

"Wasn't exactly hard," she said, and Michael could practically hear the roll in her eyes. "This guy loved the limelight. He was out there living it up pretty much twenty-four-seven in front of the press. A lot of this is probably stuff you already knew. Rumors of steroid abuse, issues in the marriage, blah blah."

"Tiny prick," Michael added.

"Wait, what?" Victoria asked in surprise.

"Nothing," Michael said, moving the conversation along. "Yeah, all that fits with what I've been hearing. Anything else of note stand out?"

Victoria chuckled. "You'll love this," she said. "I found a few interviews where Nolan talks about his movies, and oh man, does this guy have no self-awareness. He talks about these crappy action flicks like they're Shakespearean masterpieces. The guy had an ego the size of Hollywood."

"Sounds like him," Michael said with a short laugh.

"Here, let me read you a bit from one of the articles," Victoria said.

Michael listened as she began to read:

"Hollywood Star Nolan Hillhurst Talks New Movie: "A Cinematic Masterpiece in the Making."

"Nolan Hillhurst, the action star known for his larger-than-life roles and explosive performances, is gearing up for the release of his latest film, Blood and Thunder. *In an exclusive interview, Hillhurst opened up about his passion for filmmaking and his vision for the new movie.*

"Interviewer: 'Nolan, what can you tell us about your upcoming film, Blood and Thunder?'

"Nolan Hillhurst: 'Oh, Blood and Thunder *is unlike anything you've ever seen before. It's not just another action flick; it's a work of art. The depth of the characters, the intricacies of the plot—they're all woven together in a way that will leave audiences breathless. I genuinely believe this film will redefine the action genre.'*

"Interviewer: 'That sounds impressive. What was your approach to this project?'

"Nolan Hillhurst: 'I wanted to push the boundaries of what

action cinema can be. We didn't just focus on the stunts and explosions, though those are spectacular. We delved into the emotional journeys of the characters. There's a Shakespearean quality to it, a blend of tragedy and triumph that you don't often see in this genre.'

"Interviewer: 'You've compared it to Shakespeare. Can you elaborate on that?'

"Nolan Hillhurst: 'Absolutely. *Just as Shakespeare's plays were rich with complex characters and moral dilemmas,* Blood and Thunder *explores the human condition through the lens of action. It's a story about redemption, sacrifice, and the relentless pursuit of justice. It's poetry in motion, really.'*

"Interviewer: 'What do you hope audiences take away from Blood and Thunder?'

"Nolan Hillhurst: *'I want them to see that action films can be more than just mindless entertainment. They can be profound, thought-provoking, and deeply moving. This film is my magnum opus. It's a testament to what can be achieved when you pour your heart and soul into a project.'* Victoria finished reading and chuckled.

"Wow," Michael said with a scoff.

"I know. Can you believe this guy?" Victoria said. "He really thought he was some kind of sensitive artist."

Michael laughed. "Yeah, he had quite the inflated sense of self," he replied. "But this could be useful. If I can trigger that ego and make him mad with this and some of the other information I've gathered on him, it might cause a disconnect between him and Chase. Oh, Chase is the guy that he's possessing. Ava is his wife."

"Wait," Victoria said, her voice suddenly tight. "Are you telling me right now that you're working with Ava Monroe?"

"Aye, that's her name, V," Michael said.

"You asshole!" she exclaimed. "You're working with my favorite actress, and I'm here with Kate in the desert?"

"You've heard of her then?" Michael asked.

"Uh, yeah!" she replied. "We did a whole case in LA, and I didn't get to meet anyone cool, and you're helping Ava Monroe? Ugh, I hate you. What's she like?"

"Bloody terrified because her husband is possessed!" Michael exclaimed.

"I just...wow," Victoria said. "Just...you better not be mean to her!"

"I'll get an autograph for you after I've saved her life, okay, V?" he asked with an exasperated sigh.

"You better," Victoria replied. "Are you sure you don't need me and Kate to come out there and back you up?"

"No, stay put in New Mexico," Michael said to her clear disappointment. "I need to move on this fast and don't have time to wait around."

"Got it. Just be safe, Mikey," Victoria said. "You know how dangerous these situations can get."

"Always the king of safety, sis," Michael said with a grin.

"Sure you are," she replied. "Just make sure you have Ava's autograph when you get to New Mexico."

"Promise," he said. "Thanks for the help, V."

"Anytime. Good luck."

Michael ended the call and leaned back against the headboard for a moment, contemplating the next steps. With the information they had, it was time to put a plan into action and confront the spirit of Nolan Hillhurst head-on.

Twenty minutes later, Michael mounted his motorcycle outside. It was go time.

He took a deep breath, feeling the weight of the mission ahead. The engine roared to life once more, and he sped off, heading straight into the heart of the battle. The city blurred past him as he rode, each turn bringing him closer to the showdown that awaited.

This time, he wouldn't fail. This time, he'd make sure Nolan Hillhurst was sent back to whatever hell he'd crawled out of. It was time to save Chase and Ava from the nightmare they were trapped in. And then maybe he'd get Ava to sign a few things for Victoria if time permitted.

Michael Merlyn was on a mission now, and he wouldn't stop until it was done.

29

Ava set a tray in front of Nolan with his lunch on it while he sat once more in the media room, watching his old films. The old TV still lay in a shattered, twisted mess on the floor. Nolan had ordered another one with same-day delivery immediately after smashing the old one and had installed it that morning.

If he wasn't pumping iron in the gym, he was sitting there, watching those films. It was maddening, especially because he made Ava go everywhere with him now.

She had to watch the movies; she had to stand there in the gym while he worked out; she had to go to bed when he went to bed. The only time she had away from the hulking brute who had once been her husband was when she was sent off to the kitchen to prepare his meals.

That was once more plain chicken breast with a side of rice and steamed broccoli.

Nolan glanced at the tray before picking up the chicken with his fingers and taking a bite. "Why aren't you eating?" he asked, not even looking at her.

"I'm not hungry," Ava replied, keeping her voice steady.

Nolan looked her up and down and sneered. "Maybe it's for the best," he said with his mouth full. "Don't want you getting fat."

Ava felt her face burn red with anger at the comment. She considered running again, not for the first time. But she knew that it would be futile. He'd simply catch her, and it was definitely possible that things would turn violent.

Adding to her frustration was the fact that she had barely slept the night before. That harrowing nightmare she'd endured had felt so real, so horrifying. She had fully believed that, somehow, Nolan had implanted it in her head on purpose to terrify her further into submission.

The longer she stayed around Nolan, the more she realized he was a ticking time bomb of rage and hate. Eventually, that malice would be turned on her through no fault of her own. He seemed to take some kind of perverse joy in exerting dominance over her and terrifying her. How long until that escalated?

Ava told herself that she couldn't just sit around and wait for Michael or Shepherd to come and save her. For all she knew, they were laid up in a hospital somewhere, grievously injured after Nolan had beaten them both to a bloody pulp. She had to find her own bravery and help herself.

She glared at the cretin in disgust and decided it was time. She needed to make a move to save Chase once and for all.

"Chase," she called out, her voice shaking but determined. "Baby, are you there?"

Nolan laughed and put the chicken down. "Chase is a part of us now," he said, his voice dripping with malice.

Ava took a deep breath. "Chase, I know you could never give in to this," she said again, her voice pleading while maintaining its strength.

She remembered yesterday when she'd tried something similar and saw the darkness flicker away for just a second.

He was in there, and he needed to be encouraged. He had to fight.

"You're too strong for that, baby. I love you, and I believe in you. You're the strongest man I know, and you're stronger than this spirit."

"Shut the hell up," Nolan snapped. "We're not Chase. And you had better learn to respect that."

"I'm not talking to you," Ava said, her voice rising. "I'm talking to the man I love."

Nolan's face contorted with rage. He threw the tray of food on the floor and stood menacingly. Ava tried not to wince as the tray clattered along the tile. She maintained her composure even as he continued to stand slowly, towering over her all the more with every passing second.

"You need to learn your place," he said, reaching his full height and raising a hand to slap her.

Ava didn't run; she didn't flinch; she didn't move a muscle. She thought of those roles she had played, those female characters she idolized. And much as one of them would do in this situation, Ava smirked up at him. That seemed to make his nostrils flare all the more.

"You definitely need to learn, little girl," he said, his voice shaking with fury. "And I am the one who will teach you."

"I?" Ava asked, drawing Nolan's attention to the momentary disconnect he must have been experiencing.

Nolan looked alarmed for a brief second and then froze, wincing and groaning as though he were fighting with himself. He grabbed at his stomach and doubled over in pain. Ava could see that the darkness in his eyes was flickering again now with renewed intensity.

"Settle back down and learn how to be a man," Nolan growled, his voice directed inward.

"No!" Chase's voice screamed out, free of distortion, and

Ava felt her heart soar at hearing him fighting back. "I won't let you hurt Ava!"

"Chase!" she cried out, hope surging through her as her husband fought back against this invasive presence. "Fight, baby! Fight him!"

Nolan screamed suddenly, rising again a second later, his eyes once more alight with dark energy. He grinned down at her in triumph. "Chase is back where he belongs," he said through gritted teeth. "As a part of us. And now you're going to wish you'd never been born, little girl."

Ava felt a cold pull in her stomach, imagining Chase plunged back down into the horror of whatever hell was churning within his soul. She wanted to leap on this monster and claw at him, ripping chunks of him away until only her love remained. But that wasn't feasible right now. She had been brave up to this point, but now it was time to be smart.

Nolan lunged at Ava, gripping her by the throat, but she lashed out the way she had been taught in countless women's self-defense classes over the years. She kicked him right between the legs. Nolan groaned in pain and doubled over. Ava didn't wait around this time. She bolted, racing around the room and out into the hallway.

Nolan roared in anger and chased after her. Ava's heart pounded as she dashed through the house. She was barely staying ahead of him. The actress rounded corners and ducked through doorways. Adrenaline pushed through any exhaustion and kept her moving forward.

She could hear Nolan's heavy footsteps right behind her. The sound of his labored breathing filled her ears.

She darted into the living room, knocking over a lamp in her haste. Nolan was right behind her. She could feel his stolen eyes burning with fury and digging into her back. Ava's mind raced as she tried to think of a way to escape. She couldn't keep this up forever. She had to find a way out.

Ava ran into the kitchen, grabbed a chair, and threw it in Nolan's path. It slowed him down for a moment, and that gave her a few precious seconds to sprint toward the foyer.

She could see the front door ahead of her now, the sunlight streaming in through the windows.

Ava reached the door and yanked it open, but before she could step outside, Nolan grabbed her by the arm and flung her to the floor. She hit the tile hard, the wind knocked out of her. Gasping for breath, she looked up to see Nolan standing between her and the open doorway.

"This is over," Nolan said, his voice low and dangerous.

Ava's mind raced. She had to find a way past him. She had to somehow over overcome and succeed. She decided the best way to hold him at bay for now would be with words.

"What do you want with me, Nolan?" She screamed, tears pouring down her cheeks once more. But this time, they weren't tears of fear; they were tears of anger. "I'm Chase's wife, not yours. If you're taking over, why keep me here?"

Nolan's face twisted into a cruel smile. "You're here because we want you here," he said, taking twisted pleasure in each word. "You took a vow of marriage to Chase, and you're going to honor it."

He lunged for her again, but Ava was ready. She scrambled to her feet and dashed toward the stairs. She could practically feel Nolan's breath; he was so close behind her now. The sound of his every snarl and growl, like that of a wild animal, grew louder and more labored with every step.

Ava reached the top of the stairs and bolted toward one of the mansion's many guest rooms. She managed to run inside, slamming the door shut behind her just as he was about to reach for her. She locked the door and backed away, knowing that a simple door would barely slow him down.

Nolan began pounding on the wood with Chase's stolen fists. Ava knew he could easily rip it off his hinges. This wasn't about ending the chase now. It was about fear. He wanted her to feel it, and it was working.

"You can't hide from us, Ava!" he shouted. "We'll find you no matter where you go!"

Ava looked around the room, searching for something, anything, she could use to defend herself. Her eyes landed on a heavy lamp on the bedside table. She ran over and grabbed it, holding it in front of her as Chase's fist exploded through the door.

Ava took a deep breath as Nolan started punching and kicking the door to splinters. She had to calm her racing heart. She had to be strong and fight back.

The door was turned to kindling under Nolan's relentless assault, and Ava braced herself for the inevitable. Nolan burst into the room, his eyes blazing with fury as they locked on her in the same way a lion looked at a zebra.

He took a step toward her, and Ava swung the lamp with all her might. She was aiming for Nolan's head. But he effortlessly dodged the blow and grabbed her wrist, twisting it until she dropped her makeshift weapon. Ava cried out in pain as he pushed her to the floor, his hands wrapping around her throat.

"You're going to learn your place," Nolan repeated, his grip tightening. "You're going to learn to obey."

Ava struggled against him, but her vision started to blur. She could feel her strength fading, darkness encroaching on the corners of her sight. There wasn't much time left. She had to do something, anything, to break free.

It was then that she remembered Chase's left knee. It had always given him problems after a football accident back in high school. If that was a glaring weak point on Chase, perhaps it would be on Nolan as well.

With a final burst of energy, she kicked Nolan in the left knee, causing him to cry out in pain and stumble backward.

She scrambled to her feet and ran for the door, her lungs burning with every breath. She could hear Nolan's enraged roar behind her as he exploded to his feet and came back hot on her trail.

She reached the stairs and started to descend, but Nolan's clumsy attempt at grabbing her had only succeeded in shoving her roughly. It caused her to fall. Ava tumbled down the stairs. Her body hit each step with a painful thud. She landed at the bottom, dazed and disoriented.

Nolan stood over her, his face twisted with rage. This was it. This was the end. She had put up a valiant fight, but she could only hold out for so long. But, despite the fear and dread she felt at whatever was going to come next, Ava Monroe was proud of herself for fighting back against this monster for as long as she had.

"This ends now," Nolan said in triumph, his voice a menacing growl.

"You're right about that, mate," a clipped, accented voice called out from the doorway.

Instantly, Ava's heart filled with renewed hope. She recognized that voice. Even though she'd only known its owner for a few days, she'd recognize it anywhere.

Ava and Nolan turned to see Michael Merlyn silhouetted in the doorway by the midday sun.

30

Michael stepped into the foyer, his expression calm and determined. But inside, he was as close to terrified as he could be during a possession case. He had no idea if what he had planned was going to work, but he was certainly going to try.

"You again," Nolan said, tilting Chase's head as he examined Michael as the fountain of light he knew he appeared to be through spectral eyes.

"Yes, me," Michael said with a wink at the big man. "Bad news, Nollie. I'm the new landlord. And I'm here to evict you, you limp-pricked ponce."

Nolan took a deep intake of enraged breath through his nose and turned away from Ava, focusing all his attention on Michael. "The hell did you just call me?" he sneered.

And then, to Michael's horror, he turned back to Ava, grabbing her by the arm. She winced in pain, and Michael could only hope that somewhere in there, Chase was seeing t and starting to struggle.

"You think you can stop me?"

"Oh, I know I can," Michael said with a nod. He kept his eyes locked on Nolan's.

Ava looked up at Michael, and he could see the hope in her eyes. She believed in him, and he wasn't about to let her down.

Michael took a step forward. His presence radiated confidence and strength. "Let her go, Nolan," Michael said. "Your fight is with me now, mate. And this ends now."

Nolan's grip tightened for a moment before he shoved Ava aside, focusing his full attention on Michael.

"You think this is gonna be any easier than last time?" he said with a chuckle. "What makes you think you can take me? What makes you think I won't finish the job I started the other night?"

"Because I'm Michael bloody Merlyn, mate," he said with a cocky smile meant to throw Nolan off balance mentally.

"Am I supposed to know that name?" he said with a mocking laugh.

"Not yet," Michael said. "But when you get to hell, ask around about me. I'm sure you'll hear plenty of stories."

"The little man thinks he's a badass," Nolan said with another laugh.

"Oh, no, I'm a proven badass, mate," he replied. "I've washed dozens of demons down the drain, and I'm talking actual world eaters, mate. Now some silly little roided-up ponce like you. Real players."

"Talk again like you think you know me," Nolan spat.

"Oh, I know you a lot better than you might realize," Michael said.

"Enough talk," Nolan said, raising a hand and beckoning Michael forward with his fingers. "Let's see what you've got, exorcist."

Ava scrambled to her feet and backed away. This was good. Michael didn't want her getting in the way of what was going to be a fairly major scene. He just hoped she felt some comfort in knowing she wasn't alone in this fight anymore.

When Michael didn't make the first move, Nolan advanced. He walked up to Michael with a purpose, eyes blazing with fury.

Michael raised a hand menacingly and stretched out with his will. "I am addressing the entity inside," he said once more.

But just like last time, Nolan shrugged it off.

Michael sighed in annoyance. "It was worth a try."

Nolan reached for Michael, but the quippy exorcist ducked and gave the huge man a strong punch to the gut that actually doubled Nolan over and pushed him back. Nolan lunged again, screaming like an animal, but Michael dodged and kicked him hard in the chest, sending him falling back against the stairs.

Nolan stood and looked at Michael once more with wide-eyed astonishment. "How?" he asked. "How is it possible you're this strong?"

Michael simply smirked in response. "I eat a lot of protein," he said.

Nolan shook his head and narrowed his eyes, scrutinizing Michael. "No, that's not it," he said thoughtfully.

Michael knew Nolan was looking closer at his aura, sensing what most other spirits he tangled with inevitably saw there.

"There's a lot more to you than meets the eye, priest," Chase said, grinning maliciously. "A lot more. You have a darkness inside you, don't you? Hypocrite."

Michael gritted his teeth and charged. Inside, Michael felt the dark force of Jeremiah Kassidy mocking him, laughing at him as yet another spirit used their rare bond to pull at his mental strings. But Kassidy was just a passenger, and Michael was using the demon strength of the ancient spirit to put some good back into the world. The Bayou Butcher could choke on that.

Michael balled up a fist and leaped into the air, but Nolan was ready for him now. He swatted Michael out of the air with a punch that sent him to the floor. Michael rolled out of the way as Nolan stomped at him, missing and cracking the floor under his boot.

Now, it was time to get personal. "How does it feel to be in a working body, mate?" Michael taunted, reaching up to wipe a trickle of blood from his mouth. "First time in a bit, eh?"

Nolan's lip curled, and his advance stopped. He tilted his head in question. "What do you mean?" he growled with some trepidation.

Michael had an idea that he knew exactly where the exorcist was going with this. "I met your old lady last night," Michael continued. "Charming bird. Had a lot to say about you, let me tell you. But take it from me, I heard all about your…troubles. You know, instead of Nolan, we ought to rename you Peter. With a lowercase *P*, of course."

Nolan's expression darkened. "You better shut up right the hell now," he said, his voice absolutely shaking as Michael struck at the core of his manhood.

"Why so upset, mate?" Michael asked with a mocking smile. "Is it because you couldn't…rise to the occasion with your own wife?"

Nolan screamed in rage and attacked. He moved faster than Michael thought possible in his rage and began to batter him with powerful punches before slamming him into the wall. He lifted Michael by the throat and roared in his face.

"Don't talk about things you don't understand," he screamed, seemingly ready to cave in Michael's face.

Michael struggled to breathe but managed to choke out enough wind to speak again. "You're right; I don't understand," Michael said, coughing up some blood. "But I've heard it's not…uncommon. Lots of men go through it. I never have that problem, though, because I'm an actual man who knows what he's doing with a woman."

Nolan screamed and slammed Michael into another wall. Michael felt the air fly out of his lungs for a brief minute as Nolan screamed at him with such force that it blew his hair back.

"Shut up!" he bellowed.

Michael knew he had to change up the strategy. He'd pushed the Miranda button twice now. A third time would only desensitize him to the jab. It was time for another angle of attack.

Michael coughed and smirked through bloody lips. "Why be embarrassed about that, mate?" he asked. "You should be more embarrassed by your movies."

Nolan's face twisted in fury, his eyes doubling in size, utterly shocked that someone would have the gall to say that to him. Michael decided he needed to strike while the iron was hot.

"I mean, *Blood and Thunder*?" he scoffed. "What a piece of crap. I hear they show it on loop to the prisoners down in Guantanamo Bay to weaken their brainpower." Michael then laughed in Nolan's face. He knew that insecure dolts like that hated to be laughed at. As he laughed, he looked over at Ava, who was staring at him in open-mouthed horror. He raised his eyebrows, trying to tell her to join in.

Ava seemed to get the message because a second later, she turned on the acting charm and started giving a fake laugh, the likes of which anyone would believe. Nolan looked back and forth between the two of them as they laughed at his inadequacy. It seemed to break something in his psyche, and his eye started to twitch.

"You know nothing!" he cried out before lugging Michael back into the air to bash him into the floor.

Ava had stopped laughing now. Her fake laughter had been swallowed by a cry of horror as Michael's body actually cracked the tile in the floor when he made contact.

Michael grinned through the pain, through the blood trickling from his mouth. Through even the slight blurring of his vision as his insides were punished. Still, he wasn't done.

"At least your arms are huge," he choked out. "It's good that something on your body might be considered big."

Nolan's eyes went wide with rage. "I'll kill you!" he shrieked.

That was it. "I'll" was all Michael had to hear to know that this bread had been baked.

Michael noted the crazed look in Nolan's eyes as he raised his massive fist to end the fight. But he wasn't afraid now. Michael smirked in the face of the blow meant to bash his face into hamburger meat.

"I am addressing the entity inside," he said again, raising one hand with his palm out.

That time, Nolan gasped and jerked up into the air as if pulled by an invisible force. His fingers instantly opened as Michael's will ripped him into its grip and helped him helplessly suspended above the floor.

Michael allowed himself a long laugh and spat a wad of blood out onto the floor. He turned to Ava apologetically. "Send me the cleaning bill, love," he said, his voice still weary and haggard from the beating he'd taken.

Nolan looked down at him in horror as Michael stood, realizing what had happened. "What did you do to me?" he shouted, and Michael was pleased to hear fear in his distorted voice.

"You're in my power now, bitch," he said, keeping his voice calm. "You might be a master of exercising, but I'm more about exorcising."

Behind him, somewhere, he could hear Ava groan at the bad pun.

"Really, Michael?" she asked, her voice sounding as weary as his.

Michael gave her an apologetic look. "Sorry," he said. "I came up with that one on the first bloody day, and I've been holding on to it ever since."

Nolan opened his mouth to say something, but Michael clenched his fingers just a bit and the force holding him in place silenced whatever threat he wanted to spew.

"You were a man who valued power, Nolan Hillhurst," Michael said.

At the mention of his name, Nolan cringed and recoiled. Names were a powerful tool in an exorcism, and Michael used them very effectively.

"But now you're learning what it feels like to be truly powerless. You have no power here anymore, Nolan Hillhurst. I'm in control now."

Nolan screamed in frustration, desperately trying to thrash against Michael's will.

"Princeps gloriosissime caelestis militiae, sancte Michael Archangele," Michael spat in Latin.

Nolan recoiled at the words. It was a prayer to Saint Michael the Archangel, who Michael's mother had named him after.

"Defende nos in proelio et colluctatione, quae nobis adversus principes et potestates, adversus mundi rectores tenebrarum harum, contra spiritualia nequitiae, in caelestibus!"

Nolan screamed again, his body convulsing as the words of Michael's prayer burned him from the inside, further splitting him from his host.

Michael's voice grew louder, more authoritative, as he commanded the spirit to leave. "Saint Michael the Archangel," he said in English now, "defend us in battle. Be our protection against the wickedness and snares of the devil."

Nolan's screams grew louder, more desperate, and a powerful wind began to blow through the foyer. It went through Michael's hair and jacket in every which direction, and out of the corner of his eye, he could see Ava shielding herself from it.

"May God rebuke him. We humbly pray," Michael said. The Latin prayers were some of his favorite, but once in a while, he liked to throw in a little English. He was, after all, a showman at heart, and he doubted that his audience of one understood the dead language of Latin. "And do thou, O Prince of the Heavenly Host, by the power of God, thrust into hell Satan and all the evil spirits who prowl about the world seeking the ruin of souls."

Nolan's body thrashed, and a dark, shadowy figure seemed to be pulled from him, writhing and screaming. Michael's eyes narrowed in concentration, his voice unwavering.

"I command you, unclean spirit, in the name of our Lord Jesus Christ, to depart from this servant of God," he continued. "It is He who commands you, He who flung you from the heights of heaven to the depths of hell."

Nolan's body continued to thrash, and the dark, shadowy figure became more defined, writhing and struggling against Michael's will. The intensity of the scene grew, with the room seemingly pulsating with energy as the exorcism reached what Michael believed to be its climax. He felt the weight of the spirit's struggle now pressing down on him. However, he remained resolute, his voice steady and unwavering.

"You will not prevail here, foul spirit," Michael intoned. "By the power of the cross, by the power of the one who conquered death, I command you to release this man and return to the abyss from whence you came."

Nolan recoiled at Michael's words, but soon, through the

pain, he gritted his teeth and laughed. The dark entity that seemed to be pouring out had dissipated, retreating inward. Michael quickly realized that Nolan was fighting back and finding some ground. He was sinking his claws into Chase again.

Michael doubled down on his will, and the entire house shook. Nolan continued to laugh through the pain. It was a deep, unsettling sound that reverberated through the walls and made Ava flinch. Michael stood his ground, unwavering.

This was going to be a tough bond to break. But he was going to break it.

"I'm just getting warmed up," Michael said, his voice calm but firm. "I've got more than one trick up my sleeve. You know, I sometimes find that just the Catholic prayers aren't enough. Sometimes, I feel you have to tag out and let someone else come in to fire up. It's the reason the church kicked me to the curb, you see. Well, maybe you don't yet. But you will. By the Star of David, I command you, spirit. In the name of Allah, I command you. In the name of Odin, the Allfather, I command you. In the name of Zeus of Olympus, I command you! In the name of Gaia, I command you!"

The air grew thick with a palpable energy, and Nolan's face twisted in pain as he screamed. The distorted sound was echoing through the house now. Yet, he still resisted, his defiance unwavering.

"You don't have the power to cast me out of my home," Nolan spat, his voice a mix of Chase's and his own distorted tone.

But he was still saying me and not us. That was a good sign. Chase wasn't giving up in there.

"Chase needs me. He willingly accepted me."

Michael scoffed. "Hosts never know what they're getting themselves into when they agree to let a parasite like you into their soul," he said.

Nolan's eyes narrowed, a dangerous glint in them. "You bastard priest," he spat. "You'll lose! I will break out, and I'll kill you. Then Ava and I will live happily ever after."

Michael glanced at Ava, who was trembling but trying to stay strong. "Does she get a say in this?" he asked.

Nolan laughed darkly, the sound chilling as it reverberated through the space. "She lost her say in anything when she agreed to honor and serve her husband," he said.

Michael chuckled, shaking his head. "A marriage vow isn't a business transaction, mate," he said in disgust, shaking his head.

Nolan's face contorted with rage at being contradicted. "You're wrong," he growled simply.

"Ava, love," Michael said, calling over to her.

"Yeah?" she called out over the sound of the whipping wind and Nolan's otherworldly moaning.

"I need you to come here, love," Michael said as Ava climbed back to her feet, shielding her face with her arms as her hair blew wildly about. "Reach into my pocket and pull out a small vial of water. When I say so, flick the water in Chase's face."

Ava nodded, her hands shaking as she approached and reached into Michael's coat pocket. He could feel her pull out the vial and smiled. Michael then looked back at Nolan.

"Wasn't it enough that you ruined one woman's life?" he asked the hanging body in the air above him. "Why do you have to do it again?"

Nolan's eyes blazed with fury. "Miranda was a snob and a bitch," he spat. "She didn't deserve me. I won't make the same mistakes with Ava."

Michael met Ava's gaze and gave her a slight nod. She uncapped the bottle and, with a flick of her wrist, sent droplets of water splashing onto Nolan's face. He screamed in agony, smoke rising from his flesh as if it were burning.

"That's holy water, mate," Michael said. "It helps to quiet you down a bit so I can talk to the man of the hour! Chase! My name is Michael Merlyn. I'm out here with Ava, mate. She wants you back. But you have to want to come back. You have to be the one to cast this spirit out."

Chase's voice broke through, clear and without distortion. "I...," he said, and Ava practically jumped at the sound of his voice. "I won't let you hurt Ava, you bastard!"

Nolan's voice came back quickly, a venomous snarl as he thrashed wildly. "No, you can't have him!" Nolan screamed. "Chase belongs to me!"

Ava cried out, "No!" and flicked the water again without Michael's say-so.

That meant Michael wasn't ready. The water flew out uncontrolled, splashing back onto Michael's face. Instantly, Michael was accosted by a burning, searing pain as though acid had just been poured on his flesh. He screamed, smoke rising from the burns that spread along his cheek and eye as he fell to the ground, writhing in pain.

Ava screamed in horror as she watched him roll there. "What's happening?" she asked, her voice filled with fear.

Instantly, the force of Michael's will vanished, and Nolan, now free from all control, landed on his feet with a loud thud. Before Michael could recover, Nolan pounced on him, wrapping his hands around Michael's throat.

He laughed in victory now, knowing that despite everything Michael had done, no matter how close he came, he was still going to lose.

"Well, how about that?" Nolan sneered down into Michael's face. "All those prayers, all the good you try to do, and still, God doesn't want you!"

Michael struggled to breathe, his vision blurring as he fought to free himself. Ava, desperate now, jumped onto

Nolan's back. She started clawing at his face valiantly in an attempt to get him to let go, but he shrugged her off easily.

She crashed to the floor, gasping for breath.

Suddenly, a scream echoed from the front door. Michael and Nolan turned as one to see Miranda and Lenny standing there, their faces masks of horror.

Nolan's eyes locked onto Miranda's. Recognition and pure rage flared in his expression. *"You!"* he screamed in a bellowing fury as the door slammed shut behind the two with a thunderous bang.

31

"Chase, my God, what are you doing?" Lenny screamed.

He ran forward and tried to stop the young man from popping Michael's head off his body, but Nolan swatted him away with a backhanded blow that sent him sprawling across the room.

He had dropped Michael now in his rage, fixating on a singular target, the source of his ire. "Miranda," he said, his voice a guttural growl as he took a step in her direction. "What are you doing here?"

"I was worried, Chase!" Miranda said. "After that rude man came to my house last night, I couldn't stop thinking that Ava might be in the same kind of trouble I was in, and I'm not going to let it happen again!"

Michael quickly realized that Miranda thought this was Chase. She didn't know that anything supernatural was going on here. The door slamming behind her had gone entirely unnoticed in the commotion. She had no idea she was now face to face with her abusive, tormenting ex-husband.

"You abandoned me!" Nolan screamed, his voice a distorted growl.

Miranda was confused and terrified. She backed away until she bumped into the closed door. "What are you talking about?" she asked, utterly bewildered. "Chase, what's wrong with you?"

Nolan's laugh was cold and bitter. "Not Chase," he said, the unnatural reverberation in his tone clear now.

That drew wide-eyed stares from both Miranda and Lenny. Michael tried to stand but he was still having issues simply drawing breath. Ava was lying off to the side. Lenny had risen to his knees and was kneeling beside her, checking on her. That meant Miranda was alone for now.

"You don't recognize me, do you, Miranda?" Nolan asked, a mocking sneer in his tone. "Not like this."

"Of course I remember you, Chase," Miranda said, holding up a hand and trying to placate the young man. "I don't know what drugs you're on to make your voice sound like that or your eyes look like that, but we can get you help and—"

"Oh, there you go with the drugs, drugs, drugs," Nolan spat, taking another step toward her. "I thought you learned your lesson the night you flushed my stash. You remember what happened that night, baby doll?"

"Baby doll?" Miranda asked, her eyes growing wide as she looked up into Nolan's glowing eyes. "No one ever called me that, but…"

"I broke your collarbone that night," Nolan growled, gesturing back at the staircase. "Threw you down those stairs. Don't you remember? Don't you remember the way you cried? The way you looked up at me and screamed…"

"Please, Nolan…," Miranda said, completing the sentence, her face utterly horrified and transfixed by what was in front of her. "Please…Nolan…."

"Exactly," he said, growling softly now like a wolf about to pounce. "Not happy to see me, baby doll?"

Miranda's eyes widened even further through her shock and horror. She shook her head, utterly unwilling to believe what she was seeing. But it couldn't be denied. She had seen something in his eyes, in his sneer. A look that only one person ever in this world had given her. A look that she tried every day to forget.

"Nolan?" she asked breathlessly. "But…how?"

Nolan took another step forward, his face contorted with anger. "You left me, Miranda," he spat at her, pointing an accusatory finger in her face.

Michael coughed up another wad of blood as he tried to pull air down his throat.

All the while, Nolan was getting closer to his ex-wife. "You let me die."

Miranda shook her head, tears streaming down her face. "No, I didn't!" she insisted, wringing her hands together. "I tried to get away from you because you were hurting me!"

Nolan snarled. "You were always weak!" he cried out, his scream shaking the walls.

Miranda screamed and cowered as the monolithic shadow of the monster who haunted her nightmares slowly enveloped her. "Always needing someone to protect you. And when I needed you the most, you ran away."

"Holy shit," Lenny said from his place beside Ava. "No… No, it can't be."

Ava had rolled away from Lenny now and was crawling toward Michael. She laid a hand on his back and leaned in close.

"Are you all right?" she whispered.

Michael coughed again and spit, slowly trying to nod.

"Michael, you have to get up. You have to stop him. He's gonna kill Miranda!"

Michael rubbed at his throat despite the terrible pain there and cleared his throat with extra emphasis. Ava was right. Death was about to descend on this room unless he did something.

"You were a monster, Nolan!" Miranda shouted, finding her voice. "You abused me, controlled me, and then you died. I didn't kill you!"

Nolan's eyes narrowed. "Didn't you?"

As Nolan raised his arm to smash Miranda into nothingness, a brilliant white light erupted to life in the space between them. Michael and Ava looked up to see the specter of Miranda's cat, Snowball, fur a dazzling white now standing between his owner and the man who had tormented them both.

Miranda gasped, her eyes widening in shock. "Snowy?" she called out, and Michael could see fresh tears spilling down her face.

"Get out of the way, you stupid thing," Nolan growled down at Snowball.

But the cat screeched up at him, baring its fangs and claws in a protective gesture. It let out another loud screech, and the entire room filled with that same dazzling white light that had heralded Snowball's arrival.

At first, Michael wasn't sure what he was seeing when the glow subsided. It was the foyer, but from his perspective, it was rocking around. There was no sign of Ava, Miranda, or Lenny. But as the scenery shifted, Michael caught a glimpse of a pure white paw and a heavily muscled arm constricted around his field of vision.

That was when he realized it. He knew what he was seeing. Snowball's point of view. His perspective.

"It's your fault she's gone!" a gruff, slurred voice said from above.

Michael looked up to see that it was Nolan. The real

Nolan. He was holding Snowball roughly and walking with him toward the front door.

Then, Snowball shifted until he saw the space behind Nolan. And there, in the shadows, someone was moving. The figure slowly walked out into view, and Michael was floored to see Lenny, his face contorted in rage with tear streaks running down his face as he entered the foyer completely unseen. He held a dumbbell in both of his hands, and Nolan had no idea he was there.

Though the object looked heavy for him, Lenny managed to hold it up with knuckles white from his grip. He moved with a purpose; his eyes locked on Nolan's back.

Snowball's senses heightened. It sensed danger. The cat's fear and Nolan's drunken obliviousness were evident to everyone witnessing the vision. There was a sense of impending doom as Lenny approached closer and closer. Nolan continued toward the door, oblivious to the danger behind him.

The vision paused for a heartbeat, capturing the last peaceful moment before everything changed. Then, with a swift and brutal motion, Lenny screamed and swung the dumbbell. The sickening thud echoed through the room as the huge object connected with the back of Nolan's skull. Nolan's eyes widened in shock and pain, and he crumpled to the floor. Snowball's terror reached its zenith as Nolan's huge body landed on top of him, and everything went black.

After another white flash, Michael was back in the foyer, and it was clear by the way everyone was looking about, they had all experienced the same vision. Even Nolan, in Chase's body, looked stunned as he slowly turned along with everyone else to stare in open-mouthed shock at Lenny.

"No...," Nolan said, looking down at Lenny, who was still on his knees. "No, this can't be. Lenny? You? You killed me? Someone as...pathetic and....weak as you...killed me?"

Lenny looked horrified as Nolan advanced. As the big man's shadow enveloped him, he called out across the room.

"Miranda!" he exclaimed, reaching an arm uselessly toward her.

She looked absolutely mortified. Miranda held a hand to her mouth, which was open in a scream of silent horror.

"I did it for you. I did it for you. I did it for you because I…I always loved you, Miri. And I couldn't stand to see what that monster was doing to you! I knew if he didn't go away, you'd just go back to him again, so I…"

Nolan's rage exploded again as he screamed, drowning out Lenny's blubbering explanation. He raised his arms to attack, and Michael jerked himself up with one arm raised. He tried to call out, to exert his will, but only a coughing hack came up from his throat. He wasn't going to make it in time.

But then, suddenly, Nolan froze, his face twitching and jumping as his arms quivered above the helpless Lenny, who cowered below.

"Chase?" Ava called out, with her voice filled with hope.

Nolan screamed again and tried to move, but another voice came out of his mouth.

"No!" Chase screamed, cleaving himself away from Nolan's control. "You won't use me for this! You won't make me a murderer!"

Michael cleared his throat one last time and let out a cough as Chase and Nolan struggled with one another.

"Chase, fight!" Ava called out. "Come on, baby, fight! Come back to me!"

"Ava!" Chase screamed between Nolan's enraged, distorted howls.

"I am addressing the entity inside!" Michael managed to croak out of his mouth, and Nolan was once more torn into the air by the power of Michael's will.

"No!" Nolan screamed, hovering uselessly over Lenny, who

was a cringing, crying mess on the floor, curled into the fetal position.

"Chase!" Michael called out, his voice hoarse and pained but just barely audible as the wind started to pick up once more.

Chase was separated enough to fight back. That meant he was fully capable of doing what had to be done.

"Now's the time, mate! Tell him to get out!"

"I respected you!" Chase screamed. "I admired you! But you're a monster, and you're going where you deserve!"

"No!" Nolan screamed again. "You can't do this! You let me in! You can't shut me out! You need me!"

"The only person I need," Chase said, straining to be heard but with power and confidence behind his words, "is my wife!"

"You can do it, baby!" Ava called out. "I believe in you! I love you so much!"

Chase seemed emboldened by this as he fought even harder now. "I...," he called out as Michael could feel Nolan making one last effort to hold on for dear life. "Love...*you*!"

Michael could feel something in Nolan's hold snap irreparably. It was time.

"Now, Chase!" Michael called out.

"Get the hell out!" Chase screamed, and a powerful shockwave exploded out of his body. Chase's body dropped to the floor as the wind died, and Ava practically dove onto him as though to shield him from anything else that might come slithering out of the walls.

To everyone else, the phenomena had just suddenly stopped. Only Michael could see Nolan's spirit come flying out of Chase's body to coincide with the shockwave. But before Nolan could do anything, Michael reached out and grabbed him by the throat, exerting his will on him one more time.

Nolan looked terrified now, looking up into Michael's eyes for the first time, feeling completely and utterly powerless. Michael looked down at Ava and Chase. He looked over at Miranda and Lenny. All these people who this monster had upended in one way or another. But now he was never going to hurt anyone ever again.

"Michael Merlyn," Michael said into the spirit's face, and Nolan shook his head in terror. "Ask around." Without another word, Michael set his will upon Nolan one last time, forcibly shoving him back through the veil to whatever awaited him on the other side.

He remembered sitting in the library with that spirit in San Francisco just a few days ago. He had told her that he had touched the other side and knew that there was something beautiful out there. That was true.

But that hadn't been the only thing he'd felt. There was also a horror, terror, and despair that sucked in the darkness and sealed it away forever. That was the fate that awaited Nolan Hillhurst.

Michael looked over to see Chase collapsed to the floor, seemingly unconscious. Lenny and Miranda still sat on the floor, gaping open-mouthed and horrified. Both were crying, and Michael knew that it'd take some time before they could process what they had just seen.

He thought about saying something, but his throat was absolutely killing him. It was a good thing he didn't, though, because that was the moment that Chase began to wake up slowly. Ava gasped as her husband's clear-blue human eyes opened and focused on her again for the first time in days.

Neither said anything. They simply collapsed into one another and shared a desperate moment as they embraced tightly.

Michael looked around the room, noting the chaos. It

wasn't exactly a happy ending for everyone, with Miranda's horror and Lenny's guilt were still real concerns to address.

Miranda, still in shock, turned to look up at Michael. "Is it...is it really over?" she asked. "Is he...gone?"

Michael nodded, his expression softening. "He's gone," Michael whispered, and even that hurt his bruised throat.

Lenny was shaken and pale. He sat there, rocking back and forth, muttering to himself. "I never wanted this...," he said. "I just wanted to protect you, Miri. I'm sorry!"

Miranda looked at Lenny with a mix of sorrow and gratitude. "I know, Lenny," she said, crawling over to him.

Michael wasn't sure what she was going to do, but he watched her slowly reach out and pull the small man into a tight embrace. Lenny returned the hug as she whispered into his ear again.

"I know."

Ava was clinging to Chase now, tears streaming down her face. "I thought I'd lost you forever," she said, looking into her husband's face as though she never thought she would see it again."

Chase was still weak, but he was fully conscious now. He brought a shaking hand up to caress her cheek. "I'm here, baby," he said. "I'm not going anywhere. Never again."

Michael watched the scene unfold, feeling a sense of satisfaction and exhaustion. He had done his job, but the scars left behind would take time to heal. That was always the messy part. And it was the part that he conveniently never stuck around for.

EPILOGUE

Despite the emotional turmoil and physical wreckage left in the wake of Nolan Hillhurst's possession, the immediate aftermath of those horrific events saw a surprising lack of legal consequences for Lenny.

There was no evidence tying him to Nolan's death, and no one in the house that night was willing to turn against him. While murder was never truly justified, Lenny's intentions were, on some level, understandable. As far as the world knew, Nolan Hillhurst had died five years ago of a heart attack. And that was how it was going to stay.

Chase, now free of Nolan's influence, worked hard to rebuild his life and his relationship with Ava. Their marriage, once teetering on the brink of collapse, was renewed with a sense of gratitude and understanding. They took time to heal, both individually and together. And through it all, they rediscovered the love and respect that had initially brought them together.

The following day, in the sterile, beeping confines of Shepherd's hospital room, the scene was markedly different. Ava and Chase stood beside Shepherd's bed, their faces a mixture of relief and lingering sorrow.

Shepherd, his face still showing the bruises of his encounter, flashed the two of them a weary smile.

"I'm so sorry for everything," Chase said down to the celebrity medium. His voice cracked with the emotional weight of his guilt. "I never wanted to hurt anyone. I didn't even know what was happening to me."

Shepherd shook his head gently, reaching up to pat the young man on his muscled left arm. "It wasn't you, Chase," Jacob said simply. "It was Nolan. You were just as much a victim as anyone else."

"I dunno. I was quite the victim there, lad," Michael's hoarse, whispery voice said as he walked into the room.

Chase turned to look at him with wide eyes, but Ava was smiling. She already had adjusted to Michael's unique sense of humor.

"He's...what's the saying?" Ava asked Michael with a tilt of her head. "Taking a piss?"

Michael laughed and then winced, holding his throat. "Not bad, Miss Monroe," he said with a nod. He looked both her and Chase up and down without so much as even glancing in Jacob's direction. "How are you holding up?"

"We're getting there," Ava said, giving Chase's hand a reassuring squeeze. "It's been a lot, but we're stronger now."

Michael's eyes softened at that. He was genuinely happy for them. "Good to hear," he said. "It's always tough, facing down the darkness and coming out on the other side."

Ava hesitated for a moment, looking as though she wanted to ask a question. But something was holding her back.

"Don't leave me in suspense, love," he said with a smile. "What's on your mind?"

"Michael," Ava said slowly and delicately, "I have to ask.

Why did that holy water burn you? I saw it happen. Is there...I mean, are you all right?"

Michael's face grew hot and serious. He averted his gaze for a moment to collect his thoughts. When he looked up again, he once more had that gentle twinkle of amusement in his eye. "That, Ava, my dear, is a dark tale for another time," Michael said with a nod. "Suffice it to say, we all have our burdens to bear."

"I get it," Ava said. "I just hope you'll be able to handle that burden. But you have friends here. You don't have to handle anything alone.

"That's good to know, love," Michael said, reaching out to pat her on the side of the arm.

"Thank you, Michael," Ava said as tears welled up in her eyes again. "For everything. I owe you...so much!"

"Oh, stop it now," Michael said with a scoff. "I'm just doing my job. Now, I've seen you cry far too much for one lifetime, so don't go turning the waterworks on now."

"Michael," Chase said, stepping forward and offering his hand. "You saved me, man."

"No, I was just the blunt instrument," he said, reaching out to shake the young man's hand. "Your blushing bride is the one who saved you. She never gave up on you. You're a lucky man."

"I know I am," he said, looking down at Ava.

"Oh, by the way, I'm kind of a fan," Michael said, blushing slightly.

"Of me?" Chase asked, his eyebrows raised as Michael nodded. "Oh, wow, thanks, man. Well, I think now I can say back atcha."

"Aye, mate," Michael said. "And now I can tell all me mates down at the pub that I nearly got choked to death by Chase Parker. Well...by his hands anyway." Michael gave a small laugh at his own joke, but Chase simply smiled sadly. Michael chastised himself. He finally meets a celebrity he admires and he said something stupid. Typical.

"Michael, is there anything I can do for you?" Ava asked. "You've done so much, and I just feel like we should do something for me."

"Actually," Michael said, looking around the room in thought, "my sister is something of an admirer of yours, actually?"

"Oh, really?" Ava asked, blushing a bit.

"Indeed," Michael said, biting his lip in thought. "Ah, there we go!" He grabbed the medical chart off the foot of Shepherd's bed and ripped the page off the clipboard. "Would you mind signing this?"

"Hey, I kinda need that," Jacob said in protest.

"Oh, sack up, mate," Michael said with a wink. "You're fine. Ava, dear, if you could make it out to Victoria."

Ava smiled at him as she signed Shepherd's chart, handing the page back to Michael. "I hope your sister likes it," she said. "It's definitely the most unique autograph I've ever signed."

"I'm sure she will." Michael turned to look at all three people in the room. "Now them, me, and my bruised larynx are off to sunny New Mexico."

"What's there?" Ava asked.

"Apparently, the next person who needs my help," he said.

"Well, go give them hell...mate," Ava said, reaching out to pat him on the arm.

"There you go," he said with a wink. "We'll make a proper Brit out of you yet." Michael regarded Ava and Chase with a smile. "Take care of each other, you two. I don't wanna see anything about you in the bloody tabloids."

"Will do," Ava said.

"Yes, sir," Chase replied with a nod.

"All right, I'm off then," Michael said, turning to leave. But he stopped short, as if forgetting something. "Oh, and Shepherd?"

"Yeah, Merlyn?" Jacob asked from the bed.

"Don't call me for a while, all right?" Michael said with an exasperated sigh. "Like…maybe a nice long while, yeah?"

Made in United States
North Haven, CT
03 November 2024